THE
STOCK MARKET
MONK

THE
STOCK MARKET
MONK

NIKUNJ

PARTRIDGE
A Penguin Random House Company

To order additional copies of this book, contact
Partridge India
000 800 10062 62
orders.india@partridgepublishing.com

www.partridgepublishing.com/india

CONTENTS

1   The Trio—July 2014 1

2   Naren 6

3   Adarsh 12

4   Gobind—the Car Mechanic 18

5   Ripples of Excitement 24

6   The Addiction of Gains 29

7   Dhandha (Business) at Any Cost 37

8   Chemistry 44

9   Internet—the Synonym of Nirvana 51

10   I Am an Expert—Cos I Made Money 68

11   The Risk Not Understood 82

12   No Complaints 91

13   New Vistas 99

14   They All Fell Down 111

15   A Classroom with a Difference—Circa 2002 121

16   Understanding Equity 127

17   Owners Versus Shareholders 132

18   The Wealthiest People in the World 137

19   What Works in Life Works in
Stock Markets Too 143

20   Don't Make Money—Create Wealth Instead 149

21   Wealth Creation Is Boring 156

22   Think Long-Term 162

23 Why Is There Only One Warren Buffett? 170

24 Go Gabbar's Way 180

25 Going Nowhere 188

26 Seek and You Shall Find 193

27 Take a SIP—Stay Cool 199

28 Don't Chase Popularity 206

29 Rudyard Kipling Was a Stock Market Guru 212

30 Welcome, Kids 218

31 Indian Economy on a Song—Take the Plunge 223

32 Psychological Pitfalls—
   Finding the Best Performers 228

33 Markets Are Not Risky 234

34 Crowd Sees the Risk—Leaders See Opportunity 240

35 P/E Ratio 246

36 Be Anything But a Pig 252

37 Time Flies 257

38 The Last Lecture—May 2012 262

39 July 2014 271

Dedicated to Indu—my wife,

Mrigakshi and Vrinda—our daughters,

and my parents

PREFACE

The desire to succeed in stock markets or investments in general is eternal. In my eighteen years of work, I haven't met a single investor who doesn't want to conquer the markets. Each investor that I have come across has had his own views, notions, and idiosyncrasies about how to make money in the markets. This book is a random expression of my understanding of their experiences in the world of investing, especially equity markets. This book is as much about life as it is about investing. It is not a guide; it's not a how-to book either. It's an attempt at making investors see investments with lot more simplicity than they normally do, especially when it comes to investing in equities or shares. I hope I have been able to do justice to my own learning by writing this book, although I must hasten to add that my journey of learning is far from being complete.

The timing of this book could not have been better. The global economy seems to be coming out of shadows slowly over the last few years. In India we have a new government in place. Thankfully this time it's not a coalition government. From an equity market perspective, this augurs well for all of us. India now stands on the verge of an unprecedented economic boom which may lead to phenomenal wealth creation for the equity market investors. Not investing in equities could be one of the biggest mistakes at this juncture. If you are an equity investor, then this book may be able to offer you something of value to you; if you haven't invested in equities, then I hope this book shall give you confidence to do so.

Wish you a happy reading and investing!

August 5, 2014

1

The Trio—July 2014

Naren looked at an ocean of friends, relatives, and well-wishers around him, felt his chest swell with pride and satisfaction. His daughter Kanishka was getting married today. He had left no stone unturned to make this occasion a perfect one. The venue, a high-end five-star hotel in South Delhi swarmed with people who had done well enough for themselves to keep up with the likes of Naren—whose eyes reflected the youth of this evening to perfection. This setting was a dream for many but a possibility for only a chosen few like Naren, whose wealth had more zeros than many mortals could hope to acquire. Kanishka, who was getting married to a Harvard-graduated lad, had herself acquired a management degree from India's topmost management institute in Ahmadabad. Instead of joining a corporate house for a big, fat, obscene salary, she chose to work with her dad. Naren's son Kshitij had just joined a premier engineering college in Roorkee and looked forward to doing master of business administration after engineering, emulating his sister. Everything seemed picture perfect as smiles filled the hall from wall to wall. Guests were received with a warmth and graciousness that any host would be envious of. Naren's wife Lavanya, clad in a fine Benares silk sari, personally ensured that everyone was taken good care of, especially the guests who travelled from outside Delhi and India. The setting had everything, including sparkling diamonds, glittering gold, buzzing celebrities, and warmth of genuine friends who had stood by Naren's family through the thick and thin of life. Delicious food that the north Indian weddings are known for added another unforgettable dimension to the gaiety of the occasion. The guests simply couldn't ask for more.

'Naren Paappe! Oye mere yaar, kee haal chaal, aaja ek jhappi paa le,' (Naren my dear friend, how are you, come give me a hug) shouted Sardar Gobind Singh Narwal.

What followed was similar to a scene in Bollywood movies. The two friends hugged each other as if they had met after ages, despite the fact that they were morning-walk buddies for over a decade now. Gobind owned a car dealership business that had flourished over the years. Gobind's wife Paramjeet—a homemaker—looked elegant and vivacious. She soon spotted Lavanya and rushed off to congratulate her, leaving Naren and Gobind to themselves. Gobind caught a glimpse of Adarsh Chaturvedi, the third arm of this trinity, entering the hall with his wife Rachel. Adarsh belonged to Haldwani, a small, pristine, slow-paced town snuggled in the lap of the Himalayas in the state of Uttarakhand (erstwhile Uttar Pradesh). He was a chartered accountant by profession and had a practice of his own that had flourished over the years. Rachel, being a CA herself, had helped Adarsh set up his business in the initial years. For Naren these two families, i.e. Gobind's and Adarsh's, mattered more than anyone else, and the three of them ensured that they stuck together through good and not-so-good times. The three friends held each other in a triangular embrace and silently raised a toast in their hearts to celebrate this solemn occasion—an important milestone in the journey of an Indian family.

'Where is Guruji?' asked Adarsh.

'He must be on his way,' Naren answered in a tear-soaked voice.

Guruji was the most influencing force that they had ever experienced in their lives. He brought focus and order in their lives when they needed it most. He wore them together like beads on a single thread, keeping them in a divine unison. Their lives revolved around him like planets moving around the sun in their elliptical orbits. He had been their master, mentor, and tormentor too. If they really owed anything to anyone in the world, it was to Guruji and no one else. No important function, event, or ceremony would be complete without Guruji's presence, and this was one such event for them. Kanishka was the first child to get married in their families and Guruji had to grace the evening with his presence. Nothing else mattered more to the trio than Guruji's blessings, their anxiety reflected it. They were still in the triangular embrace as Guruji entered the hall, and all of a sudden, they felt his footsteps echoing in their heartbeats. All of them turned their heads in the direction of the entrance and saw a tall figure wearing a black pinstriped suit, walking in measured steps towards them. There was something magnetic about Guruji's gait, something magically electric about his presence. He filled all of them with a sense of purpose and sculpted a meaningful life from what could have been a miserable saga of failure and desperation. They called him the Stock Market Monk.

Guruji's real name was Chaitanya. They called him Guruji out of respect, compassion, and their indebtedness towards him. Despite Chaitanya being less than half of their age, the title of Guruji was stuck to him, owing to the transformation he brought about in the three of them. The trio, along with a few others present at the venue, had reached here because of him, and this fact was never lost on them. As soon as they spotted Guruji, their tears vanished. His presence was as comforting as the first monsoon showers after an endless scorching summer. Guruji made no effort to locate his hosts, as he walked past the brocaded kurtas and elegant designer saris. He was tall and handsome, not a grain of fat on his limbs. Had he not been a yogi, he could have very well charmed the audiences of Indian cinema. He looked at his gold wristwatch and smiled. He was on time and his three disciples, whom he called Three Wanderers, were as excited with his presence as a bunch of children who have been promised a trip of Disneyland. They rushed towards him and hugged him. Chaitanya embraced them wholeheartedly, shook their hands one by one, and smiled. He was no ordinary saffron-clad monk who would chant mantras at the drop of a hat. Chaitanya was happy the way he was, knowing somewhere deep within that this sainthood was god-sent. He lived in the present and enjoyed each breath, each moment, and each day. He always said, 'Each moment is a festival, celebrate it.' Naren, Adarsh, and Gobind each felt a lump in their throats, owing to reverence and gratitude towards Chaitanya. Soon their wives also joined them to meet Guruji. Rachel was not only his student but had also assisted Guruji with his work in the past. Six of them glued together, stood magnetised near Guruji, speaking to him while Naren waved at a few bearers who could fetch some water and snacks for Guruji. A few chairs were arranged, and they sat with Chaitanya, oblivious of everything and everyone else around them. The past decade flashed past them and bittersweet memories filled their minds. They had seen a lot during these years, including joys, happiness, and shades of precariousness. They often wondered if everyone had a guru who could guide them through the maze of life, carefully steering them through the complex world of investments. They had nothing to complain or worry about now, but in the past, life had inflicted a lot of misery upon them at various points of time. Given the kind of money they lost in the stock markets, they could have lost it all, had Guruji not been there. They moored the boats of their hopes on his golden shores and negotiated the tides well, when the time came and created lot of wealth for them along the way.

Rachel asked, 'Guruji! Where is Sonia?'

'She is inaugurating a new branch of Moneymentors tomorrow, so she could not be here with me. But she has sent her regards and wishes for all of you.'

2

Naren

Naren, born in a well-to-do family, inherited an export business from his father, the late Mr Jagtap Sahay. It was a small business started way back in the '80s. They manufactured nuts, bolts, rivets, bearings, and clamps for cycle manufacturers, automobile companies, ancillary units of large equipment manufacturers, and other assorted industries. Back then, the competition was sparse and the demand was robust—a rare situation that every businessman craves for. As a result, the business grew very fast hiring over one thousand employees and having manufacturing facilities at multiple locations by the time Naren inherited it. Indian currency was relatively cheaper compared to American and European currencies, and more and more businessmen looked forward to exporting their goods to foreign countries. This anxiety to export found a match in the demand from developed countries who wanted to import more and more from India. Naren had managed to get hold of some of the markets in Western Europe, especially Germany, which was known for its automobile industry. After a few years of hard work and networking, he was able to secure orders from reputed companies like Mercedes and BMW. In the early '90s, the Indian government was forced to devalue the rupee, which gave a shot in the arm to the exports.

Naren, being at the right place at the right time, saw his business fortunes prospering each passing day. His income soared year after year and a small family-run business saw the possibility of being co-owned by sophisticated investors like private equity firms. After seeking advice from leading investment bankers and reputed lawyers, Naren sold a part of his business to private investors for a whopping 200 crores in the year 1995.

Naren was an organised man when it came to work; his understanding of the business was almost perfect. From pointing out mistakes in the drawings of his engineers to making freehand sketches himself, he was always spot on. He kept a drawing board and drafter in one corner of his cabin to try his hands on nuts, bolts, threads, and assemblies from time to time. He would know as well about his inventories as he knew the receivables or the deadlines for sending out the consignments. He was very particular about the quality of his products and ensured that his manufacturing units complied with the latest regulations and applicable standards. Year after year as the business profitability improved, the private equity investors expressed the desire to increase their stake in his business, to which he politely declined.

Being an engineer, Naren had limited knowledge about financial matters but it was not insufficient. But his awareness about investments and stock markets was barely adequate. He would often hear his friends boast about investments in stocks, bonds, and real estate over dinner and at cocktail parties. The only thing which he probably understood was real estate as he had bought land almost every year over the last decade.

During his interactions with investment bankers, he often heard about stock markets and their potential, although he never dared to venture into any details as he was simply not interested. Stock markets were as alien to him as study books to Al Capone. One of the investment bankers had left behind his contact coordinates in case Naren needed any advice regarding investments. One day out of sheer curiosity, Naren fetched his visiting cards from his card folder and asked his secretary to call the banker, who was kind enough to send across a charming lady relationship manager (RM) after a couple of days. The lady told Naren about the products and services their bank offered for high-net-worth Individuals like him. Naren listened to her carefully, but despite his good intentions, most of the investment-related stuff went over his head. He wasn't sure whether it was the charm of the lady or the abundance of money he had that made him commit a small amount to her to begin with. The lady came back after a couple of days and took Naren's signature on many forms. His stock trading account became live in a few days' time and they started purchasing shares with his money. Most of the investment stuff the RM talked about was Greek and Latin to Naren but he did not want to sound foolish in front of this lady, asking stupid questions. So he kept quiet.

After a few days, the RM turned up at his office with a piece of paper called account statement and showed it to Naren. The statement listed the names of the shares and their respective purchase prices, along with their current market price. Against each stock the statement also showed the respective profit and loss, which Naren easily understood. Most of the shares were positive, albeit only marginally.

'Not bad,' said Naren to himself and thanked the RM for encouraging him to start investing.

'Sir, this is only the beginning,' the lady said and smiled.

Naren asked his secretary to make a new file to keep a record of investments. So a new file was created, and as the tradition in his office was, a swastika symbol was made on the file cover with vermillion. This was considered auspicious. The investments were doing well, and week after week, new statements came showing gains and only gains. Naren could not have been happier; he had started an experiment with only a few lacs of rupees and it wasn't bad at all. His next meeting with the RM was due in couple of days and he had already made up his mind to put more money in this game. He asked his accountant to get the details of fixed deposits that he held with various banks. These deposits, over a decade old now, ran into a few crores. There were similar amounts held in Lavanya's and the children's names as well. These deposits were a part of their personal kitty, which was composed of gold, art, and real estate. Apart from this, Naren's company also had cash surpluses which were parked in either current accounts with banks or fixed deposits.

'Sir, our investments are doing well. Just look at the gains that we have made over last one month,' said his RM. As she sipped her black coffee, she felt the caffeine feeding the ambition in her senses. She always liked coffee and the taste of victory. She knew it was the time to go for a bigger kill now; that was why she had invited Naren to the coffee shop in one of the leading five-star hotels in South Delhi.

Naren had ordered his standard drink, a draught beer.

'I must thank you for guiding me down this path. I admit that I have never gone beyond darned fixed deposits.

Thanks to you, I can talk a wee bit about stocks now,' Naren said in a confessional tone.

This was music to her ears. Before she could even respond, Naren added, 'I have decided to break 50 per cent of fixed deposits held in my name and increase the investments with your bank. I am entrusting you with my hard-earned money and I know you shall take good care of it.'

There was a certain trace of precariousness in his voice. His limited knowledge about stocks made him dependent on the bank, and his RM was seasoned enough to sense it.

'Don't worry, sir, you are in safe hands. We have a team of experts who are capable of moving in and out of stocks in time to make our clients richer than they already are.'

Although this was a typical statement made by any of the investment advisors, Naren found no reason to disbelieve her. He committed a whopping sum of 7.5 crores to her. The RM, trained for such situations, showed very little excitement and said, 'Sir, I am happy to see you gain confidence slowly. My aim is to help you make lots of money from the stock markets. Believe you me, this is only the beginning of an exciting journey. We shall keep on repeating the stellar performance that we have already shown to you, month after month.'

So in little over a month's time, Naren had taken a huge exposure to the stock markets; he was half excited and half scared because he hadn't discussed this at home. Although 7.5 crores was not a sum to really worry about, it wasn't a small sum either.

The next week, Naren received a statement which showed that his money had been invested in a few more shares. Obviously he had expected them to do as well as his earlier stocks, and to his amusement, the shares did not disappoint him.

All the shares were in green.

Over the period of next couple of months, his portfolio was up by almost 15 per cent, which meant that he had made almost Rs. 1 crore in just three months or so. This called for a little celebration with his family.

He took Lavanya and kids out to dinner that night.

'Guys, I have earned four Mercedes cars in the last three months by investing in the share market. In other words, I have made one crore in stock markets in the last three months,' Naren said.

This shocked Lavanya, who almost knocked a water glass off the table.

'What are you saying, Naren? What is this? How come? Investing in shares? I don't believe you.'

Naren told the entire story. Their kids did not fully comprehend the situation although they knew what a crore meant.

'Although this is not comparable to the money that I make in my business, here I don't have to employ hundreds of people. A few crores and one relationship manager, that's all. Imagine if I invested a few more crores here, I could have made more,' he said.

Lavanya picked up her fine crystal glass and raised a toast to Naren's success. The bearers knew they were in for a hefty Friday-night tip.

3

Adarsh

Adarsh had married Rachel in 1990 against his family's will. The fallout of this adventure was that he had to leave his parents' home in East Delhi. He did not have enough material resources initially, but he believed in their collective capabilities. Both of them were qualified chartered accountants (CA) working with small accounting firms. The money wasn't great, but the learning curve was steep enough to equip them with acute financial wisdom. Adarsh could smell a balance sheet from a distance and make an accountant pee in his pants. He knew how companies cooked up their accounts, played with key numbers, used depreciation to their advantage, undermined their profits to short-change the government. After two years in the job, he started his own company—a small consultancy firm advising clients on accounts, taxation, and other corporate matters. As it usually happens, the business took its own time to shape up. Over the next couple of years, they were barely making both ends meet but had earned the loyalty of a few clients, who would swear by them. By 1996, the growth trajectory of the business started steepening.

He would often go do down memory lane, think about the humble beginnings in 1992, when they started their practice in a small chamber in the dingy lanes of

Chandni Chowk in Old Delhi. Well, it wasn't exactly a chamber, but a CA could not say that he was working out of a cubbyhole. He did not mind working out of this tiny, cramped, and dark office as it was strategically located, from a business perspective. He had access to Bhagirath Place, the largest wholesale market for electric goods, and to Chawdi Bazaar—a specialized wholesale market of brass, copper, and paper products, established in 1840, it was the first wholesale market of Old Delhi lying to the west of famous Jama Masjid and Sadar Bazaar, where one could buy anything from Diwali crackers to the political party flags at the time of elections. Adarsh could not have found a better place to start his office from.

Willpower was the wind in his sails, honesty and dignity—the two oars which helped him negotiate the unkind tides that formed life's fabric. He wasn't like other CAs who would connive with income tax officers to milk their clients to get their share of pound of flesh. He never advised clients to avoid the taxes. He rather helped them keep the tax liability to the bare minimum by smart and careful planning. He believed that no amount of taxes could make a rich man poor, so there was no need for anyone to avoid taxes at all. He paid his on time, every year without fail.

In the initial years, Rachel travelled with him to his Old Delhi office to share some workload. She had got enough blisters on her soles while boarding the unceremonious Red Line buses of Delhi, occasionally taking a tonga ride from Pahar Ganj to Chandni Chowk and walking endless miles to reach where she was today. She stood firm in tough times, displaying courage, passion, and a relentless zeal for life.

The quality of their work spoke for itself; their clients gave good references to make their business flourish over time. They slowly made transition from a pure account-keeping company to a comprehensive consultancy firm where they guided their clients beyond mere bookkeeping. Today they were responsible for maintenance of accounts, taxation, and internal audit for some of their clients. Over this period, Adarsh had also acquired a degree in law, which gave him a formidable advantage over many competitors.

Once the business or their practice stabilised, Rachel withdrew herself a bit and focussed more on her home, viz. taking care of the kids' education and overall upbringing. She was just as efficient a homemaker as she was a qualified CA. She made the transition from office to home as smoothly as an Olympic cyclist changing lanes without troubling the other fellow cyclists. She planned everything from breakfast to dinner, from ration to fuel consumption, from helping the kids with homework to choosing hobby and sports classes for them and from day-to-day expenses to planning the investments for her family. Not a single penny would go waste in her home and everyone was made to respect money. She always told everyone, including her two daughters, that money was a scarce resource and one should always handle money matters wisely. Even after being confined to the four walls of her home, she kept herself updated on global political and economic developments through newspapers and TV channels. She was a voracious reader, and once the kids were sent to school, she would religiously read two newspapers, watch stock markets, and also read a book—generally a biography, autobiography, or some spiritual journal. She thought it was important for an individual to grow spiritually after a particular age to make his/her existence a worthwhile proposition and effect positive change on the society. Like Adarsh, she was also a regular yoga practitioner. Her activity levels reflected her good health; her demeanour showed her spiritual inclination. She tied her family members in a bond of meaningful existence. She taught her kids to pray, chant mantras from Holy Scriptures, read storybooks, and play a lot without compromising with studies. She also helped Adarsh make bridges with his parents over the last few years. After retirement, his parents had moved back to their ancestral place, a small village tucked in the foothills of the Himalayas in Uttarakhand. Every year Adarsh and Rachel would visit them for fifteen to twenty days along with their daughters in the summers, when Delhi climate became unendurable. Adarsh had bought some twenty-five acres of land just outside his village and converted it into a farmhouse. He made his parents leave their old home and move into this plush, cosy, and comfortable place which offered a nice view of valleys and snow-capped Himalayan range. So Adarsh and Rachel had everything: money, family, and happiness. While work demanded more time from Adarsh, the kids placed huge demands on Rachel's time, owing to their studies and growing age. Life was cruising along nicely; they had nothing to complain about.

It was during one of long drives to their farmhouse that Adarsh told Rachel about opening a share trading account with a bank, on Naren's advice.

'What? A trading account—why? What's the need?' Rachel asked in a tone that lacked her usual softness, inching more towards being called furious.

Adarsh knew that the drive now was more about arguing and convincing than admiring the scenic beauty along the route. 'We need to benefit from what's happening around us. Naren has made more than a crore already in the market and I feel it's time for me to take the plunge too.'

'I shall speak to Lavanya and see what Naren is up to. Till then you won't open any account,' said Rachel, growing impatient. She hated Adarsh being fascinated by others' money.

'I have already opened the account, dear Rachel; it's no big deal—only a small experiment.'

Rachel was quiet. She decided to speak to Naren and understand the matter in detail. She was handling the investments on her own and was doing quite well. They had some mutual funds, bank and fixed deposits, shares of a few blue-chip companies and tax-free bonds of the Reserve Bank of India in their portfolio. Somehow keeping a lid on her anger and frustration, she told Adarsh not to operate the account till she spoke with Naren. Adarsh agreed and smiled slyly, looking at his daughters who were enjoying their video games on the back seat of their newly acquired sedan.

The next week, they went to Naren's place, which was only a stone's throw from their house. Naren was all praises about his trading expedition, and his passion knew no bounds as he spoke about his gains. Adarsh was spellbound—as if he was listening to a master preacher. Rachel was feeling uneasy as she looked at Lavanya, who was busy pouring tea for all of them.

'Rachel, don't worry unnecessarily, Adarsh is a grown-up man. He knows what he is doing and then Naren's also there with him,' Lavanya said.

'We know our limits, darling, not a penny more than one crore,' said Adarsh.

Naren, who was enjoying his tea, spoke again: 'Trust me, Rachel; I shall take care of him personally. I have requested the bank to assign the same RM to both of us and they have agreed to it. Now for Lavanya's sake, please praise the momos.'

Rachel could not help smiling at this even though she was feeling helpless. She made it clear to Adarsh that he wouldn't venture beyond Rs. 1 crore, even if he could afford to. Adarsh agreed like all faithful husbands do. He had the carte blanche from the home ministry, the expertise of his friend Naren, the services of his RM, and a favourable environment in the stock markets. He could not go wrong and he expected himself to learn the tricks of the trade along the way as he understood the balance sheets so very well. 'Don't tell me that Gobind is also there with you in this,' said Rachel.

'How could he not be?' said both of them simultaneously.

Both Lavanya and Rachel gave their husbands mysterious looks.

4

Gobind—the Car Mechanic

Gobind Singh Narwal did not remember his school days as they weren't worth it. His parents worked hard to earn a decent living but could not achieve much materially. All they left behind for Gobind and his six siblings were a small house in the congested JJ Colony and a car workshop in West Delhi. Money was a scarce resource and food a luxury in a family where human values and ethics mattered more than anything else. Being the eldest of the children, Gobind had to take charge of the workshop at an age when he should have been reading storybooks and learning to ride a bicycle. He missed out on his teens when destiny catapulted him straight into adulthood with a spanner in his hand. All he remembered of the past was a hammer's constant tonking against the metal of vehicles, grease-stained hands, and endless hard work. Despite being poor, he never resorted to shortcuts. If a hose pipe could be repaired, he would happily do that; if a radiator leaked, then he knew exactly what needed to be done, same as with shock absorbers and other car parts. He would never ever short-change a customer. With his hard work, he slowly grew the size and scope of his workshop over the years. The number of mechanics, labourers, and customers increased gradually, yet the pace wasn't satisfying. He was hardly making a few thousand rupees every month. He always had this feeling of having little less or deserving more, until a miracle happened.

One evening when he was returning to home after a long hard day, he saw a group of ruffians who were trying to rob an elderly gentleman. It took Gobind only a few seconds to comprehend what was happening. A few young men were beating an old man, trying to snatch his bag, which probably contained cash. They were brandishing knives openly. It seemed that they could kill someone if they had to. They had dragged the passenger out of his car, beaten his driver to a pulp, and almost succeeded in robbing him until Gobind arrived on the scene. Gobind tackled the goons one by one and beat them black and blue with his punches and kicks. He took out his kirpan (a knife which most Sikhs carry) and swore to kill them if they did not vanish immediately. The goons got scared and fled. Since the driver was not in a position to drive, Gobind drove their car and took them to a nursing home first. Later on, he dropped them home. The gentleman named Jagtap Sahay stayed in a mansion in South Delhi. He wanted to return the favour by paying Gobind lot of money, but the latter refused to accept even a single penny. He however insisted that Gobind have dinner with his family and introduced him to his son Naren, who could not thank him enough for his courageous deed. Sahay family knew that Gobind had stood between their patriarch and his death that night. Although Gobind refused to take any money from them, they wanted to return the favour in a very special way.

Jagtap's cousin brother was chairman of the largest car manufacturing company in India. It was only a matter of one phone call and a deposit of a few lacs of rupees for the

Sahay family that Gobind was awarded a car dealership for the entire West Delhi. The land for showroom was also provided by the Sahay family on which Gobind insisted to pay a rent every month. Gobind had no control over his tears when the inauguration of his showroom took place. The first car was purchased by Naren and Adarsh bought the second. Overnight his life shifted from a dingy, potholed, and broken road to an expressway, and he found himself sitting at the steering wheel, hungry to shift gears.

India was growing; real estate prices were going up, especially in areas surrounding Delhi. Demand for new cars was increasing day by day. Earlier car buyers would look for a well-maintained second-hand car but now, thanks to money that they had, everyone wanted to drive a brand-new car purchased from a showroom. Lady Luck seemed to have blessed Gobind at the right time. Before beginning to take the profits from his business, he returned every single penny the Sahay family had invested in him, which brought him closer to Naren.

Being a mechanic himself, Gobind made sure that his service centres provided excellent services to the customers, unlike other car dealers who used their workshops to make more money out of their customers. His fortune continued to swell and money kept flowing in. In five years' time, a poor mechanic who once found it difficult to survive was knocking on the doors of riches. Although his life remained simple, goddess Lakshmi kept him company and showered all her blessings on him. One dealership became two and two became ten, when all of a sudden, Mr Jagtap Sahay passed away. Gobind felt that he lost his father again. He stayed with Naren throughout the thirteen-day mourning period; after all, he was almost like a brother to Naren.

Gobind married Paramjeet—daughter of a grain merchant from Amritsar. She filled the vacuum in Gobind's home and life. After two years of marriage, she gave birth to twins—a boy and a girl. They could not have asked for more. There were grand celebrations in the family. Gobind's sisters were gifted heavy gold jewellery, costly silk saris, and lots of cash. Donations were made to gurdwaras, including Bangla Sahib, where Gobind went every week without fail. They visited the shrine of Vaishno Devi in the state of Jammu and Kashmir and sought blessings from the goddess. Paramjeet found a nice friend in Lavanya and treated her almost like an elder sister. Both families would often meet on weekends over a lunch or dinner.

Gobind's grip on business matters improved over a period of time, thanks to Naren's guidance. Naren used to take lot of interest in Gobind's business and always considered Gobind's family as his own family. Their bond grew stronger as the time passed. Their financial fortunes also moved in sync, although Gobind did not have as much money as Naren. Gobind bought a house in the same block where Naren stayed; in fact, it was Naren who spotted the property and asked Gobind to purchase it. They were closer than ever now. Gobind never lost an opportunity to seek guidance from Naren, whether it was a business matter or a small family affair like choosing school for kids, a holiday destination, or deciding the food menu for a function at home. His world revolved around Naren in almost everything he did, except the occasional peek under the car bonnets that came for servicing at his service centres.

Gobind knew nothing about money except the erstwhile shortage part. Now that he had plenty, he tucked away a handsome amount in bank fixed deposits that earned him interest; he also purchased commercial properties for his business, and Paramjeet, otherwise a lady of simple means, consumed gold voraciously.

It was Naren who introduced Adarsh to Gobind.

'Leave all your accounts worries to him, he is a champ, Gobind,' Naren had said.

No questions were asked and no fees were discussed either. Gobind had appointed Adarsh's firm as his accountant cum auditor cum tax consultant in less than a minute and he never ever repented this decision. Adarsh brought order to an otherwise unorganised business where books were kept only for the sake of bookkeeping. Taxes were paid but never planned. Adarsh personally ensured that financial matters were regularised within no time. He not only helped Gobind save lot of money in taxes but also helped him get the right software and people to man his financial matters. Needless to say, no tax evasion was suggested even remotely. Gobind slowly started to understand the meaning of pre- and post-tax profits, utility of gains and losses, and the benefits of paying the accurate taxes regularly. What Gobind lacked in sophistication and finesse was made up by his instincts and sheer guts that one often required in business. Naren's guidance, Adarsh's financial acumen, and Gobind's guts took the business to new levels, where Gobind rubbed shoulders with the elite, walked with the privileged few, and flew high with the ambitious clan.

Life was going good and he had no complaints to make to anyone. Often when he looked back, he would see the faces of Mr Jagtap Sahay and Naren. They were god-sent angels who lifted him from lanes of poverty and comfortably placed him in a zone of luxury and comforts. Each night before going to sleep, he remembered Naren and Mr Sahay before he thanked God for all his blessings.

5

Ripples of Excitement

Naren had first met up with Adarsh during a corporate meeting. Adarsh was representing the investors who were willing to buy a stake in Naren's business. Generally these meetings and negotiations are dog-eat-dog types and 'I know more than you, stupid' kind of meetings, where both parties negotiate hard, forgetting human values quite often. To Naren's surprise, the element of human ego was almost absent from the meetings he held with the opposite party, and one of the reasons for this happening was presence of Adarsh, who led the negotiations from the front, placing each party's interests and benefits on the table in a transparent manner. His client, an original equipment manufacturer (OEM) was gaining a lot by doing backward integration and also got a foothold in the booming Indian subcontinent. Naren, on the other hand, was getting a fat reward for running a family business professionally and efficiently. He would not only get more capital to expand his business but would also get access to expertise of his prospective partners. Adarsh had mentioned to his client that paying a premium for a pie of this business was justified, given the benefits they would derive out of this venture. There was no thumping of tables, no corporate tongue-lashing and no swearing for each other's blood, and absolutely no throwing of tantrum on both the sides. Naren was so impressed with Adarsh that he had made a decision in his mind to appoint Adarsh his auditor and financial consultant after the cooling period was over, and he managed to do it. Later on, they realised that this feeling was mutual when Adarsh told Naren that even he was positively moved by Naren's no-nonsense approach.

Adarsh came on board as a tax and financial consultant and the impact of this decision was soon evident on Naren's business.

Although Naren had amassed a lot more in terms of money and zeros in his bank account, Adarsh never felt he had any less, maybe because of his acumen. In fact, this thought of having less than Naren never passed his mind. Life cruised along fine for both of them, year after year of piling up luxuries and every other element that could make life comfortable and worthwhile. Lavanya and Rachel never interfered in their relationship, although Rachel had never approved of this stock market adventure of theirs. Lavanya was indifferent, and the kids always thought that their parents had more money than they could ever count.

Adarsh made his beginning in the stock market very cautiously, not moving beyond few lacs initially, while Naren had a bigger stake in this game since beginning. Stock markets were bubbly, giving both of them more reasons to stay happy and cheerful.

Such is the charm of gains in the stock market. They fuel the investors with more ambition each passing day.

That these investments were becoming an obsession for both of them was reflected in their behaviour and mannerism. They would often slip to a quiet corner during a family dinner or a corporate function and discuss about their shares, count their gains, and make plans about minting more money through stock markets. Their investments were doing well and the stock market indices were zooming day after day. Their conversations were now less about family and business, more about stock markets and shares. They would regularly watch business channels that showed real-time movement of share prices and counted their chickens throughout the day. Their respective businesses were doing well which gave them more time for their stock market adventures. These initial gains not only made Adarsh soon reach the threshold of his one-crore limit but also prompted him to invest more without telling Rachel.

Gobind used to wonder what these two talked about. He did not understand what a million dollars was or, for that matter, what a healthy balance sheet meant. All he knew was that Adarsh and Naren were far more intelligent than he was. Since the three of them did most of the things together, Gobind had immediately agreed to be part of this adventure. Paramjeet did not take active interest in Gobind's business, so there was no question of her being opposed to Gobind's share market foray. She knew Gobind was hard-working and intelligent enough to take care of his money, plus Naren and Adarsh were anyways there with him.

So here they were, three friends from well-to-do backgrounds, their businesses booming, fortunes soaring, not many liabilities and too much money at their disposal. Experimenting a bit with the equity markets with a part of their money wasn't something that they got too much hassled about. The timing could not have been better as stock markets were beginning to grow decently.

What more could a novice ask for?

Naren, Adarsh, and Gobind were enjoying the ride to money, glory, and success. This was in early 1998, when Indian markets started following their global counterparts the way kids followed the Pied Piper in the town of Hamelin in Germany. Infotech was the name of the game and hordes of Internet start-ups and software development firms were starting their operations and raising money from investors to fund their growth. India, being one of the developing markets, offered cheap yet skilled workforce that was helping some of these firms service their customers. A lot of software firms were either sending their engineers abroad to work on foreign assignments or they were using their Indian offices to service their customers based mainly in the US and Europe.

Only a few years back, the Indian stock market investors did not know much beyond Bank (State Bank of India), Lever (Hindustan Lever), and a couple of metal and cement companies. But now these new software and technology companies were slowly eating the mindshare of investors who believed that ways of doing business would change forever with the advent of the Internet. As a result, any company related to this field found its business flourishing and stock prices zooming. The Internet and software wave had captured the fancy of investors across the globe which reflected in the buoyancy of global stock markets.

Naren and his two friends were part of that group of investors who were enjoying this joyride of increasing stock prices. They couldn't have asked for a better start.

Many investors try their luck in stock markets, but only a few are able to make money. The trio belonged to the latter category. At least their beginning suggested that.

They began on a very strong footing, like Sachin Tendulkar opening the innings in a one-dayer and scoring a century within the first ten overs, setting a platform for the other batsmen to come and slog. This was an overwhelming start, leading them to think about stocks most of the time. Naren was busy with the post-stake sale integration with his new partners, shuttling between Delhi and Berlin quite often. Adarsh had his hands full, owing to the fierce level of activity on the tax-filing front, and Gobind knew no rest as everyone in Delhi wanted to have a car desperately. The money-spinning machine was working overtime for the three friends, and there was no reason for it to stop as whatever they got into made money for them. They saw the graph of their investments move only one way, thanks to their dynamic and intelligent relationship manager. Her presence in their lives was synonymous to prosperity.

And with the early gains pouring in, the game had barely begun.

6

The Addiction of Gains

Naren had started his investment experiment in April 1997. Adarsh came on board three months later in July. Gobind, who was last to join the gravy train of gains, started his journey of fortune in the month of November. The three of them had different levels of understanding when it came to their investments. Naren understood this game better than the other two because he was the first one to start a portfolio; the other two simply followed him. Technically, Adarsh was more qualified to understand this field, but he didn't bother much beyond a point, as Naren had full control over the situation. Every time Rachel asked him about the status of their investments, she got a detailed statement from Naren's office. Gobind did not bother at all; he knew he would never understand stock markets no matter how hard he tried. Naren kept track of their investments and he knew nothing could go wrong. Anyways, he had invested only a small amount of Rs. 2 crores. He did not know the exact numbers, but he knew that Adarsh and Naren had a far bigger exposure to the stock market in comparison to his.

Naren used to meet his relationship manager, now their relationship manager, every week. Her name was Sonia. She was one of the few students who were picked by the bank from their MBA school campus as management trainees.

After completing her probation, she was moved to the priority banking division, which handled large customers of the bank and provided specialised services in investments and banking. She was given a list of existing customers by her boss, with an agenda to sell more and more investment products to them so that the bank could make more revenue. Her salary and incentives were linked to the revenues she made. Typically a relationship manager (RM) had to earn revenue of minimum three times (called 3X in industry parlance) of her salary to justify her cost. Whatever he or she earned above this threshold of 3X was divided in the ratio of 75:25, with 75 per cent going back to the bank and 25 per cent coming to the RM. She was not only required to increase the wallet share from the bank's existing clients but also carried targets for acquiring new customers. The bank monitored her targets on a quarterly basis, and so far, Sonia had been doing exceedingly well. At the end of the first year she had a book worth Rs. 25 crores divided into mutual funds, insurance, deposits, and stocks.

The bank made revenue of 2 per cent on mutual funds, 1 per cent on stocks and in excess of 20 per cent in the case of insurance. So, most of the RMs preferred to sell insurance. Sonia was different. She was methodical, organised, and sensible when it came to guiding her clients. For her, moneymaking was important but not critical. She never compromised with the client's interests, no matter how much revenue she or the bank lost. She maintained good relations with her clients and followed a strict regime of client engagement. She knew their financial needs and goals like the back of her hand. Being young herself, she used her profession as a means to advance her own learning.

She was a voracious reader and used to share her knowledge with her clients too. Reading kept her updated about the developments in the dynamic world of investments that was changing by the minute especially in the time of the Internet era, when information was only a click away. Sonia had been working only for a couple of years when things started heating up in India. Stock markets were buzzing with activity, and new mutual funds were getting launched. As a banker, she had access to so much information that she had no time left for herself after reading. She would carry a lot of material back home, often reading late into the night. She would wake up early morning and hook up to the Internet through her dial-up MTNL connection. She would read about equity markets and mutual funds in the USA. She believed that Indian markets would also follow the same growth trajectory as American and European markets. She would download interesting articles and mail them to her clients. When she visited her clients, she would carry a copy of the articles she had mailed to the client, with the relevant portion of the text duly highlighted with a marker. No matter how much she studied, she was still inexperienced and she knew this fact well. She worked very hard to learn the tricks of the trade. She met all her clients once a month, but the rate at which she was acquiring new clients, it was becoming difficult for her to maintain the monthly frequency. Every morning, she spent one hour reviewing her client portfolios and analysed their performances. She had to send a monthly report to each client as part of the bank's agreement with the clients. She did this religiously every month, keeping all internal approvals in place before time so that the clients didn't have to wait. In two years' time, her book size had grown to Rs. 60 crores. The bank had earned roughly Rs. 0.75 crores from her book last year. Her salary being only Rs. 5 lacs per year, she had to only make revenue of Rs. 15 lacs for the bank, and the rest was divided according to the formula. This year she was in for a bonus of Rs. 15 lacs (minus taxes) which was more than 200 per cent of her salary, thanks to her three new clients, who accounted for a lion's share of her book.

Although this kind of bonus was a luxury, her top three clients being 75 per cent of her book meant concentration of risk in her book. If these three clients were to walk away, her book would reduce to a number that would make her survival difficult in the bank. She thought of not only acquiring more new clients but also strengthening relationships with the trio so that they wouldn't give her a nasty surprise one day. While pondering over the summary of her client book one morning, she observed interesting things. This is what her book looked like:

31 July 1997					
Name of the Client	Bank FD	Direct Stocks	Equity Mutual Funds	Insurance	Total*
Naren Sahay	5	7.5	1	0	13.50
Adarsh Srivastava	2	0	3	0.15	5.15
Gobind Singh Narwal	4	0	1	0.15	5.15
others	10	1	1	1	13.00
Total	21	8.5	6	1.3	36.80
%age	57.07%	23.10%	16.30%	3.53%	100.00%
*amount in Rs. crores					

31 January 1998					
Name of the Client	Bank FD	Stocks	Equity Mutual Funds	Insurance	Total*
Naren Sahay	5	15	9.50	0.50	30.00
Adarsh Srivastava	2	5	1.00	0.00	8.00
Gobind Singh Narwal	2	4	1.00	0.00	7.00
others	2	2	9.00	1.00	15.00
Total	11	26	21.50	1.50	60.00
%age	18.00%	43.00%	36.00%	3.00%	100.00%
*amount in Rs. crores					

She didn't need to be Ramanujan to analyse the shift in her client preferences over the last year. Her fixed deposit book had shrunk significantly and the direct stocks book had grown from 8 crores to 26 crores, a jump of 200 per cent, thanks to the booming stock market. A whopping 79 per cent of her book was in direct stocks and mutual funds now, so she wanted stock markets to keep doing well. Although she wouldn't make as much revenue on stocks as on insurance, this could open the floodgates of fortune on her. The trio was responsible for it and she knew it very well. While Naren was the biggest of the three, other two were also significant, looking at the money they were making. Probably they had money parked in other banks which was hidden from her. This shift in preference also meant that her future depended a lot on how the equity markets behaved in future. Her mutual fund book that grew by approximately 250 per cent was mainly composed of sectoral funds that invested in the infotech sector where boom was in bloom. She wasn't sure of whether to be happy or worried about this fact. She had to do something to add stability to her book and to her client portfolios. As she was experiencing these mixed emotions early in the morning, she saw her mobile phone flash. She had received an SMS which read, 'You are about to become the youngest banker to achieve 70 crores of book size in the first two years of joining the bank and win the prestigious Phoenix award—Boss'.

Winning the Phoenix award was a dream come true for every banker. Only five bankers from each country qualified every two years for this contest. They were flown to the global headquarters of the bank to be felicitated by the chairman of the bank. Everyone wanted to qualify but only a few achieved this distinction, and she knew this award was up for grabs this time for her. She set up a meeting with Naren. She needed ten more crores from her clients and trio could come in handy for this purpose.

She felt an irrepressible impulse to win this contest.

For the moment, everything else took a back seat; everything stopped mattering as Phoenix became the sole reason for her existence. She would worry about stability later; for now she had to win the contest at any cost.

She was surprised to see both Adarsh and Gobind with Naren. This was the first time she met the three of them together. They met at a plush business club at a five-star where Naren had a membership. After exchange of greetings, the conversation moved to investments, and Sonia couldn't help noticing the swagger in Naren's tone.

Money was talking. She smiled.

'Sonia, thanks a lot for being our RM. We are so happy being with you,' Naren said.

'Thank you, sir.' Sonia looked at the other two and gestured politely.

It was Adarsh's turn to speak now. He asked, 'What do you feel about markets from here on, do you think infotech companies' stock prices can keep moving up like this?'

Sonia knew about Adarsh's academic background and his strength and capabilities with numbers. She was ready for this question.

'Sir, it's not so much about the stock prices. We believe that the Internet is going to change the way we live and do our business. Efficiency levels shall move up and a huge disintermediation shall take place, posing a challenge for traditional brick-and-mortar models. Stock prices are only a by-product of this huge social and economic change. Earnings of the companies shall grow multifold as use of the Internet shall reduce costs of doing business. This is only the beginning. The real fun is yet to come.'

Adarsh was a man of details. He did not like vague and far-sighted statements to affect his life and investments. He wasn't satisfied with Sonia's response; his face clearly showed it.

Sonia continued, 'Sir, this is not a price movement phenomenon. New businesses are cropping up in the field of technology. Everything from our mobile phones to our aeroplanes is going to be controlled by software written by engineers. Look at the way our lifestyles are changing, and most of it is because of either technology or the Internet. From an investment perspective, one has to identify and invest in these new businesses today in order to reap the benefits tomorrow. To provide you more insights into this sector and related investments, you must come to one of these sessions that we organize for our investors. We invite investment experts from various mutual funds who give a pep talk about investing in this sector.'

Still not convinced, Adarsh decided not to push further. He would find someone who was more mature and knowledgeable than Sonia. Gobind and Naren did not ask much to Sonia for different reasons. Naren had made too much money from her advice and Gobind worshipped Naren, so there was no reason to disbelieve or doubt her. Naren had made up his mind to increase his stock market exposure by another 7 to 8 crores, and Gobind also wanted to contribute something, so as to come closer to Adarsh's investment amount.

'Both of us are providing you an additional ten crores, you may see how it needs to be allocated among mutual funds and stocks. We leave it up to you,' Naren said with a smile.

Sonia was happy. Although she did not like Adarsh's expression, the additional ten crores from the other two meant that the prized Phoenix contest was in her pocket. As soon as her meeting ended, she messaged to her boss— 'Additional 10 crore investments from clients. Phoenix tamed.'

Her clients were getting addicted to stock market gains.

She was already making shopping plans in her mind. London was calling and she was ready to fly.

7

Dhandha (Business) at Any Cost

'Owing to the steady progress you are making, I am recommending you for a double promotion, although I must not be telling you this as I am your boss.'

Sonia felt a tide surge in her veins. Her eyes acquired a mystical glint in anticipation of success. She had hardly spent any time in the bank and she was getting promoted way ahead of her peers. This meant a lot for her career and life.

Her boss continued, 'People like you are invaluable to the management. They not only ensure a bigger, better, and more prosperous future for our stakeholders but for themselves too. When you visit the headquarters later this year, you shall feel the might of the institution that you are working with. Our bank's rich heritage of best practices in customer services has made us earn the trust of millions of customers across the globe to put us a cut above the rest.'

She was spellbound at the eloquence and charm with which her boss spoke. His baritone voice was one to die for and his mannerism encouraged involuntary emulation. He was tall, dark, and handsome. His understanding of the banking industry was thorough and comprehensive. His control on operations was immaculate and his track record enviable by any standards. He was the youngest zonal head in India and for the right reasons. Sonia was slowly drowning in her own fancy when her boss's voice fell on her eardrums again.

'Sonia, the reputation carries a price tag only a few can afford. Our priority bank customers come to us because they can afford our services and pay our fees. They are those blue-blooded human beings who have excess of everything, including money. They have built their businesses by making obscene money from small customers like us. They need to be given absolutely the best services and, in turn, charged exorbitant fees. Because for them, anything cheap is infra dig. They are the bastions of capitalism who practice socialism only on page 3. We need to make sure that we make our margins from their money and lead a lifestyle like theirs by milking them for the services we provide,' her boss added.

'Make the most of it when the going is good, like these days, when markets are on song, even if it means that you have to compromise on the asset allocation.'

Sonia did not mention that she was already making a compromise by not alerting her clients who had gone overboard in direct stocks. She was a little surprised to see her boss talk like this. She always thought that he was a highly principled banker, which obviously was a wrong notion of hers, as now he was asking her to compromise on the vital elements of investment management and advisory. She bore a confused look, and her boss seemed to have read her face.

'Sonia, dilemma is for fools and idealism is for idiots. There is no perfect solution to determine a balance between the client's and our interests. We all have to achieve the economic objective of the bank first and mould the interests of our clients accordingly. If we were to become Mahatma Gandhi, then we shall have to wear handwoven cotton clothes and not pinstriped suits. Who hasn't made compromises at critical junctures in life? Did Arjuna not compromise when he killed Karna, while the latter was trying to pull his chariot's wheel out of mud? Did Rama not compromise when he hit Ravana's navel because of the information provided by Vibhishan? Winners are remembered for the final result and not for the proverbial cul-de-sacs they often find themselves in. Think beyond Phoenix; take a look at the bigger picture. Your capabilities and potential can take you places. I looked at your book and found out more information on your larger clients. You have a group of three clients who are worth at least 300 crores. They have large deposits with other banks which you need to target ASAP. Sonia, you haven't learnt the tricks of the trade yet. Direct stocks are the largest proportion of your book and the bank makes the least amount of revenue on them which also means there is a great scope for improvement in your quarterly incentives. I suggest that you do the following. One, move some part of your stocks to mutual funds, where we earn much more. Two, introduce margin trading to your clients, so that your direct stock grows multifold immediately. Three, get them to break their deposits with other banks and move this money to our bank. Four, make your clients buy and sell shares regularly. We make money every time they buy or sell. Five, make these guys feel precious and rich every time you meet them and sell them insurance where we make more than 20 per cent.'

Sonia was really impressed with the legwork that her boss had done. She was also aware of the combined wealth of three of her largest clients but she hadn't made any real attempt to increase her wallet share with them. She was happy with the book she already had. Although she did not completely agree with her boss's ideas, she could pick and chose what suited her most without hurting her clients. She did not know much about margin trading, so she decided to find a stockbroker who could help her understand this. She was OK with her clients moving their deposits from other banks to hers as it had no risk element involved. She knew she had undersold insurance, so a big fat policy for each of his clients could easily be recommended. They wouldn't mind the bank milking them a bit.

Her boss spoke again. 'Sonia, don't use heart in matters where brain can do a better job. Keep emotions and feelings aside in business matters. If you have to rise through the glass ceiling and touch the sky beyond clouds then you have to become a hard-core professional who stays at the edge of cutthroat competition. I see you among the top ten RMs globally. You have that zing and spark, dear, believe me.'

She was so excited to hear this.

Could she really be among the top ten RMs as her boss was saying? She did not show any reaction though. She kept listening to her boss carefully.

'My dear girl, you need to chalk out a detailed plan to make your three jokers eat out of your hands. You need to convince them to increase their exposure to the markets through margin trading. This is your key to the corporate stardom that many of the RMs dream about day in and day out. I have decided to attach a stock market analyst with you. He is a bright young man who shall help you with his research and expertise. He shall also monitor your client portfolios actively and provide buy and sell calls. He shall accompany you for the client meetings should you need his services. But remember one thing, Sonia. He is an analyst and not a salesperson like you. He may have his own ideals but I want you to keep the bank's commercial objectives in mind. I shall call him in now.'

He quickly walked towards his large mahogany table and pressed a button on his desk phone. He punched four keys and Sonia heard a beep on the speakerphone. After a few seconds, an energetic voice answered the phone.

'Chaitanya, can you please come in here?'

'Yes, boss,' was all Chaitanya could say before the boss disconnected.

Sonia saw an Adonis in his late twenties walk in through the door.

Her heart skipped a beat involuntarily.

Chaitanya was a good-looking man who could set a girl's heart on fire by winking from a thousand-mile distance. She felt strangely magnetised by his appearance. They would soon work as a team, meeting and entertaining clients together. Excitement was an understatement for the state of mind she found herself in. She could already feel little bubbles of mystique softly bursting inside her. Her eyes gleamed and she wondered if Chaitanya could read her feelings through them.

'Sonia, this is Chaitanya,' the boss spoke softly.

Sonia who was by now frozen in her reverie was blank and offered no reaction.

'Sonia, meet Chaitanya—one of our best research analysts,' he spoke again but got no response.

The boss walked across the large table and touched her shoulder in a manner that appeared subtle but was strong enough to dislodge her from the cloud nine she was floating on. Sonia felt as if someone had passed a stream of electric current through her veins.

She was startled, embarrassed, and apparently a little disappointed with herself. She thought she revealed too much in those few seconds but quickly recovered from her hallucination. She got up from her seat and extended a hand to Chaitanya.

'Hi, I am Sonia,' she said in a tone which was more professional than feminine, although she wanted it to be the other way round.

No one spoke for the next few minutes except their boss who sang encomiums about Chaitanya and his abilities.

'Sonia, Chaitanya is one of our brightest analysts. He has a strong understanding of local as well as global markets. He has spent couple of years on our treasury desk in Singapore and carries tons of relevant experience when it comes to investing. His understanding of the Indian stock market is second to none, and he has an uncanny knack of picking the winners from a group of shares. The bank's proprietary book has benefited a lot from his stock picking. He has a passion for numbers and carries a strong analytical skill set. I think you two shall be a formidable duo. Both the bank and your clients should benefit a lot from this move of ours.

'Chaitanya, now I don't want to tire myself out by introducing Sonia to you. You already know enough about her, don't you? I anyways have to rush for a meeting with the country head. So you guys help yourselves in knowing each other,' the boss said.

Chaitanya smiled and nodded positively. It meant the meeting was over and it was up to them to decide the future course of action. Both of them exchanged their mobile numbers and decided to touch base soon.

8

Chemistry

No matter how hard she tried, she couldn't stop herself from sending a message to Chaitanya. Nervous fingers followed her heart's instructions, turning a deaf ear to whatever little her brain had to offer.

'I am EXCITED to be working with you as a team. It shall be fun. Sonia.' She typed and pressed the Send key on her sleek Nokia handphone. She held her breath for a few moments as she expected a quick reply. Nothing happened; no 'beep beep' sound came back. Seconds became minutes and minutes turned into hours and still nothing. She was unsure of her action now. Puzzled, she went to sleep still harbouring a hope in her heart. She kept tossing in her bed the whole night, and various thoughts crossed her mind. Needless to say, all these thoughts were about Chaitanya.

Was she in love already?

She jerked herself out of bed as her alarm went off early, at 5 a.m., found her way to the switch, and flicked the light on. She remembered her parents and their deity by closing her eyes for a minute or so and started her morning lazily. Last night's thought still hung on her mind like a reluctant Delhi fog. She was feeling really stupid having messaged Chaitanya.

Did she act too soon? Shouldn't she have held him at some distance for some time rather than letting her anchor down at the drop of a hat?

'Stupid, stupid, stupid, Sonia—you are completely stupid,' she found herself muttering under her breath. Nervously she picked up her mobile phone from her study table and checked for the messages.

There was no reply from anyone. Not that anyone mattered. She wanted a reply from someone who hadn't bothered to respond.

She was so upset with herself that she wanted to throw her phone out of window. This dumb piece never beeped when she needed it most. She wanted her phone's beep to keep pace with the lub-dub of her heartbeats but a phone was a phone, an electronic device without any emotion whatsoever. She felt bad and desperate.

'Did I do the right thing?

'Did he see my message?

'Is he ignoring me?

'What will he think of me?

'Did my message reach him at all?

'Will he reply?'

Questions jumped in her mind like corn kernels in a popcorn maker. Each new question took her frustration to a new peak. She was beginning to think that she had committed a huge mistake by taking this chance. She shouldn't have sent that message to Chaitanya. Now that the bullet had left the barrel, she could not do anything. Her worst fear was that she still had to face Chaitanya.

'Gosh! How awkward will that be?' She talked to herself.

She was bobbing up and down in the ocean of desperation amid the tides of fear and anxiety that were tearing her apart. No shores were in sight till the 'beep beep' sound went off. She ran to her phone and immediately checked the incoming message. It was indeed from Chaitanya.

'I am equally thrilled with the prospect of working with you—Chaitanya☺.'

Sonia looked skywards and thanked her angels. She read the message at least a hundred times and thought of responding to it but something held her back. Something inside her asked her to exercise restraint, which was indeed difficult for her.

Then throwing all caution to the winds, she picked up her phone and typed again.

'When do we meet to chalk out the action plan?'

'4 pm at office canteen,' pat came the reply.

By now she had decided to play the game of heart. She had never felt like this for anyone until now. Her fingers sportingly kissed the keypad of her phone to type another subtly tingling message.

'Looking forward to it, although 4 is too late. How shall I wait until then?' She let her guard completely down now and sent this message. She knew the reply would come and it did come.

'There are a few things in life that are worth the wait and I hope this is one of them. Waiting shall be difficult for me as well. :)'

She couldn't believe her luck. This wasn't happening, until she pinched herself.

'Am I dreaming?' she wondered before replying. She thought hard about her next step and found herself even more confused than she initially was.

'Can we meet at some other place? Office canteen is drab and boring.'

'Let's meet at the coffee home opposite Mohan Singh Place then. ☺'

'Nope, I don't like that place. It's too noisy.'

'What about coffee shop at the Meridian?'

'That's too costly dear,' Sonia replied.

'Then think of a quiet and cost-effective place and lemme know. I have to rush off for a couple of early morning meetings. See you at 4 ☺'

Sonia answered happily, 'Aaarite, I shall. See you at 4 but you have to find a place and let me know.'

She was floating few levels above the cloud nine and her joys knew no bounds. The popcorn turned into snowflakes and filled her with dreams of Santa Claus who had personally come to deliver love's bounty to her doorstep. Even if it was her first meeting with him, she was getting an unusual feeling about this. She knew this was only a beginning of something more exciting, something more romantic and something more worthwhile. Chaitanya would not only add more meat to her efforts professionally but could also bring much more happiness to her personally. She looked at the armoury of her cosmetics and smiled like a teenage girl, surprised at the pace of her heartbeats.

Was she thinking too much too soon? She didn't care as long as her spirit guided her in the right direction, on the path of love.

She was pleasantly surprised to see Chaitanya already standing at the door of Gaylord Cafe, next to Rivoli cinema in Connaught Place. They shook hands and greeted each other with expectant smiles. Chaitanya had booked a table for two; this certainly pleased Sonia. She knew the difference between a respectful man and a chivalrous lad.

They started their discussion with Sonia giving a brief account of her client book, product-wise and client-wise breakdown and background of a few of her leading clients. Chaitanya could spot the unmistakable quiver in her voice, the blush on her cheeks, and the subtle expectation in her eyes that belonged to a woman filled with desires.

He in turn told her about his work in great detail. Sonia was impressed by the way Chaitanya spoke and explained. He weighed his words in his mind before speaking. To Sonia, his mouth was like an ATM; what came out was only what was necessary—not a penny less, not a penny more. He was passionate about his work, understood his responsibilities, and thought a lot. He had never worked with individual investors earlier, so he was keenly looking forward to this opportunity. He carefully took notes in his black spiral notebook, jotting down even minute details about the clients whom he was going to meet shortly. He asked many questions in order to further his understanding of the clients' background and behaviour. Sonia was even more impressed now. She observed Chaitanya's mature handwriting, his meticulous way of using the blank spaces in the notebook, and his ability to focus. No wonder he was a leading analyst in the bank's team. She observed that he was very quick with numbers and was noting down percentages wherever required. He asked her about the history of transactions and Sonia provided him with a bundle of printouts which she had brought with her. He would go through them later to understand the pattern of investments of Sonia's clients.

Sonia felt good; she felt strangely complete in his presence. She often looked into his eyes while sipping her coffee and noticed Chaitanya's discomfort whenever they made eye contact. She liked his expression which was a hybrid of confusion and masculine blush (if any existed). They spent two hours together, mostly discussing the clients, markets, and the bank. She wondered how time flew in his company. Chaitanya paid the bill and they left soon thereafter. Sonia was so lost in her reverie that she did not even discuss about the future course of action with him. Ideally she should have done so. But she was thrilled at this work-in-progress item because it meant meeting Chaitanya again and having soft goosebumps. It was getting darker and neither of them wanted to go back to the office.

'Can I drop you somewhere, Sonia?'

Sonia couldn't help smiling at her luck. 'I am going home, so you can surely drop me somewhere, in case you are also travelling in that direction.'

'Where do you stay?'

'Sarvodaya Enclave near IIT Delhi.'

'Great, I stay in RK Puram, so I can take a small detour and drop you home,' he said casually.

It was almost a thirty-minute drive. Chaitanya dropped her at the corner of the street and waited till she entered her building. They waved at each other and smiled too.

Chaitanya heard a 'beep beep' sound on his phone; he knew who it was even without looking at the screen. While waiting at a crossing, he picked up his mobile and checked the message.

'Thanks for coming, your company means a lot—Sonia.'

He smiled. He was beginning to like her.

'I am equally privileged to know and work with you ☺,' he typed and sent.

Over the next few days, Chaitanya studied Sonia's client portfolios. He looked at the trades, holding period, number of shares, mutual fund holdings, fixed deposits, and other information that was provided in the printouts Sonia had given him. He combined this with the information that Sonia gave orally. He made comprehensive notes on each of the clients, carefully classifying them in various risk categories. He wanted to know more about them in order to help them more effectively. Since three of her clients constituted the bulk of her book, they were the most important ones for the time being. He had to meet them, know them, and probably help them along the way. To him they were the golden goose for Sonia who could bring more revenues to the bank. He called up Sonia and asked her to fix up meetings with Naren, Adarsh, and Gobind.

The meetings were set up for the coming week.

Snowflakes were slowly turning into mild volcanoes, teasing and testing Sonia day and night.

9

Internet—the Synonym of Nirvana

The world of the Internet was coming into being slowly but surely. More and more dot-com companies were being born in the USA. Everyone was convinced that these companies were going to change the way people lived, shopped, ate, travelled, enjoyed themselves, and everything else that one could think of. The Internet was a medium that could potentially change the future of countries and societies at large, and this was reflected in the number of infotech and dot-com ventures that were started during those years. A lot of these companies found their way to the capital markets trying to raise money from individual and institutional investors. The excitement that first started in the USA found its ripples reaching Indian shores very soon. Although a few Indian infotech companies had tapped the market with their initial public offernigs in early nineties, they had not made much impact on the investors' minds. It was only towards end of 1997 that investors found themselves tracking these stocks day and night. Institutional investors like mutual funds began to participate in this sector, providing retail investors an opportunity to be part of this excitement.

National Stock Exchange of India (NSE)—one of the leading stock exchanges in India—launched the CNX IT index to help investors track this sector. This index had a base value of 1000 on 1 January 1996 that managed to reach only 1041 after one year, i.e. 1 April 1997, barely rising by 4 per cent over this period. However, the action picked up during 1997 when this index started taking bigger leaps. By the end of June 1997, the index was at 1574 points, gaining by a whopping 50 per cent during this period and by another 52 per cent by the end of December 1997, reaching 2399. During the last quarter of the year 1997–98, the CNX IT index increased by almost 1000 points to reach 3422, which meant that the index increased from 1041 to 3422 during the financial year 1997, a gain of almost 229 per cent, which most of the investors hadn't seen earlier. This surge in stock markets brought unparalleled exhilaration and excitement to everyone, including Sonia, Chaitanya, Naren, Adarsh, and Gobind. Naren was the most excited among the three friends.

CNX IT index was composed of twenty stocks from the IT sector, which represented the IT sector in India. As the stock prices of these companies increased, the index also increased. As the index went up, the volumes increased too. As per an estimate, only 1.12 lac shares were traded in CNX IT on 31 March 1997 and the turnover was approximately Rs. 1 crore. In one year's time, this increased to 18 lac shares and 64 crores. However, during 1998, these figures went up multifold to 76 lac shares and 424 crores. This only meant one thing—the interest and participation in the IT sector was going up in India, just as it was happening in USA. The ripples of excitement turned into a tide that leapt with intensity unseen hitherto. More and more investors wanted to jump into this ocean of ecstasy to enjoy the tides of enrichment.

It was during this period that Naren was introduced to Babu Bhai Calcuttawala—a stockbroker who was known as BBC in his close circles. He bumped into BBC at a dinner and cocktail party hosted by the bank for its clients. One of the leading mutual funds was launching an infotech fund, which would invest the money in Infotech sector shares. The bank arranged a presentation by the fund manager for the select clients of the bank. If such a presentation was organized about a year back, it would have been quite difficult for the bank to get enough customers to attend the same. But things were different now. Since the stock markets were doing well, clients were more than willing to attend these functions, to know more about markets, particularly infotech share prices, and to get an occasional tip about some share which could double their money in two months' time.

Generally a fund manager would talk about the infotech sector at large and then give a spiel about why India was a unique opportunity. He would talk about the growth that had already taken place and give examples of a few stocks that had already earned millions for the investors. Names like Wipro, Infosys, and Satyam had already found their way into a common investor's stock market lexicon, and every time these names were mentioned, the audience would feel at home as if these three were the money plants growing in their own backyards. These three had made their IPO investors fairly rich by now.

Then the best part would come. Some new names would be discussed which would be slated to become the next Infosys and Wipro, and spin millions of rupees for the investors. Lofty share price projections would be shown on the large screen to attract people. Good things were said about the infotech revolution and how it would bring a comprehensive change in not only the way businesses were done but also how our societies functioned. The Internet was the next big bang which would lead to new creations. That would sweep a bigger change than most of the investors anticipated, which only meant that one could reap a bonanza by investing in infotech funds like this one.

BBC listened to the presentation quite patiently and asked a few pertinent questions when the session was thrown open for discussion. Being a stockbroker, he had to use a bank for holding not only his proprietary funds but also client funds, and the balances usually ran into crores. Although BBC did not need a bank's advice for stock market investments, Sonia had still invited him. He could become a large customer for insurance or mutual funds. The trio of Naren, Gobind, and Adarsh did not ask any questions to the fund manager as they did not have any, partly because they believed in the potential of the infotech sector and partly because they completely trusted Sonia. If this fund was good for them, she would anyways let them know. Sonia was going to recommend investing in this fund anyways as she needed more revenue for the bank and a fat bonus for herself. There was no risk in it since markets were doing well.

'Sir, meet Chaitanya. He is one of the analysts working on the treasury desk of the bank. He shall be working along with me to help my clients. Chaitanya, please meet Mr Sahay, Mr Srivastava, and Mr Singh. They are my largest clients,' Sonia said as she introduced them to each other.

'Pleased to meet you, young man, I believe we have a meeting with you next week. And, Sonia, you may address us by our first names,' said a smiling Naren.

'Yes, sir, I shall. But it may take some time,' Sonia said.

'I look forward to meeting you, sir. Meanwhile could I get you something to drink?' asked Chaitanya.

The trio politely declined by saying that they would take care of themselves.

'Sir, let me introduce Babu Bhai Calcuttawala also known as BBC in the broking circles. He is one of the leading stockbrokers in India and has a large research team covering most of the stocks. Their speciality is picking up the small stocks early,' Sonia said. The trio had noticed Babu Bhai asking questions to the fund manager. They thought that BBC must know a lot about stock markets since he was a broker who spent lot of time watching markets and trading in stocks. Sonia left BBC with them and moved to attend more guests. The conversation started with self-introductions and exchange of cards.

BBC noticed Gobind's card and said, 'Mr Singh, I am a regular customer of your company. I purchased my first car from your showroom in Green Park.'

Gobind swelled with pride and smiled ear to ear, saying, 'I hope you are happy with our services.'

'Absolutely and I would like to provide you my services someday, we have lot of customers who come to our office for trading in stocks,' BBC said.

'We are happy with the bank for now. They have been advising us on the stocks and the mutual funds too.' Adarsh spoke with a tinge of scepticism, which was noticed by BBC.

'We are the suppliers of research to most of the banks and they act on our advice to suggest to you the stocks to be bought or sold,' BBC said with great enthusiasm.

Naren anticipated a tug of war developing between Adarsh and BBC. He pulled Adarsh's arm and said, 'Let's get another peg of whiskey.' Both of them moved to the counter that served liquor, leaving Gobind with BBC. From the corner they stood in, they could see Gobind having a prolonged discussion with BBC. Since it was Gobind who did most of the talking, they assumed that the discussion was about cars, not stocks. Soon, Sonia joined Gobind and BBC, and now it was difficult to assume what was being discussed between the three of them. Adarsh and Naren decided to join the party.

'Babu Bhai, you have been there in the markets for more than fifteen years now. What do you think about the current markets?' asked Sonia.

'Sonia, let me not discuss my work here. I am here to enjoy a sumptuous meal and have a good drink.'

Sonia persisted, 'Babu Bhai, you are so busy in work during the weekdays; I can only get hold of you during such occasions only.'

'Leave markets alone, dear. I shall tell you a few names. Buy them in your personal portfolio, and maybe in a year's time, you can prepare for your retirement. I have recommended these shares to a few of the large banks and mutual funds,' BBC whispered, a trace of alcohol evident in his voice.

'Babu Bhai, I know you would hate me for asking this. But please tell me what you feel about the infotech shares?' asked Naren.

'Naren ji, infotech sector is a money-printing machine. Jab tak himmat hai, chhapte raho.' (Keep minting while you have courage.)

The conversation ended there, and all of them left shortly thereafter. Chaitanya dropped Sonia home. The trio left in Naren's Mercedes. Naren first dropped Adarsh and then Gobind. After Adarsh got down, Naren asked Gobind about his conversation with BBC. Gobind mentioned that BBC was telling him about stock markets and the infotech sector in particular.

'What did he say?' asked Naren.

'He told me about a trading strategy used by most of the smart investors, who want to restrict their exposure to stock markets and yet participate in the upside without committing full amount. It's called margin trading,' Gobind said.

'What did you say?'

'I didn't say much. I told him that I don't know much about all this and that our money is being managed by you with the help of the bank's relationship manager.'

'Hmm,' Naren said. He was thinking hard.

Soon, they came to Gobind's house. He got down.

'Bye, Naren,' he said and went away.

Naren thought about something and checked BBC's card lying in his pocket. He would call him tomorrow.

Sonia and Chaitanya were beginning to feel the intensity of their relationship—their mobile bills were a living testimony of this fact.

Chaitanya looked at the portfolios of all clients managed by Sonia. Most of them were doing well, thanks to a buoyant equity market. Although he didn't worry about the stock markets, he realized the portfolios were quite susceptible to adverse stock price movement in one single sector. The entire equity exposure was towards the infotech sector, which theoretically presented a risk. Another anomaly in these portfolios was that there was virtually no investment in tax-efficient debt mutual funds, which provided a decent return of 15–16 per cent per annum at that time. He had to discuss this with Sonia before he met her clients, which was scheduled after ten days as Sonia had to travel to London to receive her award from the bank chairman.

'You make the changes that you want to. I have full trust in you. We shall communicate the same to the clients,' Sonia had said.

'Thanks, Sonia.'

Chaitanya prepared detailed restructuring plans for her client portfolios. They needed to present and discuss the same with the trio before implementation as these were large clients for the bank. The meeting took place at Naren's office, which functioned as headquarters for the trio's investments.

'Sir, as I told you, Chaitanya shall be working closely with me on your portfolios. He has studied your portfolios in detail and made certain recommendations. He shall explain it to you now,' Sonia said.

'Madam, there is no need to discuss. We trust you and shall go with your suggestions. You can make the changes you feel are necessary to be made,' Gobind said.

'Hang on, Gobind, let's hear him first and not jump to conclusions.' Adarsh spoke politely.

Naren agreed with Adarsh and asked Chaitanya to start, while tea was served along with a variety of cookies.

'Sir, right now I am making recommendations on the asset allocation of the portfolios. Ideally each portfolio has to have a judicious mix of debt and equity assets. Mr Sahay's and Mr Srivastava's portfolios are bit overboard in terms of exposure to equity assets. They have more than 80 per cent exposure to equity at this stage. Mr Singh's portfolio is underexposed to equity currently. Also, the debt portion of the portfolios is invested in bank fixed deposits, which are tax inefficient as one has to pay the full tax on them,' Chaitanya said.

This pleased Adarsh, who always thought that they must be saving some tax being paid on the interest income generated from fixed deposits. Naren kept quiet but listened to Chaitanya attentively. There was a strange magnetism in his voice.

Chaitanya continued, 'Further, our equity exposure is entirely towards the infotech sector. This, to my mind, is a risk that is increasing by the day. We must have exposure to other sectors as well. I have only these two observations at this stage. I shall look at the individual stock and MF holdings later and suggest more changes if required.'

Chaitanya's summary was brief, succinct, and sharp.

'Brevity is the soul of wit,' Sonia thought and smiled. Chaitanya was proving to be worth every penny.

'Chaitanya, we are planning to increase our investments with the bank. That means you shall have more money on your hands. Since we are happy with the returns we have made so far, we won't mind allocating more money.' Naren spoke at last.

'Thanks a lot, sir. That's indeed kind of you. May I ask each of you individually, what is the objective behind your investments, if you don't mind?'

The trio hadn't thought about this one. They were taken aback by the stupidity of this question. Anyhow they didn't mind answering.

'I want to make more money,' said Naren.

'I invested because my friends were investing. So I am just trying my hand out there in the market,' Gobind said.

'I want to make use of my skills to make more money. I understand finance and feel that I can actually make some money in the markets, which is not a bad thing to do,' Adarsh added bit nervously.

Sonia was a little surprised too. She didn't expect Chaitanya to ask silly questions to such large, high-net-worth investors. Honestly she was also taken aback by the casual answers provided by the trio. She was none the less happy that additional investments were being made. This only meant more revenues for the bank and her. They wrapped the meeting up with a promise to come back with recommendations soon.

'Chaitanya, I am surprised at the way you spoke to these investors. You can't ask silly questions to people who have cumulatively put more than fifty crores with us. They are grown-up men, not thumb-sucking kids.'

There was an unmistakable trace of irritation in Sonia's voice. Chaitanya kept quiet.

'They have filled a detailed questionnaire at the time of signing with the bank. I am sure you have seen for yourself.' She gave him an 'I am surprised at your stupidity' kind of look.

'I am sorry, Sonia. I needed to hear from them so that a comprehensive financial plan can be drawn for them. All of us should know our investment objectives very clearly, and I am not sure if these investors are clear about their objectives. I think they have come in the markets for fun. They are happy because they are making money currently. The situation can change tomorrow. Today's grown-up men can be irritating monkeys on our back tomorrow.'

Sonia's mobile phone rang. It was Naren.

'Sure, sir, it shouldn't be a problem. I shall speak to him and let you know.'

'Who is it?' Chaitanya asked.

'Mr Sahay. He wants a meeting with BBC.'

Sonia called BBC immediately; a meeting was fixed for the trio. She dialled Naren's number and told him the same. She was bit surprised to hear what Naren said.

Chaitanya observed this and asked, 'What happened?'

'Mr Sahay wants to meet him alone.'

This left Chaitanya a bit flummoxed as well. He was thinking hard and aloud now. He had to make detailed plans for not only the trio but for the other investors also. He had to look at each and every share they held, each mutual fund scheme they had invested in, and at the shares those mutual funds had invested in turn, to assess the risk in the portfolios. If all client portfolios were similar to the trio's portfolio then he would look at exiting some of these stocks or mutual funds and adding some other investments. He was genuinely disappointed at the answers provided by the trio. He thought they knew what they were doing. The meeting with BBC also set a little warning bell going off in his mind, although he did not say anything to Sonia.

He thought Naren's meeting with BBC was not such a good idea.

Naren met BBC in his office. There were many people bustling around, staring at the TV screens that showed live markets. A few were sitting with the computer operators giving them buy and sell orders. A few others were chatting with each other, probably discussing stock markets. Naren walked though the mass of people—noise, trades, hopes, dreams, expectations, and financial aspirations taking shape on the liquid crystal screens all over the place. BBC's cabin was the end of a long corridor. He sat across a large table which had a bigger heap of papers than Naren had ever seen. There was a computer screen on BBC's right-hand side and a TV in front that alternated between showing live markets and pictures from various sections of his office through a closed-circuit TV camera. A few telephone sets were ringing amid this mess, keeping BBC connected with markets, investors, and fellow brokers. BBC always wore a pristine white safari suit, white leather sandals, and brushed his hair back from the brow. His fingers showed more gold than skin which not only contrasted well with his dark colour but also spoke about the money BBC was making. He constantly chewed betel leaf along with his favourite tobacco, which his personal staff ensured was available in plenty all the time. His face offered no reason to be termed as graceful or good-looking. Naren felt out of place in such a setting, but then he didn't come here to stay forever. He had come here to open a specific trading account, to be personally monitored by BBC. He knew through his contacts that BBC had strong connections within the broker community and large institutional investors.

Without bothering to check with Naren, BBC had already asked his staff to serve water, tea, and biscuits in his cabin. He was a broker after all, not a sophisticated businessman like Naren.

'Yes, Mr Sahay, what can I do for you?'

BBC didn't have the necessary etiquette to hold long and interesting conversations. It was not his fault. He came from a Gujarati background, where every second meant money and every minute meant sixty times more money. He did not get sufficient education to work on his mannerisms but had enough training to earn money without studying too much.

'I want to open an account with your firm. You shall personally monitor this account. I shall start with five crores and take it up to twenty-five crores if you make profit for me. No one, and let me categorically say *no one*, except you and me would know about this account, not even the bank who has referred me to you,' Naren said in a crisp tone soaked in superiority.

BBC wasn't one to take someone's arrogance in his stride but an amount of twenty-five crores was too big to be ignored. He ignored Naren's bullshitting and kept on smiling. Neither Naren nor he wanted to stretch this meeting any longer.

'Mr Sahay, someone from my office shall contact you for the paperwork and other formalities in a couple of days. We shall set up an account as soon as possible,' BBC said.

'Thanks a lot, now I have to go for a meeting,' Naren said as he got up to leave.

BBC smiled at his good luck. Twenty-five crores meant a lot to him. The brokerage income of this amount meant a lot of money finding its way to his pockets. If for a small insult and ignominy, he could have more such clients, he would thank his angels.

He picked up a biscuit from the untouched tray, dunked it in his teacup, and savoured the taste.

BBC ran retail as well as institutional businesses. He had fifteen branches spread across Delhi and UP, where small individual clients (called retail clients in industry parlance) walked in for doing trading in stock markets. He would charge them a small brokerage on buying and selling. Apart from retail investors, there were jobbers who worked on a limited set of stocks and arbitrageurs who bought on one stock exchange and sold on the other, only to profit from the price difference in the stock prices quoted on two different exchanges. Few investors did margin trading with his firm, which meant they put up only 15 per cent of the money, the rest, i.e. 85 per cent, being contributed by BBC's firm. The margin trades were squared off or carried forward on fortnightly basis. This was flourishing business for BBC; markets were doing well making investors richer week after week, fortnight after fortnight. BBC not only earned brokerage on such trades but also made handsome interest income on the fund that his firm lent to the investors. Then there were investors who did delivery-based business. They took delivery of stocks, kept the share certificates with them, and later on sold them to some other investors by executing a transfer deed.

Naren had signed for margin trading. Since he had to pay only 15 per cent up front, his exposure to the markets would be approximately seven times the margin money. So 5 crores meant taking an exposure of approximately 33 crores and

25 crores margin money would mean an obscene amount in excess of 150 crores. Naren was quite keen on playing the big boys' game, even if it meant taking bit of risk. BBC bought four stocks—Bolton Technologies, Santafour Software Ltd, Vindhyachal Futuristic Communications Ltd, and Raftech Infosys—in his portfolio, investing Rs. 25 lacs in each. Naren paid only Rs. 15 lacs to start with. At the end of the first fortnight, his portfolio showed a marginal increase of 1.5 per cent, this meant he made slightly less than Rs. 1.5 lacs, adjusted for the brokerage, in fifteen days' time. He just wanted to dip his toes in the unchartered waters before taking the plunge and this wasn't a discouraging start.

The second fortnight was slightly better, as Vindhyachal Futuristic Communications Ltd, popularly known as VFCL, moved up by 7 per cent and the other stocks also showed marginal gains enabling Naren to net nearly Rs. 2.15 lacs, adjusted for the brokerage.

Naren got a call from BBC's office requesting a meeting. They met at Taj Mansingh coffee shop to discuss their future strategy.

'Infotech business is doing very well in India, and foreign investors are taking lot of interest in these companies now. Since our currency is relatively cheaper, the foreign investors known as FIIs find our markets very attractive. The total market cap of India is approximately Rs. 1,500 crores, a figure of $50 million, which is peanuts for FIIs. One of the companies on our portfolio is expected to announce a stake sale shortly. I expect the stock to go up significantly,' BBC said in a rehearsed tone.

Since Naren was happy with his first month's gain, he asked BBC, 'So what should we do?'

'Buy more VFCL. I suggest you increase your exposure to this company by a couple of crores now and we can review our position after fifteen days.'

'OK, ask someone to pick up a cheque of forty-five lacs from my office and make it three crores. Let's review after fifteen days,' Naren said casually, waving for the bill.

Nothing happened in the VFCL counter for next one month and the stock stayed where it was. Naren felt a little uneasy until the news came in papers in the first week of the third fortnight. An Australian billionaire had picked up 5 per cent of VFCL for $50 million, valuing the company at $1 billion. The stock zoomed up, hitting the upper circuit (a limit of 15 per cent price movement in a single day). Upper circuit meant that no more buying could be done in the stock for that day.

Naren's gain for the fortnight in which VFCL did a bit of Sergey Bubka pole vault was close to Rs. 50 lacs, which was slightly less than the total amount of Rs. 60 lacs he had paid as margin to BBC's firm so far.

This margin business was fun. Just contribute a small amount and play big games.

After the encouraging toe-dipping, Naren decided to go knee-deep now. He called BBC and asked for another meeting at the same place only to increase his exposure to ten crores. This meeting lasted a little longer than the last one had. He took BBC's opinion on markets, economy, and stocks. He found BBC to be shrewd, mature, and practical. His abhorrence for BBC was unconsciously being replaced with a strange bonhomie. Moneymaking can make you like an idiot and hate a wise man, although BBC wasn't an idiot by any means.

'We shall see the performance of our stocks for couple of months and then make a decision about increasing or reducing exposure. Meanwhile let me know if you get more tips like VFCL, where there is an opportunity to make a quick buck,' Naren said.

BBC could see the seed of the greed being sown in Naren's psyche. He knew what it meant. This time, BBC paid the bill and carried on. He knew that the future meetings would be even longer than this one. He didn't mind spending money on his clients as long as there was a scope for the next meeting.

10

I Am an Expert—Cos I Made Money

Chaitanya took a week's time in studying the client portfolios in detail. He wrote down his observations and made final recommendations regarding each portfolio. He then asked Sonia to fix up a meeting with the trio. Naren was busy travelling overseas and Adarsh was tied up with audits. There was no point meeting Gobind without the other two, so Sonia decided to wait till Naren returned. Finally after fifteen days' wait, they got a meeting.

Naren felt buoyant and energetic after his US trip. He had met many clients who were keen to invest in India and specifically in his business. He categorically mentioned about the enthusiasm that US equity markets were showing regarding the Internet and software boom. He had met a few fund managers too, who further boosted his confidence about stock markets. He was on his high horse, galloping with the winds, refusing to come down at any cost. Although Sonia tried to interrupt him, Chaitanya heard him silently.

'Let's hear what the young man has to say about our portfolios,' Gobind spoke, cutting Naren's flow; Adarsh nodded too.

'Show us the magic wand, Chaitanya; take us to the path of obscene money, make us richer by a few more crores,' Naren chuckled in a haughty tone with a trace of definite arrogance. Sonia observed it. She felt a little uneasy at this sarcastic monologue of Naren.

Chaitanya was brief once again. He said to Naren, 'Sir, as I had told you earlier, your portfolio and Mr Srivastava's are adequately exposed to the equities at this stage. However, the entire exposure is in the infotech sector. I recommend that we reduce it at least by 25 per cent and add other sectors which are trading at attractive valuations. I will not recommend having more than 50 per cent exposure into equities at this stage. Mr Singh's portfolio is underexposed to equities, so I recommend increasing the equity portion to approximately 50 per cent of the overall value. Debt funds are doing well and interest rates are going to fall, so we must add these funds to our portfolio. This way we can book some gains from equity markets and park them safely in debt funds. These funds can generate an annual return of 15 to 16 per cent.'

He continued, 'The mutual funds that we hold in our portfolios have also invested in similar stocks as we have purchased in your trading portfolio. This increases our risk further. I recommend that we add other sectors by either buying stocks directly or by adding mutual funds that do not invest in the infotech sector. We have already made more than 150 per cent on our direct equity and mutual fund portfolio, so a little caution won't do us any harm.'

He shared a list of mutual funds and stocks that he felt were appropriate to be included in the portfolio. Sonia felt a strange uneasiness inside her.

Gobind listened patiently and so did Adarsh. Naren's sharp reaction came immediately after Chaitanya stopped talking.

'How long have you been in the markets, Chaitanya?'

'Sir, four years.'

'Well, then allow me to impart some wisdom to you. I think the infotech sector is going to zoom not only through the roof but also through the stratosphere. I know brokers, fund managers, and other large investors who have the same opinion, and here you are asking us to exercise caution and add sleeping dud sectors to our portfolio. The global excitement is to be seen to be believed. I interact with many traditional businessmen; they all tell me how technology is changing their businesses each passing day. The stock prices shall at least treble from here.' Naren spoke with a sense of newly acquired expertise. His aggression was partly formed by his gains with the bank and with BBC and the experience of his recent overseas trip.

'There is going to be no looking back from here. You can take a stamp paper and take my signatures on it,' Naren said.

'We were actually thinking of increasing our direct stock exposure with you guys,' said Adarsh. Gobind played spectator to this bizarre show of pomp and muted wisdom.

'Sir, we have made these recommendations based on our research and understanding formed over the years. Our team has people more experienced than me and Sonia. Our suggestions are an output of collective thinking and experience,' Chaitanya persisted.

Naren cut loose again. He said, 'Young man, go back to school and take classes in basic investing. I am sorry to say this, but you don't know anything about momentum, about skimming the markets by playing smart, making it big when the opportunity is right there at your doorstep. I am in the company of men who have more grey hair than the minutes you have spent in the markets and they are certainly wiser than you. You guys only handle only a small part of my portfolio. You don't know that I have made more money in last fifteen days than you would ever make in your life. Don't give me this spiel about risk management and the bullshit about debt funds. I am simply not interested.'

Naren's tone was demeaning and disrespecting. There was no doubt about that. Chaitanya felt bad but he knew that investors could get carried away by the profits they made in the markets. This was not Naren speaking; it was his money that did the talking. Chaitanya kept quiet.

Naren would have gone on, had Adarsh not stopped him. Adarsh said, 'Let's think through this and touch base after couple of days. Sonia, why don't you call us the day after? And we shall decide on the future course of action.'

Sonia felt for the first time that she was losing her grip on the trio. They might not mean anything for Chaitanya, but for her, they meant a healthy and prosperous future. She had never seen Naren disagreeing with their advice so strongly. She knew something was awfully wrong. She couldn't not believe Chaitanya either. Although her own understanding of markets and stocks was adequate, she was nowhere near Chaitanya when it came to equities. Markets were roaring, stocks were zooming, and her investors were cruising along fine, then why rock the boat?

She found herself caught between a rock and a hard place.

If she agreed with Chaitanya, she could lose her clients. She could end up losing her love the other way round. She needed to use her common sense and strike a balance with everyone to keep things moving.

One thing that stuck in her mind was Naren's saying that the bank was managing only a small portion of his portfolio. She was shocked to hear this. Suddenly she remembered having fixed Naren's meeting with BBC. She had forgotten to follow it up.

Everything was clear to her now. BBC was guiding Naren and she didn't know about it. She felt like a fool, having let her client fall in BBC's bag so easily. She would seek the boss's advice.

'Sometimes the client is right, sometimes he is wrong, and sometimes he is wrong yet right. We need not correct him, as correcting may not get us the desired result. Any corrective action or even a faint hint of it may damage client's self-respect. If that happens, then you are sure to lose the client forever. Respect the client, his idiosyncrasies, and philosophies—no matter how silly they may seem to be. We are professionals, not his family members. Strike a balance between what you seek and what the client wants to achieve. After all, it's his money. Chaitanya, make a few cosmetic recommendations which do not change too much in their portfolio. Sonia, you focus on getting more money out of them. We are tight on revenues this quarter and I need you guys to help me. And, Chaitanya, it would be better that you avoid meeting the trio for couple of weeks,' the boss said.

'But, boss, this may not be appropriate from an investment viewpoint,' Chaitanya argued.

'Correct or incorrect, right or wrong, appropriate or inappropriate, everything is relative. There is nothing in this world that can be termed being completely right or wrong. That's why I am asking you to strike a balance. You never know what may happen tomorrow. We may suggest a trimming of their portfolios and the index may go up by 100 per cent. The clients shall blame us. And let me remind you, we are not alone in all this. The clients want it too, my boy.'

Sonia, who was quiet until now, said, 'I think Boss is right. We needn't infringe upon the clients' ideas and thought process too much.'

Chaitanya felt uneasy at this corporate gibberish. Boss was only worried about the bank's revenues and Sonia about her client book.

'Who worried about the clients?'

No one actually . . .

Chaitanya had no other option but to toe the line. He made a few half-hearted changes in the clients' portfolios. As the boss had suggested, these were only cosmetic in nature and didn't do much to change the core of the portfolio. Another meeting was set up with the trio, and the focus of this meeting was to go with the flow and not rock the boat. Sonia told the trio that Chaitanya was unwell and could not make it to the meeting.

Gobind knew the real reason though.

Naren was floating on the clouds. His exposure with BBC had gone up to fifteen crores of margin money now, and he was minting money every day, every week, and every fortnight. All of his trades were rolled over to the next cycle as he never felt the need to encash his positions. After all, he didn't need the money. Moreover, such encashing would lead to unnecessary payment of taxes, which he didn't want. He kept his secret from everyone including his friends, family, and his bankers too. Adarsh and Gobind had no reason to worry; their portfolios were ringing in cash too.

'Sir, we looked at your portfolios in detail and have made certain recommendations accordingly. We need to add some amount of debt in your portfolios, which we shall create from your fixed deposits with the bank. Equity portion shall remain the same. The bank feels that markets shall remain bullish for a few years and there is no need to come out of equities now. In fact we would recommend buying more equity funds and stocks, should you want to bring more money in,' Sonia said.

A victorious Naren couldn't help smiling at her suggestion. Gobind was indifferent. Adarsh didn't want to spoil the atmosphere. He had committed an additional sum of Rs. 2 crores along with Gobind, who also contributed additional investment of Rs. 2 crores to his portfolio. It was Naren who made the biggest contribution. He added Rs. 5 crores to his portfolio and a broad smile to Sonia's face.

'How much is our portfolio worth now?' asked Naren.

'Sir, a little over 80 crores, including the additional amount you committed today,' Sonia answered.

'That's a lot of money. Make sure you guys handle it well. I trust you and the bank, but we need to ensure that the best of your team is on top of our investments.' Adarsh spoke for the trio.

'Yes, sir, I understand what you mean. Don't worry— your money is safe with us,' Sonia spoke with confidence. The meeting was over.

Sonia was meeting Chaitanya in the evening at a cafe that had just opened in Chanakya Puri area.

In Sonia, Chaitanya saw a charming, smart woman who knew her ways very well. He could also see the fissure which was beginning to show in their professional views.

During their meeting cum date that evening, Chaitanya said, 'Sonia, I am not going to be with you in this. I shall ask Boss to take me off this assignment. I am not cut out for such things. I am an investment person who knows only two shades, black and white, and nothing else. I don't think these investors are doing the right thing, and more importantly, we as a bank are not helping them either. We are just worried about our own survival, compromising the clients' interests.'

'Oh! Chaitanya, can we talk about this later, please? Right now I need a little celebration around my success. Didn't I tell you that trio has invested some more money with the bank and their total exposure is more than 80 crores? That's big, isn't it?'

'Sonia, please don't me count in this celebration. I don't want to spoil your mood but I genuinely feel that we aren't doing what we should be doing.'

'Chaitanya, I am trying to juggle various things myself, and believe me, it's not easy. Anyways let's not discuss this matter further, else we shall end up fighting, which I don't want to do. Tomorrow is Friday, let's have dinner together,' Sonia spoke softly.

Chaitanya agreed to the dinner. Although he did not have much to do this evening either, he needed some time for himself. He went to the office with Sonia and then slipped out quietly to walk around in the Connaught Place area—once known as the heart of New Delhi. Named after the Duke of Connaught, Connaught Place was always bustling with activity. Popularly known as CP, Connaught Place had a uniform series of colonnaded buildings devoted to shops, banks, restaurants, hotels, and offices. Often creating confusion, the outer circle was technically called Connaught Circus (divided into blocks from G to N) and the inner circle Connaught Place (divided into blocks from A to F). There was a middle circle too. In 1995 the inner and outer circles were renamed Rajiv Chowk and Indira Chowk respectively, but these names were rarely used. At the centre of these concentric circles was a huge circular lawn where one could see people sitting, sleeping, and milling around. Beneath this lawn was the famous Palika Bazaar of Delhi.

Chaitanya walked along the long corridor of the inner circle, losing himself in the enormous crowd that came from various directions, crossing the intersecting roads that sliced CP in equal parts. Lost in his thoughts, he kept walking till he reached the other end and took a right to reach Madras Hotel—his favourite restaurant, one of the few places in CP where one could have authentic South Indian food. He not only liked the food but also the down-to-earth setting that this hotel offered. He had a plain dosa with sambhar and coconut chutney, a meal that was always value for money.

He was feeling as useless as a dead fly in a bowl of milk that could be taken out with a slight flick of a finger. He wasn't angry; he never got angry. He was disappointed with everyone including Sonia. He couldn't do much at this stage as he didn't want to lose anything or anyone. He finished his early dinner and walked back to the office, stopping at a roadside book hawker, picking up a couple of books—*The Money Game* by Adam Smith and *The Warren Buffett Way* by Robert Hagstrom.

Chaitanya was a voracious reader since his childhood days when he read comics, short stories, and religious scriptures too. He had finished reading the Ramayana and

Mahabharata by the time he reached fifth grade in school, thanks to his parents who always carried books for him from their school libraries.

Chaitanya was concerned and a bit worried about the bank's investors, especially the trio, who were a bunch of good people with caring families. He felt a strange knot in his stomach, a soft little storm churning within him, rising from his abdomen, reaching nowhere, leading to an unfamiliar anxiety. He wanted to read more about stock markets, investing, and more importantly, the current frenzy in the Indian and global markets.

A few miles away from Chaitanya's place, Naren was enjoying his success in stock markets. His bets with BBC's firm were doing well, making him richer day by day. He had started tracking a few companies himself, by reading the newspapers and TV channels. Although he did not understand much about infotech and software, he became familiar with a few companies. This familiarity combined with the rising stock prices of these companies led to a sense of expertise to Naren. Since he was making money in these stocks and tracking their development, he believed that he knew these companies. Some part of the information also came from BBC, who would tell him about which fund house was buying what. Which company was placing stakes with FIIs? Which stocks were driven by operators? An investor could make money by simply playing on the news. After Naren made money in a few stocks suggested by BBC, he started trusting him more and more. He had still not informed Gobind and Adarsh about his secret affair with BBC. He thought of informing them soon though. The bank portfolio was doing well too, but this soon would become a much smaller part of his portfolio as he was planning to put more money with BBC. He thought about the suggestions Chaitanya made regarding their portfolios but soon rejected them as he was confident about the performance of the infotech sector. Even if the stock prices fell, he would have enough time to liquidate his positions and encash. He thought about his business; it was throwing more cash than ever and Naren had nothing to complain about. His family was fine, kids growing by the minute like a dream, and Lavanya was as caring as ever. His friendship with Adarsh and Gobind was an asset that many rich people were deprived of. He had absolutely nothing to worry about. He had asked his staff to place a TV with a cable connection in his cabin. He wanted to track his investments more closely, since the bets were large. This would also help him track global markets, which were now having a bigger linkage with Indian stock markets. Lot of investors were watching the NASDAQ composite index those days. NASDAQ composite was the primary index of the NASDAQ stock exchange, the second largest stock exchange after New York Stock Exchange. Founded by Bernard Madoff in 1971, it was the world's first electronic stock market.

Naren became one of the millions of the investors who were tracking NASDAQ composite to stay ahead of other market participants thinking that they were the only ones tracking it. Stocks and stock market slowly became a larger part of his life. He would talk to BBC daily to check the value of his portfolio. He would check the net asset values (NAV) of his mutual funds every morning in *The Economic Times*. Often he would try to strike up a conversation with his senior employees and tell them about stock markets. He would call Gobind and Adarsh a couple of times a day and update them on the happenings in the stock market. While he was in office, his attention would constantly flip between office work and the stock market. He would often quote the stock prices in his conversations with his friends, family, and even with some acquaintances who didn't know anything about equities. He started getting invitations for more and more parties, which gave him opportunity to know more investors who were dabbling in the world of equities. At one such party, he overheard the name of Chetan Parekh, a man who started as a stockbroker but had now become a famous equity investor owing to large stakes he held in a few infotech companies. The investors referred to something called C-10 stocks, which confused Naren. He asked BBC about it.

BBC said, 'Chetan Parekh is the man with the golden touch. Whatever he touches becomes gold overnight. He is the man in the big league, followed by everyone including brokers, retail investors, FIIs, fund managers, operators, and high-net-worth Investors. The man is worth more than a few thousand crores as of today. He is an example to be followed sir. In a nutshell, he is the god of stock markets.'

'Which are those stocks?'

'Naren bhai, few of the stocks that we have purchased in your portfolio are from his list only. So don't worry, you have got the best stocks in your portfolio,' BBC spoke.

'What about your portfolio, Babu Bhai? Do you also own these stocks?'

'Sir, I can't survive if I don't own them. If, being a stockbroker, I don't follow Chetan Parekh, then I have not future in this business. I own only C-10 stocks,' BBC lied.

Naren felt relieved hearing this. He owned stocks which were also owned by the expert investors, which brought a semblance of safety to his mind. He asked BBC to add more stocks from the C-10 stocks to his portfolio immediately. He committed another 15 crores to BBC over the cocktails, taking his exposure to 25 crores of margin money (exposure of 150 crores) in the second month of their relationship. BBC couldn't help but smile. His firm made 0.75 per cent every time Naren bought or sold a share. Rs. 150 crores meant a commission of Rs. 1.12 crores, if all the stocks were bought once. He would make a similar commission when the customer chose to sell those stocks. Imagine if the stocks worth Rs. 150 crores were bought and sold five times a year, the commission would soar to Rs. 5.6 crores. BBC did this quite often, in the name of profit booking. He would sell the shares and buy a larger quantity next day, making a small risk-free commission on every trade, which customers like Naren didn't mind as they were making money thanks to the upper circuits that their stocks were hitting frequently.

BBC threw a party to celebrate his firm's ten years in the business. He had invited more than two hundred people, including his clients, employees, fellow brokers, and a few relatives too. Wine and liquor flowed like water. There was cheer all around. Investors stood in small groups obviously discussing stock markets as if everything else in India had come a cropper. Naren, who didn't know anyone, found it hard to kill time. All of a sudden, he felt that he saw Sonia among the crowd, almost like a blur in the corner of his eye. But she vanished too quickly to be really present there.

Naren dismissed this thought. He must have seen someone else. How could she be there?

Maybe he was drunk.

It was late into the night. Naren left as the clock hit 12 a.m. Tomorrow, he would disclose his secret to Adarsh and Gobind.

11

The Risk Not Understood

'Guys, I am going to tell you something which will sweep you off your feet, a little secret that I kept from you. I am sorry for this, but I didn't want to expose both of you to any risk at this stage, so I experimented on my own to begin with. 'Naren spoke with the enthusiasm of a twenty-year-old boy.

'I have added another dimension to our investing adventure, and let me tell you, this is even more exciting than what we are doing with the bank. The thrill, the rush of adrenalin, and the feeling of triumph is simply great.'

The suspense was building up; both Gobind and Adarsh were on the edge of their seats, trying to anticipate what was coming next.

'You remember the party thrown by the bank? Which all of us attended?'

'Yes,' both of them said synchronously.

'I met someone in that party who has almost done magic with his advice.'

Still clueless, Adarsh and Gobind asked, 'What magic, Naren?'

'Magic of investing—the man has got everything it takes to beat the markets and make lots and lots of money.

This guy has been advising me on equities for the last few months and made me richer by a few more crores.'

'What? You have been investing in market without letting us know,' Gobind said.

'Yes, I have been and I am sorry for this,' Naren spoke with a slight trace of guilt.

'That's not fair, Naren,' Adarsh said.

This time Naren's tone was a little louder.

'C'mon, guys. You know I am not cut for smaller things in life. Trading portfolio with the bank is like swimming in an aquarium whereas I am born to glide with sharks and tame the storms. With all the excitement going around in equities markets, I felt bogged down with the bank's advice. I felt as if my wings were clipped while there was this entire sky available. I wanted freedom to spread my wings and I am glad I have found it. Since there was a bit of risk involved, I didn't want to trouble you guys without checking it out myself first. You have the right to be annoyed with me.'

Naren spoke with flair. He gave a full account of his first meeting with BBC and how the relationship evolved afterwards. He also disclosed the amount at stake without trying to convince Gobind and Adarsh to join him in his new adventure.

Adarsh did not react much but felt left out. Gobind was half dejected, half excited, secretly thinking of opening an account with BBC already.

'Have you informed Sonia?' Adarsh asked.

'No, I haven't. I don't think there is any need to inform the bank about it. Anyways that guy Chaitanya would be squeamish about this whole thing. The bank would never like their clients doing business with other players. Moreover,

I have not reduced the bank's share to provide for BBC. And we decide for ourselves, not the bank.'

Naren continued to speak as if he was talking to kindergarten kids.

'Initially, I picked up a few shares to test the waters. BBC's advice was bang on. I made money week on week for three weeks before I decided to increase my bets. What's funnier is that you don't have to put up the full amount up front. You have to pay just 15 per cent and the rest is contributed by his firm. You have to settle your trades on fortnightly basis and pay the net amounts. This also gives you an opportunity to play bigger bets as for every 100 bucks being put you can take an exposure worth 600 bucks. Isn't it great?'

'But, Naren, that increases your risk also six times,' Adarsh said.

'I know what you mean, Adarsh. But this is different. You are being advised by people whose job is to trade and invest on full-time basis. They understand the markets like the back of their hand, plus they are very well networked. They know who is buying what. They also know who is selling what. They are in touch with big foreign investors, mutual funds, big brokers, and investors like us. They have a finger on the market's pulse, that's why they are always ahead of the curve. They can act faster than the kids whom the bank has appointed to advise us. In fact I think they are the ones who run this market.' Naren continued to pour wisdom on those two.

Adarsh and Gobind found no reason to interrupt or discourage Naren. After a few more minutes, dinner, and drinks, the trio vowed to be together in this adventure as well. Adarsh and Gobind agreed to open accounts with BBC without letting Sonia and Chaitanya know about it.

Despite their minor differences in professional life, Sonia and Chaitanya were cruising along fine. Their individual liking for each other grew each passing day. They would catch up with each other whenever they found time—in the canteen, while on calls, meeting for lunch and dinners, and on the drive back home each evening. Slowly they got addicted to each other, and when Sonia had travelled to London as winner of the contest, Chaitanya found himself missing her. They spoke to each other over the phone every day and exchanged passionate emails which only brought them closer. They decided to marry each other, if Sonia's parents agreed. Chaitanya had lost his parents in an accident a few years back. He had no one to seek approval from.

While the trio had opened another chapter in the book of investing, Chaitanya was reading about Warren Buffett. He found both the books interesting. Both laid a lot of emphasis on quality, discipline, and the need to control the risk in investing. Hagstrom's book discussed Warren Buffett's investment style and philosophy in detail. Adam Smith's book dealt more with investor behaviour and psychology. Despite their vastly different contents, both the books seemed to highlight the need of separating oneself from the crowd, if one were to succeed in investing. Another trait of the successful investor suggested by both the books was investing for the long term. Warren Buffett held the stocks he liked for extraordinarily long periods of time. He had had stocks in his portfolio held over a period of 30 to 40 years also. Chaitanya found this really interesting. Most of the investors he had dealt with so far had shown no inclination of holding stocks over longer periods like these. Smith's book also discussed market frenzies and manias that could grip the investor's mind temporarily and induce them to make inappropriate investment decisions.

Chaitanya superimposed the ideas from those two books on the Indian equity markets and the prevalent investor behaviour. The excitement was slowly turning into madness. More and more investors were participating in the equity market by buying direct equities and mutual funds. Mutual funds were launching new schemes to invest in the infotech sector. ICE was the new buzzword on the street. ICE stood for infotech, communication, and entertainment. The stocks in these three sectors were soaring upwards, defying gravity and common sense and even investment wisdom. With soaring stock prices, investor confidence was also assuming new heights, making them increase their exposure to equities. Equity markets were a funny place to be in. Everyone was judged on the basis of the gains made during a particular time period. Investors who made more money were supposed to be wiser than others and vice versa. A big party was going on, and it seemed everyone had an invitation to this extravaganza. Moneymaking had become an easy thing, probably the easiest thing. Something wasn't right. Something was bugging Chaitanya for some time now; he wasn't comfortable with the pace of growth of stocks although he was also witnessing it for the first time. Anyone who had anything to do with the stock market was quick enough to give a word or two of advice at the drop of a hat. Chaitanya decided to dig deeper to find out the truth behind this madness called the infotech boom.

What he found out was simply shocking.

1. The whole stock market was divided into two parts, the old and the new economy stocks. Old economy stocks were the traditional businesses like manufacturing, transportation, utility, services (apart from ICE), banks, housing finance companies, construction companies, and everything else that did not belong to the ICE bucket.

2. The only stocks that were rising for the last year and a half were ICE stocks.

3. Most of the mutual fund houses in India had launched infotech or Internet funds to collect thousands of crores from investors.

4. The top ten stocks in the top ten mutual fund portfolios were exactly the same.

5. The whole market was going berserk behind a group of ten stocks called C-10 stocks. These stocks had already more than quadrupled in a very short period, but investors thought they would keep going up forever. The investing community was fixated on new ways of valuing stocks that were different from what Chaitanya knew.

It was a bubble that was growing larger and larger; it could be burst with the slightest prick of a tiny pin.

Traditionally a company was valued on the basis of its earnings or the dividends it paid to its shareholders. Many

Internet companies that were part of the new economy were mere start-ups and did not have any earnings in the initial years. These companies spent lot of money in their early years to create a business platform and attract eyeballs (number of customers browsing through their websites). Number of eyeballs became a proxy for earnings and cash flows. These companies were raising money in the IPOs from the primary markets where millions of people bought their shares hoping to double their money fast. To Chaitanya this was like tulip mania, which happened in Europe sometime when prices of tulip flowers became so high that people started selling their valuable assets and even homes to buy tulip flowers, hoping to make money from them. Chaitanya took all the C-10 stocks and tried to value these companies on the basis of their earnings. He was shocked to find that none of the stocks justified the price that they were quoting at. Their prices had gone much beyond what the fundamentals suggested. This was like a time bomb ticking continuously, waiting to explode; only the date, year, and the precise time were not known to him or anyone else, for that matter. He needed to alert Sonia and the trio sooner than later.

Would they listen to him?

He didn't know that. He thought of trying anyway.

But what would he say?

That the stock prices may fall?

When?

By how much?

Why?

He didn't have precise answers in his mind. All he knew was that these stocks didn't deserve the prices they were quoting at. He somehow felt that the prices would not sustain for too long, and when the prices fell, there would be a widespread carnage. He could see a time period where everyone would turn a seller causing these stocks to hit lower circuits, thus making it difficult for the investors to exit. He decided to speak to Sonia first, as talking to the boss would be futile. He called up Sonia. They decided to meet for dinner at Sonia's home after two days.

Sonia wasn't much of a cook. She kept this in mind while ordering the food from a nearby restaurant. She wanted to have dinner outside, in some plush restaurant, but Chaitanya insisted on meeting at her place so that they could chat comfortably.

Both of them being vegetarians, the food was a simple mix of a dal (cooked lentils), a dish of paneer (cottage cheese), green salad, assortment of breads, pickles, and fresh lime soda. The evening was pleasant. Cool breeze coming from northern side window—a harbinger of winter—filled the room with a subtle chill that obviated the need of switching on the ceiling fan. Céline Dion complimented the setting with her chartbuster 'My Heart Will Go On' from the movie *Titanic*. Both the song and the movie had become a rage with the public at large across the globe.

'Chaitanya, we won't talk about the office, clients, or the markets today,' Sonia spoke while placing the dishes on the table.

'Hmm,' Chaitanya said.

'There is a life beyond them. Sometimes I feel that we need to find more time for ourselves between these fierce, fast-paced, mechanical hours that seem to symbolise corporate life.'

'Hmm, I agree.'

'Dad and Mom are coming over. They want to meet you soon. This also means that they have agreed.'

Chaitanya didn't say anything. He felt green shoots of love mushrooming in the depths of his heart too. Often he thought about their future, pictured themselves as husband and wife, and smiled. He had never experienced love, so he didn't know what it was like. Perhaps it was an addiction to someone, someone who filled the gap that you knew existed somewhere but were unable to spot, an acceptance in humility, an arrangement that lasted beyond thoughts and time. Although he never said those three words to Sonia, both of them knew very well that they were made for each other.

'When are they coming?'

'Next month. We shall take a few days off to go to Shimla with them. Please apply for leaves in advance.'

'Yes, madam.'

The food was as scrumptious as a dream. They ate well and cleaned the dishes together. They spoke about marriage arrangements, shopping lists, and choice of place for honeymoon, enjoyment, and everything else except the markets, clients, and office. Soon it was time to go. Since Chaitanya couldn't discuss markets with her, his concerns simmered inside him. He decided to keep them to himself till he got another chance.

He said goodnight, kissed Sonia softly on her forehead, and drove off.

12

No Complaints

For Sonia, life was cruising along fine. She was floating on clouds of comfort, romance, and luxury. Her career was on an upswing, thanks to the double promotion that she just got. Her client book was growing as steadily as the zeroes in her bank balance were. Her clients were loyal to her. They trusted her advice and did exactly what she advised to them. This was an ideal situation for a banker. If you had clients who could swear by you, then any target could be achieved even before it was set. Her bosses were happy with her too. Her London trip was a testimony to this fact. Although her targets were being increased quarter after quarter, she wasn't really worried about it. Her biggest client group, whom she called the trio, was doing well not only on the investment side but also in their respective businesses. Naren was looking at raising more money from private equity Investors, while expanding his business in Europe and South Africa. Gobind had opened two new showrooms, one in Peera Garhi in West Delhi and the other in Moti Nagar in the central part of Delhi. Delhiites were thriving, thanks to booming real estate prices, aspirations and their dreams making cars a staple item in the middle-class recipe. Adarsh's intellectual property was taking him places across the country, and he was acquiring new clients by the minute, raking in unprecedented moolah. He found himself crossing Indian borders quite often for business and pleasure.

Only Chaitanya found his life stuck between a rock and a hard place. While he was pleased with the way his personal life was shaping up, he wasn't particularly comfortable with the way things were moving in stock markets. Everything he read in the books so far was being blown to smithereens by the winds of greed. Fundamental tenets of investing that seemed to have worked for some distinguished investors globally found no place in the modern-day encyclopaedias of stock market gurus. Not that he knew about the future, but there was something that nagged him every day. Something was about to undergo a huge change. He remembered seeing the movie *Titanic* a couple of years back at a South Delhi multiplex. Directed by James Cameron, the epic movie starred Leonardo DiCaprio and Kate Winslet, who fell in love with each other on the ill-fated maiden voyage of the *Titanic*. Chaitanya admired the attention the director paid towards the minute details in creating a grand epic that went on winning many Oscars. What stuck in his mind was that a ship considered to be very safe once sank to the bottom of the Atlantic, to be written off in the depths of oblivion, leaving behind only memories and nothing else. He remembered a scene from the movie in which the heroine raises concerns about the number of lifeboats being inadequate, should there be an emergency. But her concerns were brushed aside by the pompous fellow passengers and a not-so-concerned captain.

Chaitanya couldn't help comparing the stock markets with the *Titanic*, the only difference being that there were no lifeboats whatsoever on the ship of Indian equities.

What if this ship sank too?

He had nothing beyond this to complain about. His life was going to enter into a new phase, with Sonia as his partner. He was already making plans to move to a bigger place after marriage. He had contacted a couple of property dealers, who showed him many apartments that were available for lease and outright sale as well. He and Sonia liked a particular three-bedroom flat that had large windows with a garden view. Between the two of them, they had enough money to purchase this flat. After a few days of deliberations and discussions among themselves and Sonia's parents, they finally purchased this property. Apart from the shopping for the marriage, they now had to devote time towards decorating and designing their new home. An interior decorator was hired, paid an advance, and monitored regularly to get the work finished in time.

Sonia's parents visited them as planned. They got engaged in March 1999 amid a few friends and relatives from Sonia's side. Chaitanya had no one. The marriage date was fixed for the coming winters, when most of the marriages took place in Northern India.

The trip to Shimla with Sonia's parents was fun; it was their first official break as a couple, although they were not allowed to stay in the same room. Sonia and Chaitanya got to know more about each other during this trip. They took long walks along The Mall twice every day, having tea at an old coffee home in the morning and occasionally enjoying pani puri on the Ridge in the evening. They climbed up to the Jakhu Temple on the top of a hill where there were more monkeys than humans. They sought blessings of the monkey god for a better, prosperous and peaceful future. They drove down to a place called Tatta Pani (warm water) on the banks of the River Sutlej, driving along the serpentine hill roads. The greenery was captivating, the peace enamouring, and the easy pace of life put the commercialised civilization to shame. They dipped their toes in the cold Sutlej stream, sitting on a small rock, holding hands, praying silently for a lifelong association. Chaitanya found himself at peace here although Sonia checked her email occasionally and took a few calls on her new cell phone. To Chaitanya there was something magnetic about these mountains. He could hear his breath talking to him; even a whisper seemed like a song of spiritual romance. He vowed to keep coming back to this place whenever life was kind enough to permit. One week ended faster than they had thought. Soon they found themselves back in the din and bustle of Delhi, the clamour of traffic, buzzing mobile phones and skyrocketing stock indices.

They saw Sonia's parents off at the Palam airport soon after returning from their trip. Away from the freely growing fern, smiling flowers swaying their heads in clean fresh air, and deodar trees reaching for the boundless firmament, life became a slave of the routine; the ghost of worries hounded Chaitanya's mind yet again.

Powered by the profits he made with BBC, Naren made some courageous calls. He liquidated almost all his fixed deposits and invested this money with BBC. His existing exposure of 150 crores of margin money was already worth more than Rs. 400 crores. He topped this amount with another 50 crores (exposure of 300 crores) that came from the fixed deposits. In a nutshell, Naren had a combined exposure worth Rs. 1200 crores in the markets. Adarsh and Gobind chipped in 5 to 10 crores each. This was a large exposure by any means. Many other private bankers and brokers started chasing the trio, who did not acquiesce to their requests. BBC became dearer than a brother to Naren. He devoted most of his time tracking markets now, even ignoring important business matters sometimes. His investments were making more profits than his business was. Gobind took a note of this fact, discussed this with Adarsh and once also broached this subject with Naren, who conveniently said, 'Don't worry, Gobind, I am in full control of my business all the time.'

Naren knew that wasn't true, yet these words came out of his mouth unconsciously. The IT index was zooming fearlessly. From a modest 1000 three years back, the index stood at whopping 14000 in March 1999. While the index had grown more than fourteen times, a few stocks, including the C-10 stocks, had multiplied the investors' money more than thirty times. Money was being spun each day between 9.30 a.m. and 3.30 p.m. The ticker tape running at the bottom of TV screens became a synonym of passion, job, business, pastime, and even lifeline to some people, the trio being one part of this milieu. They were enjoying the never-ending joyride that brought thrill and money. The three of them booked luxurious penthouses with a leading developer of Delhi, in an under-construction building. The construction work had just started, but the coloured brochures that the builder showed were enough to entice people who had lots of money and wanderlust for quality living. The possession was due sometime in 2003. The three of them had chosen the top three floors, Naren being on the topmost and Gobind on the lowest of the three.

Adarsh was stuck between the engineer and an erstwhile car mechanic turned a business tycoon. Everyone was busy in their own ways. Naren had too much on his plate; the stock market was becoming a passion for him. Price rise brought an unprecedented happiness to him. He increased his bets steadily with BBC. He mentioned to Sonia that he wasn't happy with Chaitanya as he was too conservative to play in equity markets. Naren believed that equity markets were for the brave and the bold. He even saw shades of indecision and timidity in Gobind and Adarsh too. That was why Naren made all the investment decisions on behalf of the trio. He was the boss chosen by a silent, nonexistent election that took place when he started venturing into equity. Both Gobind and Adarsh commended his strong-mindedness and courage. Often, Naren would dictate to them when it came to markets. He was also told them often about how the stock prices would pan out over next week or next few months. To him, equity was a game of perfect timing, where smart players were better informed than the others. That was why the bigger guys made more money than the others. According to him, one needed the right kind of networking for surviving in the marketplace. Naren was often meeting fund managers now. He was one of the largest investors in the entire North India; bankers, mutual fund sales managers, fund managers and other brokers were making a beeline for a slice of his portfolio. He loved to interact with people who knew about equities, often wanting to have an upper hand in the conversation. He could argue with anyone on anything related to equities. If someone talked about fundamentals and long-term investing, he would brazenly tell them about how he made a fortune in the market by sheer courage and timing. He told everyone that—how he always kept an eye on prices by watching the market live. Anything unusual triggered a buy or sell action. He was soon questioning the portfolios that mutual fund managers were running. He compared their returns with the performance of his portfolio, found faults with any investment recommendation that came his way. He believed in himself, his understanding of the equity market and the functioning of the infotech sector too. He bought, believing that his stocks' prices would go up, and up they went, making him feel that he knew these companies. Some people in his office also took his advice when it came to investing. He attended many parties thrown by various banks as these gave him a chance to interact with the who's who of the investment world, the demigods who knew everything about tomorrow. From the peak he was standing on, the mortal world looked too small, too insignificant compared to what he already possessed. On one occasion, Naren publicly argued with a fund manager who spoke negatively about the ICE stocks. Naren called him names in front of at least two hundred people and said, 'This rat doesn't know anything about stock markets. He is talking about fundamentals when momentum is the name of the game.'

Meanwhile his fortune continued to soar. His business flourished further and a new set of private equity investors valued his company at 110 million dollars. Naren decided to offload another 20 per cent that could fetch him Rs. 100 crores looking at the prevalent rupee-dollar equivalence of 46.5 rupees to a dollar. The deal was supervised by Adarsh, who made sure that Naren didn't lose his midnight sleep over fluctuating currency and fickle-minded lawyers.

Naren could smell the money finding its place in his bank account. Even Sonia was aware of this deal. She wanted this money to be handled by the bank.

But Naren had other plans. He called up BBC.

13

New Vistas

It was September 1999. Naren enquired about the commissions that BBC made on his trades. Apart from this, BBC charged interest on the margin money at 18 per cent to his clients. Naren did the calculations, only to find this a incredibly lucrative business. Although his own business was doing well, it didn't have the element of instant gratification like stock investing had. Naren called BBC to set up a meeting. Now he didn't need Sonia to fix it up for him; BBC was closer to him than he was to Sonia. He didn't feel it necessary to inform either Gobind or Adarsh as they would have definitely opposed his proposal. They met up at a revolving restaurant in Connaught Place; from here they could see virtually the whole of Delhi within a radius of ten kilometres.

'I have sold a part of my business to foreigners. I have few more crores to be channelled into stock markets.'

BBC's eyes lit up, as if one had plugged two live fireflies in his eye sockets. Being a seasoned campaigner, BBC kept a lid on his excitement and asked Naren what was there in his mind.

'I want to become a business associate with you. I like to invest a part of my money in markets and lend the other part to other retail investors to earn interest income as well as brokerage, just like you do.'

'That's a wonderful idea. A man of your might should be more than just an investor guided by fools like me. Business is in your DNA. You shall do very well in stock markets because you understand it so well now. In fact sometimes in past I have relayed your advice to my investors and they benefited a lot from it. Now, don't ask me a commission for your advice, dear.'

Both of them laughed heartily at this. BBC had to go somewhere. He promised to get back to Naren with the required legal documentation to formalise their relationship.

Naren trusted BBC by now. He signed all the papers without batting an eyelid, and the next day, Rs. 100 crore was transferred to BBC's company account for a bigger game of fortune. Out of this, 50 crore (exposure of 300 crores) found its way into the same stocks that Naren was already holding; the rest of the money was used by BBC for lending to the clients. For this portion, BBC also agreed to share brokerage as well.

Naren was as excited as an electron in a heated cathode ray tube. He felt he had too much money to take care of. On top of it, the money was multiplying faster than he had thought. Cash registers were ringing, thanks to his investments and now his new business partnership with BBC. His exposure with BBC was over a whopping 1000 crores and another 170-odd crores with the bank. He made so much money in the stock markets that the gains stopped mattering to him. It all started with a small experiment about a year back.

He wanted to celebrate his success, so he decided to throw a small party for friends and relatives.

Chaitanya was bowled over by the invitation. Normally it was the bank who invited clients to parties. It was as rare as dewdrops in the desert to receive a party invitation from a client. There was no mention of any reason for this celebration. The card was a plain invitation to dinner and cocktails. Surprised, Sonia and Chaitanya decided to attend as Naren was too big to be ignored. Normally they carried gifts for clients on their birthdays, anniversaries, and other important events; since they didn't know what the occasion was, they decided to go empty-handed.

The party was organised in a five-star hotel. There were about a hundred people in the hall. One would assume that they all were close enough to be invited there. Chaitanya saw Adarsh and Gobind, their families, many strangers, and surprisingly BBC too.

What was he doing there?

How come Naren befriended BBC?

Chaitanya's mind was racing. He tried to connect the dots, moving backwards in time. It must have been during one of those countless parties that the bank threw, when Naren bumped into BBC and the rest must have followed. This jigsaw puzzle had only one block; even a blind man could have put it together without the slightest of effort.

Naren's voice boomed on the speakers fixed in the walls and false ceiling of the hall. Not too loud nor too faint, just perfect to be received in harmony on the eardrums—a hallmark of luxury of a five-star.

'Friends, I have invited to you all to celebrate something very special today, something that I fell in love with, something that I didn't know existed until a year back, something that brings lot of excitement to me, something that I have grown infinitely passionate about. This passion has now led me on a path of new business possibilities.'

Everyone was silent, listening to Naren, raptly.

'Most of you who know me as an engineer shall be surprised to hear about this new passion of mine. This became possible because of two persons who are very much present here and whom I shall always be grateful to.'

'Before I spill the beans, I want to ask everyone to guess about this new passion of mine.'

There was a few seconds' silence before someone from the crowd said, 'Real estate.'

Someone else said, 'Art collection.'

Another person said, 'You must be starting an IT company.'

There was a loud uproar of laughter followed by silence again. A few more guesses were made but no one could guess accurately.

Naren spoke again.

'Guys, don't rack your brains anymore. Let me first tell you about these two persons who are responsible for this decision. They are Mr Babu Bhai and Ms Sonia. Sonia, who works with a leading bank, got me on this path initially. She has been helping me with my investments for the last year and a half. Babu Bhai is a friend, mentor, and a stockbroker too.'

Everyone including Sonia, Chaitanya, Gobind, Adarsh, Rachel, and the invitees were more puzzled now. They didn't have a clue whatsoever.

Naren's speech continued unabated. He was confident, fluent, and charming with his words, indulging the crowd—holding everyone on the edge.

'Friends, I have started a new venture with Babu Bhai, partnering him in his stock market business. Needless to say, stocks have become my passion over the last couple of years. I had absolutely no idea that I would become a stockbroker one day. I am as surprised as you all are. Yet I am excited, rejuvenated, and enthusiastic about what is going to happen in this country and especially the stock markets. My conviction in equity forced me to make this decision and I want to celebrate it with all of you. This is all from my side, I don't want to stand between you and the liquid nirvana that's placed on the bar counter for all of you.'

A loud laughter broke out instantaneously.

'I thank all of you for sparing your time and coming here,' Naren spoke to an audience who had already begun to hound the bartender.

Naren's face beamed with radiance. His energy levels reflected a childlike enthusiasm. His eyes bore expectations of a prosperous future.

Chaitanya was disappointed, Adarsh and Gobind were shell-shocked, and strangely, Sonia was indifferent. Gobind and Adarsh took Naren to a corner.

'You didn't even bother to inform us, forget consulting. Is this what our friendship is all about? Keeping big secrets from your close friends?' Adarsh said.

'Naren, ai koi chnagi gal nahi haigi.' (Naren, this is not a good thing.) Gobind spoke in a soft tone, expressing his anger none the less.

'Gobind, Adarsh, listen to me. This happened sooner than I realised, like falling in love. I became so obsessed with this idea that I was scared to discuss it with anyone, fearing that everyone would discourage me. I am sorry for letting you guys down. Now that you know about it, I want you guys to help and support me in this also. Come on; let's raise a toast to this new beginning.'

The bullet had left the barrel. Adarsh and Gobind didn't press further, moved towards the bar where a mini scuffle was on. They had to wait for a few minutes to get their drinks. The bartender was busy as a water supplier in the Thar Desert.

Naren excused himself, spotted BBC, and caught up with him.

'I hope you like the party, Babu Bhai.'

'Naren bhai, maza aawi gayo.' (It's fun.) 'Let me get you a drink now. You deserve to get drunk tonight.'

BBC and Naren walked arm in arm, like two inseparable friends, their gait hopeful, their confidence infectious, and their friendship sprouting like a promise.

Gobind and Adarsh definitely felt left out. Even Lavanya couldn't help noticing this. She quickly moved over to where Gobind and Adarsh were and engaged them. She spotted their families and attended them.

Chaitanya felt lost. He didn't belong here. Everyone seemed busy, indulged, and falsely pretentious too. He was painting a picture of the future in his mind. He knew something wasn't right, something out of place and context. He found Sonia missing, wondered where she was. He waded through the crowded hall to search for her; his anxiety came to an end when he saw her talking to BBC. He dismissed it as regular banker-client banter.

But it wasn't.

What appeared from a distance wasn't true at all.

Chaitanya congratulated Naren for his new venture, wished him luck, and noticed that Naren did not treat him as warmly as he had treated Sonia. Chaitanya felt suffocated in this setting of pomp and cacophony. He waved to Sonia and signalled at his watch. Sonia, who appeared to be a bit busy, gestured that he should wait for some more time. Chaitanya had no other option but to follow her command.

As he was feeling lonely, he decided to step out of the hall and take a walk around the swimming pool area, where a few kids were having fun in the water. He pulled a chair and sat comfortably. He felt a lot better now. Soon he heard Gobind's voice calling for him. Gobind, who was carrying drinks in both hands, came to Chaitanya and offered him one of the drinks, which he told him was fresh watermelon juice. Chaitanya, being a teetotaller, had no issues in accepting the same.

'What are you doing here alone?'

'Nothing, I was getting bored inside. Actually I am not a party animal,' Chaitanya said.

Gobind replied, 'Mai bhi.' (Me too.)

'Naren ai theek nahi kitta, ai stock market sadde te palle nahi pad di.' (Naren is not doing the right thing, I don't understand the stock market at all.)

Chaitanya kept quiet. He observed Gobind. There was a trace of sincerity in his voice, a genuine concern for Naren, which most of the guests did not have.

Before Chaitanya could reply, Sonia called on his mobile and told him that she was ready to leave. Chaitanya finished his juice, waited for Gobind to finish his drink, and then sought his permission to leave. As he turned to leave, Gobind spoke. 'Chaitanya Paappe, may I have your mobile number please?'

'Yes, sir, why not? This is my card carrying my contact details. My personal email ID is written on the back. You can contact me any time you want.'

Gobind accompanied him to the hall, where Sonia was already waiting for them. They left shortly thereafter without meeting anyone else.

Sonia was smiling, humming a song that Chaitanya knew little about. Chaitanya was curious; he wanted to know how Sonia knew BBC. He tried hard but couldn't resist asking her about the same. Sonia told her about everything since they were going to be life partners; she told him that she was in cahoots with BBC, getting a referral fee from him on every trade that Naren placed with him. In a light-hearted manner, she also told Chaitanya that she got a fat one-time commission from BBC when Naren got into a partnership with him. The amount was obscene, much beyond what she was earning with the bank.

Chaitanya was shocked. He thought he knew Sonia but realised he didn't. His face turned as red as molten lava coming out of a crater; he asked Sonia to stop the car immediately and stepped out. He felt cheated; he knew what Sonia did was unethical. Being a bank employee, he had to report this incident to the management which would certainly affect his relationship with Sonia, maybe endanger their marriage too.

'Will you please say something?' Sonia asked, still sitting behind the steering wheel. She looked at his face and immediately knew that she had made a terrible mistake by telling Chaitanya.

'I am sorry, Chaitanya, but I did it only to secure our future. Anyways, the bank was losing business because of BBC,' she added.

Chaitanya kept quiet, his eyes turning crimson in the dark of the night; anger filled him beyond tolerance. He did not want to create a scene by shouting at her.

He kept his calm and said, 'I shall report this to the management tomorrow morning even if it affects us. Goodnight, Sonia.'

Sonia was furious; she was embarrassed too. She pressed the clutch, shifted the gear lever from neutral to first, and zoomed away, leaving behind a black streak of rubber marks on the smooth South Delhi road. Chaitanya had decided to take a long walk back home. His house was a good six kilometres away. He thought about the words he said to Sonia. Perhaps he shouldn't have said them at this hour especially when she was driving alone. He thought of calling her but stopped. Maybe it was his ego that came in the way. He kept walking, absent-minded, different thoughts clogging his mind at the same time. He had barely covered two kilometres when he heard his mobile beep. He knew who it was from, only he didn't want to check and respond. He had already begun to feel a dilemma being born in his mind. No matter what, he would do the right thing tomorrow when the bank opened. He was tired when he reached home; he needed a sleep. Before going to bed, he checked the message on his mobile, it read: 'I am sorry. I shall resign tomorrow first thing.'

Sleep eluded him. He picked up his mobile and typed a message to his boss. He looked at the picture of his parents and bowed to them. A new life waited for him.

The next morning, Sonia found her desk phone buzzing. It was her boss. She was scared to death. With shaking hands, she picked the receiver only to hear the boss shouting on the speaker, 'Sonia! Come here immediately.' She had no other option but to follow his command and take the long walk to the gallows. As she knocked on the boss's door, she could feel her knees creaking and a fear creeping on her nerves. Not certain of what she would say, she walked in.

'What the hell is going on, Sonia? What are you guys up to? I am shocked and frustrated with what Chaitanya has done.'

He threw a paper in her face and said, 'Read this gibberish.'

Sonia could not believe her eyes. Chaitanya had tendered his resignation, citing personal reasons.

'I don't know why he's done this. I really have no clue,' she spoke, sobbingly.

'I had a detailed conversation with him this morning. He has not only brought shame to the bank but he has also shattered my faith. I never thought that he would turn out to be so dishonest. How could he do that?' he said.

The boss gave a detailed account of what Chaitanya had told him. Sonia found tears rolling down her cheeks. She listened to the boss as guilt kept rising deep inside her. She wanted to run out of the boss's cabin and call Chaitanya as soon as the boss stopped.

'Well, you can't do much now. Don't tell the trio anything as they do not know anything about this fraud. I just hope that they never learn about it. I know about your relation with Chaitanya, I don't know what shall happen now. I can only wish you luck. You can leave now,' he spoke.

Sonia ran out of the cabin and dialled Chaitanya's number. His phone was switched off. She kept trying but all she heard was 'The number you are trying to reach is switched off.'

She went to the parking lot and picked up her car. She drove as fast as she could. Her fears came true when she found a lock on Chaitanya's door. She sat down on the stairs and cried aloud. She held her face in her palms and closed her eyes.

After waiting for a couple of hours, she gave up. She typed a message to Chaitanya, requesting him to call her back.

But she knew he wouldn't. Her sin was too big to be forgiven—his sacrifice too big a burden to be carried all her life.

She prayed for his happiness and went home.

It was all over because of no one but her own self. She cursed herself to death.

A few days later, she received a small packet addressed to her. She recognised Chaitanya's hand immediately. She tore it open to find a letter and a small box carrying the engagement ring she had slipped on Chaitanya's finger not so long ago. She was blank as she read the letter.

Dear Sonia,

After what happened that night, one of us had to go away. I am returning the ring, so that you can start a new life and find someone for yourself. I don't know where destiny shall take me. Don't waste time searching for me. If we ever meet again, it shall be by accident, not appointment. I won't lecture you on morality as I know life shall teach you in her own way. Just one thing, be honest with your clients if possible.

I wish you luck and a purpose-filled, clean life.

Goodbye!

Chaitanya

Shell-shocked, she clutched the ring in her fist, almost twisting it out of shape. She felt too weak to pick herself up from this moral dilapidation. She was sinking in her own mud and she didn't want anyone to save her. She decided to tell the truth to her boss and move on. Once she had finished with the boss, she would inform the trio as well. This was the least she could do.

14

They All Fell Down

'Don't be emotional, Sonia. I can save you if you wish.'

'Sir, you won't understand,' she said and walked out of his cabin.

But walking away from the bank wasn't that easy. HR department took a declaration from her that she wouldn't contact her clients for a period of six months or else she could be sued. Having no energy to fight and no desire to survive, she surrendered to her fate. She served her notice period and handed over all her clients to a new relationship manager. She had no option but to wait for six months before she could do anything for her clients. She decided to leave Delhi and stay with her parents for a few days, after which she would go to the hills, searching for Chaitanya.

Time and tide wait for no one. The trio forgot Sonia and Chaitanya pretty soon. Markets were booming and they were making money faster than they could breathe; they didn't need anything else. The new relationship manager kept on servicing them. Slowly the trio moved a major portion of their investments from the bank to BBC. This also helped Naren's new business prosper. Things could not have gone better for them. It was like a party that didn't seem to end. C-10 stocks didn't know any gravity; they kept on soaring day by day, making the trio more and more confident. Their cumulative exposure in stock markets was approximately 1300 crores, Naren contributing more than 98 per cent of it. The market value of their exposure was more than 3000 crores, thanks to the stock market boom.

The dream sequence continued until one day, a scam was unearthed in a couple of co-operative banks in the state of Rajasthan and Andhra. It appeared that these banks had dished out huge loans to a few individuals who used this money to ramp up prices of a few stocks. Markets came down a little bit when this news came out. The prices of C-10 stocks also fell by a trickle but recovered quickly.

'Naren, what do you make out of this little scam that's being talked about?' asked Adarsh.

'Frankly speaking, I don't know much about it. From whatever I read in the papers, it doesn't seem to be of much importance. See how markets recovered today,' spoke Naren.

'I agree with Naren. Anyways, with both of you being there with me, I am not worried about my money,' Gobind said merrily.

'Fill my glass, Adarsh, and don't be a worrywart. Everything is fine. Even if markets fall, we shall have enough time to walk out with more than handsome gains. BBC is with us. I know all his moves. He has put in lot of money in the counters that we are holding. We shall do exactly what he is doing,' Naren said.

'Rachel is asking me to take 50 per cent out,' Adarsh said as he poured soda and whiskey in Naren's glass.

'Don't worry, I shall speak to her, but if you want to take money out you can do so. It's your money after all,' Naren spoke with confidence.

Naren took out his mobile and dialled BBC's number. He spoke to him at length and assured Adarsh and Gobin d that everything was indeed hunky-dory. After finishing a couple of drinks more, they left.

After one week, markets fell again but recovered quickly. C-10 stocks were holding their own firmly, keeping Naren content and confident. His relationship with BBC grew stronger and stronger. He used to spend a lot of time with him, chalking out strategies for stock market investing. His regular business was also doing fine. He was due to travel for a month or so, meeting his clients across Europe. He had planned to take the family along as well. He needed a break; this could a good opportunity to celebrate his success in stock markets. One day while he was finalising his travel and stay arrangements, BBC called him.

'Naren bhai, I want to meet you as soon as possible. There is something exciting I want to talk about.'

'Sure, Babu Bhai, whenever you say.'

'Then let's meet at Taj Mansingh at 5 p.m. today.'

'Okay. See you, Babu Bhai.'

Naren ordered his standard drink; BBC settled for a chai.

'Naren bhai, a few large brokers are facing a temporary cash crunch as they have taken aggressive positions in the stock market. They need cash against the shares they are holding. We can make as much as 3 per cent per month.'

'Is this kind of lending safe?'

'Yes, it is absolutely safe as we shall be getting their shares as security. Moreover, these guys are highly reputed in the broking circles.'

'So what do you want me to do? Sell my shares and create cash for lending?'

'No, no. Why sell the shares? I think you can liquidate some of your fixed deposits and also use some cash that you can spare from your business. Your fixed deposits anyways don't earn much. Moreover, we can take the interest in cash also, so that we don't have to pay taxes.'

'How much are they looking to borrow?'

'They need more than a hundred crore but we can chip in whatever we think is appropriate.'

'I think I can spare about fifty. Give me a couple of days before I organise this. As I am travelling for a month beginning next week, I would like to finish this matter before I go, although I would like to receive interest by cheque only. No cash dealings with me,' said a beaming Naren.

BBC settled the bill and they went their ways.

The money was arranged before Naren left for Europe. He knew BBC would take care of things in his absence.

One week after Naren left, markets fell again; this time they did not recover the next day but continued to fall for three to four days in tandem. Naren called BBC.

'Naren bhai, it is nothing but a small correction. We should not worry about it. In fact we should buy more. This is a normal in a bull market.'

'Let's watch the markets for a few days and then we shall take call, Babu Bhai.'

Markets kept on falling. A few days later, the details of the scam were revealed to the public. It was not a small matter as the banks had lent more than a few thousand crores to stockbrokers, who used this money to manipulate stock prices. BBC kept on telling Naren not to worry, and Naren didn't worry even if he had lost about 15 per cent of the gains he had made so far.

A string of bad news came from the overseas markets also, where a few infotech companies that had raised millions of dollars from the public went belly up; their stock prices came crashing sharply. The losses of 15 per cent soon became 30 per cent. Investors believed that markets would recover, and they did, leaving investors, traders, and everyone involved with the stock markets even more confused.

'See, Naren bhai, every time the shares are falling, buying is coming in, especially in C-10 stocks. He is too big to fail, you know. I suggest we buy on every dip.'

Naren trusted BBC. He told him to do what he thought was right and decided to enjoy his vacation. He trusted BBC, and moreover, BBC had invested his own money too.

Naren enjoyed his vacation while things continued to worsen in India. A couple of brokers were arrested in connection with the scam while a few bankers were questioned by regulators.

Naren finally came back after a month-long vacation only to find that the stock market had crashed by over 40 per cent from its peak and investors of infotech stocks were becoming familiar with a new animal called lower circuit.

Brokers whom Naren had lent to went bust. The stocks they had provided as security went down in price as well, meaning that Naren could not recover even a fraction of the money he had lent to them. BBC's own portfolio went down in value day by day as bad news kept on pouring in. Naren wasn't able to think at all until the day came when even thinking could not help.

Chetan Parekh was arrested and the C-10 stocks fell more than 95 per cent over a period of time, giving no time to the investors to exit. From a position of having no sellers, stock markets came to a stage where there were no buyers. Everyone wanted to sell but shares kept on hitting the lower circuits. This meant that once the stock had fallen by 10 per cent, no more trading could be done in that stock on the day it hit the circuit. What had taken years to build took only a couple of months to be destroyed, leaving everyone dumbfounded, clueless, and helpless.

Naren was in a state of shock; Adarsh and Gobind were no better. Naren's exposure in the markets was obscene. By paying margin money of approximately 150 crores he had taken an exposure of 1000 crores in the market. Now the value of his stocks had gone down below 100 crores, which meant that his entire gains were wiped out. But he was still required to settle his account and keep paying the margin to BBC. He came to a stage where he had virtually no cash except the fixed deposits held in Lavanya's name in couple of banks. The money he had lent to the brokers could not be recovered as well. Since the mutual funds he had invested in also held the same stocks, their NAVs also fell in line with the stock market. There was no hope for Naren anywhere. Adarsh and Gobind were no better, although they were not as devastated as Naren was.

They had no one to seek help from, no one to look forward to. They remembered Chaitanya's advice now, but it was too late to do anything.

After lot of deliberation, they were able to convince Naren to sever his ties with BBC and not to roll over his trades any further. Adarsh helped him sell a huge chunk of his business to pay off the money Naren owed to BBC's firm. Their world that began with a bang ended in a whimper.

Slowly their life started taking a new course along the terrain of reality. One day while cleaning his drawers, Gobind found Chaitanya's card buried under papers. He took it out and flipped it to find Chaitanya's email ID written on the back.

Sonia went in search of Chaitanya in vain. After a few months, she gave up and came to Delhi to meet Gobind. She had a debt to settle; she would then go and stay in the place where she and Chaitanya were supposed to live as husband and wife.

Gobind got the help of a colleague to write email to Chaitanya. He just wrote two sentences: 'Chaitanya Paappe, we have lost everything in stocks. We need you. Gobind'.

PART 2

A Journey Begins

15

A Classroom with a Difference—Circa 2002

A man stands in a classroom, with whiteboard markers of various colours in his hand; a blank board faces a group of students that is composed of businessmen, homemakers, bankers, chartered accountants, traders, doctors, and college-going teenagers. The man's face radiates like a full moon. The classroom is silent because students are meditating. After exactly two minutes, an alarm would go off and the class would start. These two minutes are precious for everyone as they try to meditate, leaving behind their worries and anxieties, driving their mind to a state of blankness where nothing exists, nothing is felt, and nothing matters, as students focus on their breath moving in and out. These two minutes are liberating as the students unplug themselves from their routine, unaware of everything including the boisterous traffic outside the building where the class is held, thoughts of relatives unwell, family members waiting back home, business targets, boss's rant, the worry of breadwinning, upcoming exams, and numerous other things that clog a common mind all the time.

The man's eyes are open. He observes his ten students, who have enrolled for this unusual course that has no fixed tenure, no syllabus, no textbooks, no exams, no results to be declared, no certificates to be given, and no grades to be marked and sent to parents—a course unknown to the teacher as well. For many students, two minutes seem long enough to focus, long enough to sit still and not think of anything. A few students silently chant the Gayatri mantra, a few others repeat *om*, a few think of their deities, and a few have nothing else to focus on but the miseries of their past, silence being their bond for these two long minutes, hope their master. The man knows this journey is going to be difficult. He has to make his students change the course of their lives by changing their thought processes, shed their old habits to wear a new garb of discipline that could potentially change their future, embrace simplicity in a world that's growing more complex each passing day, and above all, make them believe in the importance of their karma without worrying about the fruition. Most of the faces are unknown to him. He doesn't know how these students came to know about this class. He did not advertise anywhere, he didn't tell anyone, and no visible references were received by him. Somehow the students have found their way to him. He is happy to see three familiar faces amid these students. Like other faces, these three faces also have worry lines streaked across their foreheads, black spots under their eyes, and a long, painful story of losses etched all over their conscience. A look of dejection reflects their broken strength and their deflated ego. But all this doesn't worry the man. He is as determined as Krishna, who won the battle of Kurukshetra for the Pandavas even before a single arrow was nocked on the bow. Two minutes are over; the class shall begin now. The man speaks for the first time.

'Friends, welcome to Moneymentors. My name is Chaitanya and I am going to be with you in this class till the time we achieve our goal. I am not a teacher, I am not a guide, I am not a master either. I am a student like you all are. Together we shall learn, grow, and prosper spiritually, if not materially. This class has no lecture schedule, as I do not know what to teach to the students who are older to me, who are wiser than me, who have seen more life than I have. Still I shall try my best. I have no different skill set from your own; it's only a matter of chance that I am standing here in the capacity of a teacher. Let's all unlearn and learn from each other and make this experience worthwhile. I request you all to introduce yourself to the class. You may tell little more than your names and also state the expectations that you have from this class or me.'

The first student is a homemaker named **Kantha Subramanian**. She belongs to Madurai, a small town in Tamil Nadu. She has a typical accent which most of the North Indians identify with the south. She speaks fluently though. She takes about three minutes to recount her experience with money and stock markets. She has lost a few lacs of rupees in the recent stock market fall. This has affected her married life as the money belonged to her husband. She wants to restore normalcy in her married life by recouping her losses from the markets and also probably make some more money. Simply put, she is here to make money and learn about stock markets.

The second student is a college-going teenager. She has a crisp voice full with energy. Her name is **Simmi**

Kharbanda. She stays in Lajpat Nagar; her grandfather was a refugee from Pakistan, who found a place here and raised his family with honour and pride. Her father is a food grain trader having his shop in Chawdi Bazaar. He has lost more than fifty lacs in stocks, thanks to a rogue banker. She is here to make up for this loss by investing in the markets again.

'I want to make more money than my father lost and make him feel proud of me,' she says.

The third student is a middle-aged paediatrician. He has his own practice in Greater Kailash part two, famously known as GK-II to all Delhiites. He hasn't lost money anywhere. He has heard that big money can be made by trading in stock markets, so he is here among all of them. If he likes the experience, he would like his son to take these classes as well. His name is **Naresh Kohli**.

The fourth student, **Balwant Jakhar**, hails from the holy land of Kurukshetra in Haryana. He is a retired IAS officer. His wife loves to go to kitty parties. Most of her investment ideas come from such get-togethers. He is an honest person who has made just enough to lead a healthy retired life. His wife has helped shave off a few zeros from his bank balance by dabbling in equity markets, thanks to her kitty group. He is trying to do the balancing act by attending this class. Someday he hopes to make his wife attend these classes too.

The fifth, sixth, and seventh students are acquainted with the man. He knows them well.

The eighth student is a writer, a dreamer, and a wanderer sort of a person. He is here purely for philosophical reasons. He has neither money to lose nor losses to recoup. He says he is here because of destiny. He was destined to be part of this class, so he came here; otherwise, who notices an ordinary 3×6-foot billboard from the window of a racing, crowded Blue Line bus? His name is **Mrigendra Biswas**.

The ninth student is a middle-aged lady named **Mridula Satija**. She is a branch manager of a public-sector bank. Her losses in the stock market have brought her here. Like others, she too wants to make quick buck in the markets, of course with the help of her teacher.

The tenth student is a young man in his late twenties. He works for a mutual fund. Now that he has lost everything he earned since he started working, he wants to redeem his pride by making money in the stock market. His name is **Sumant Mishra**. There is one more student in this class, whom no one knows about, except the trio of Naren, Gobind, and Adarsh. This student has opted for distance learning.

The man smiles as the introductions come to an end, subtly clears his throat, and says, *'I do not know anything about stock markets and moneymaking. Yes, I know a little bit about businesses and maybe life too. This may help because I feel there's a lot common between the markets and life. I shall try to make the best use of my experience and your life experiences to learn more. If we can learn sincerely, everything shall fall in place. I can't make any promise to those who hope to make money, hope to recover their losses, or seek to find a quick-fix solution for their stock market misdemeanours but I can offer some hope to those who want to adopt equity investing as sincerely as their religion.'*

The students are not able to understand anything. They look at each other, find the same expression of confusion writ large on each face. No one speaks though; there might be something exciting, something interesting and more rewarding down the road.

'Let's start tomorrow. Before you leave, I shall just say that investing is not about making money. Good night.'

Students begin to leave one by one in hope of finding something interesting tomorrow. The trio of the fifth, sixth, and seventh students also leaves just as everyone else. The man sits alone for a while, not sure about where to begin, how to teach these students meaningfully and do some good to all of them. He thinks about the past he chose to walk away from.

16

Understanding Equity

Anxious students arrive on time—their minds as open as their notebooks, hope guiding them through the maze of confusion they carried home the previous evening. Meditation time has gone up to three minutes today. It shall go up by one minute each day until it reaches fifteen minutes, and after that, it shall remain constant. Three minutes pass somehow, with students struggling to focus on any single point. Horses of thoughts race wild, mind toggles between the eternal and the mundane. The alarm goes off at last. Chaitanya speaks.

'Friends, I am happy to see you turn up on time. This is a good beginning. I thought a lot about how to start this journey with you all and I feel we shall do a great favour to ourselves if we begin by understanding the very meaning of the word **equity***. So, tell me what equity is.'*

It seems a simple, easily answerable question to most of the students. A few students raise their hands, mentally transporting themselves back to school days, feeling nostalgic. Chaitanya nods and they start speaking one by one.

Mrs Subramanian: Equity is nothing but shares and share market. Share prices go up and down and sometimes people make money, sometimes they lose.

Sumant Mishra: Sir, equity means shares of a company that are issued by the company in share markets, to enable investors to trade in them. Earlier, these shares used to be physical share certificates, now they are available in dematerialized forms also.

Balwant Jakhar: Equity means shares of a company.

Mridula Satija: Literal meaning of equity is fairness, although in the context of share markets, it means owning shares of a company either through primary or secondary markets.

Chaitanya looks around for the right answer but there are no more raised hands. The trio remains as quiet as an island after the passage of a storm, thanks to the losses they incurred in the past. The trio is here because of the insistence of Gobind and Rachel, or else they would never come to a class meant for middle-class students. Plus, what could be taught about equities in a classroom? They believe that nothing can ever bring back the money they have lost. They are sitting here physically pretending to be a part of this class, speaking nothing, feeling nothing, and hoping absolutely nothing.

Chaitanya says, 'Equity in the context of stock markets means 'ownership interest', simply put, people who own shares are the owners of the company. Let me try to explain this with a simple example of a chessboard that has 64 squares. Imagine these 64 squares to be the shares of the company. Say each share is worth Rs. 10, the value of the company is Rs. 640 (64×10). Suppose Mrs Subramanian buys 32 shares of this company from the market, she owns 50 per cent of the company. So in simple words, Equity means ownership and shareholders are the owners of the company.'

'But, sir, how can we own the company by merely owning the share certificates of the company? Owners practically run the company and are responsible for profit and losses. We do nothing except owning these shares and trading these shares in the market,' says Mrigendra.

'Although we as shareholders do not run the company on a day-to-day basis, we are still the owners of the company, entitled to the dividend payments made by the management. We may come back to this point again, for the time being, let's know that shareholders are the owners of the company and their ownership percentages are determined by the number of shares they own in a particular company. I would request Adarsh to spend some time with all of you and explain the ownership concept in more detail later.'

This wakes up the trio out of their slumber; they feel they should be more attentive at least, if not participative. Naren finds this class boring and too basic by his standards. Adarsh too feels the same; Gobind finds it enlightening though.

'Let me come to the second point now. How do the owners of a company earn money? Come on! Who shall answer this one?'

'Owners of the company make money when their company makes money, I mean when the company earns profits. A part of this profit may be given back to the shareholders as dividend or may be redeployed in the business itself for future growth,' says Adarsh.

Naresh Kohli, speaking for the first time, says, 'But I feel shareholders make money by buying and selling shares in the market.' His voice finds a few other supporters, who also nod in affirmation. Most of the students feel that people buy and sell shares for making money out of them, even if they are the shareholders or so-called owners of the company.

'Thank you, Mr Kohli, for raising this point which is very relevant from our perspective. This journey can't begin without understanding this point in depth; forget about completion of the journey. Most of the participants in the share market do think like you. Let me ask all the students here, if they agree too.'

Most of the hands except Adarsh's go up in unison, supporting the paediatrician's belief.

'I believe that all shareholders are equal. They all prosper when the company makes profit. This growth in profit reflects in share prices over a period of time. Before going into the details about equity and ownership, let me ask you another simple question. What do you mean by the creditors of a company? How do the creditors earn money? And how are creditors different from shareholders?'

Adarsh, raising his hand firmly, says, 'Creditors earn a fixed interest on their investments. They generally provide loans to the company and charge a certain rate of interest on this loan. They do not get a share of profits, but do get a fixed interest on their loans as per a schedule.'

'Can we simply say that shareholders own the company and make money when the company makes money and creditors make a fixed amount every year irrespective of the company making profits or not? I hope this is understood by everyone here.'

A few of the students find themselves becoming more alert as the discussion progresses. What they thought would be drab and boring is slowly becoming interesting. But the moot question of making money from the stock markets is still not answered. They still do not know how this shall be addressed. Meanwhile, Chaitanya continues.

'Now we know that the shareholders are owners of a company, although to a smaller extent, I want all of you to contrast the behaviour of the owners of a company—I mean the owners who run business on a day-to-day basis—and the persons who become shareholders of a company by merely purchasing the shares of a company from the stock markets. Think hard and try to find out as many differences in the behaviour as possible. We shall deliberate on this in our next class. I request all of you to think about this as much as possible. A few students like Mr Sahay, Mr Gobind Narwal, and Mr Kohli, who run their own businesses, shall be able to help us in this respect. I would also request Ms Simmi Kharbanda to speak to her dad and try to get some insights in this matter. With this we conclude today's session.'

To their own surprise, the students are beginning to enjoy seeing things with a different perspective and hoping to learn something new. Today's session was slightly different from what they had thought. They never thought that by owning simple, stupid share certificates, they were entitled to be the owners of the company. Although holding a few shares doesn't make any difference to the management of a company, it makes lot of difference to the person who has bought the shares from the market. The difference is the thought process.

17

Owners Versus Shareholders

After the customary meditation time which has now become four minutes, the students look forward to their teacher, their mentor, their guru who shall somehow teach them all about shares and the share market, maybe provide them with some golden rule book which carries a ready-made recipe for moneymaking. The guru smiles and starts immediately, without any ado.

'I hope all of you have had some time to ponder over what we discussed yesterday. Let's move forward from where we left off. I want someone to volunteer and start the discussion.'

Students look at each other reluctantly, hoping the other person will start, just as it happens in any classroom, until Gobind Narwal raises his hand and is allowed to speak.

'Sir, as I understand this matter, the owner of the business owns the business. He is the maalik, ultimately responsible for running the business and the results that come out of it, while the person who buys shares from the market is only worried about his share prices. One person is fully responsible for the business and the other is not at all bothered, and why should the investor be bothered at all? He is only a shareholder, after all. You cannot compare these two persons as their relationship with business is totally different and their thinking is different too.'

'Does anyone else want to say something? Ms Kharbanda, did you have a chance to speak to your father?'

'Yes, sir. I spoke to my father and asked about this. He says pretty much the same things as Mr Gobind has said. He says the owner builds the business from scratch, runs it on a day-to-day basis and tries to grow it over a period of time. Some businesses typically run for generations, especially in India. My grandfather used to be a grain merchant too. His business got handed over to my father when he passed away. He also says that in larger corporations, businesses are run more professionally than the smaller family-owned businesses, as there are many shareholders in these companies.'

'Can I request Mr Sahay to say something here?'

Naren is a little puzzled and quite lost too. Forgetting big losses is not easy and certainly his losses aren't small. He finally speaks.

'I agree with both Gobind and Simmi. They have explained the roles of the investor and the owners in very simple language. Both have touched upon the fact that the owner is ultimately responsible for the business outcome, while a small shareholder may not be. The owner eats, breathes, and lives on his business. For him business is everything, but for the investor who has purchased the shares of a particular company, the motive is somewhat different. He only wants to make money in these shares and is really not worried about the business. If the management does a good job resulting in profits for the company, the shareholders also benefit. So all I would say is that the owners are business focussed but the investors are price focussed.'

Students are impressed with Naren, the first time the class applauds for anyone. Chaitanya joins them in clapping and is smiling too. He has been able to break the ice with the trio, which is an important milestone in this journey.

'*Thank you, Mr Sahay, Miss Simmi, and Mr Gobind, you all have enlightened us with your thoughts. You made three very important points. **One**—the owner is the Maalik. **Second**—larger businesses have more shareholders or stakeholders than family-run smaller businesses, hence they tend to be run more professionally, and **third**, which to my mind is really a crucial point, that **owners are business focussed, while the investors are only price focussed**. I am indeed thrilled and enthused with this beginning and hope that all of you are enjoying this journey with me.*'

'Yes, sir,' all of them say.

'Would anyone else like to say something?'

Mrigendra Biswas raises his hand and says, 'Sir, Mr Naren Sahay has made a very important point here, which is philosophically very appealing to me: the fixation owners and investors have with different objectives.

'*Thank you, Mrigendra. It's important to have different perspectives in a group. This leads to greater level of exploration and learning too. Mr Kohli, would you like to add something to what these gentlemen have spoken?*'

'No, sir.'

'*Let me ask you another question. How many of you believe that these fixations on the part of owners and shareholders are correct? Please raise your hands.*'

Almost all the hands go up in the air in a jiff. Chaitanya wasn't surprised to see this. In fact he expected it to be so.

'*Good to see that we all think alike. Let me throw a spanner in the works and challenge this thought especially from a stock market perspective. I do not think the shareholder's fixation on the price is appropriate. Can you tell me why? Anyone?*'

All is quiet now; no one wants to accept the challenge thrown by the master as they believe he knows much more than them, that he is an expert on shares and the share market. No hands go up, making the master speak again.

'*Go back to where we started and think about business again. Think about what a share represents. As you know, a share is nothing but a small part of the business. It is a unit of an enterprise. Think what would happen to a share's price when the business does well and when it doesn't. Also think about your investment, whether you have invested your money in shares or in the business itself. On a larger neutral level, you shall see that by investing in shares you are actually investing in a business. Sumant, if a business can be seen only in terms of the number of shares, just as our chessboard is, then tell me what drives the value of a share. Or simply tell me how the prices shall move up or down.*'

'Sir, when a company does well, the value of its share should go up, and when it doesn't do that well, then the prices may go down also.'

'*Very good. So what is driving the price?*'

'Sir, the earnings that a company has or the profit a company makes drives the price.'

'*Should an investor then focus on price or something else that drives the prices? Price is only a by-product of something else which is more important. Is it correct to say that if businesses do well, the stock prices move up ultimately?*'

Everyone nods positively. They began from a simple concept of defining equity and now they are led to an important point, i.e. what drives the share prices? They all are getting a vague sense of direction now. The master wants them to first understand the game they are playing. The game of equities is actually a game of earnings, while most of the investors play this game on the turf of rising or falling prices. The trio also finds this class adding value to them, shaping their thought process like it should be. Adarsh looks at his watch, fifteen minutes more to go, but he doesn't want this class to end today. He is enjoying the feeling of being childlike, curious at an age when his kids are old enough to be meaningfully curious themselves. Being a student again is after all not so bad. He can feel the positive palpitation in Gobind and, more important, in Naren as well. It is Naren who has lost the maximum, probably lost more than the money itself. He has lost business reputation, his killer instinct, and his ability and confidence too. Adarsh recalls how worried he and Gobind once were. Not that they have come a long way from that point in life but he can see signs of positive changes in Naren. He is truly thankful to Guruji. He is sure of reaching somewhere, sometime with Gobind and Naren with him. To him the destination is not important, the journey is.

'Dear all, I want you to do a simple exercise. Try to find out about the richest people in the world. Get me their names and also the sources of their money. How much money they have made is not important to us but how they have made it is very important for all of us. That is all for today. Good night.'

18

The Wealthiest People in the World

The students are prepared today, their eagerness writ large on their faces, their excitement quite manifest. Meditation time stands between these initial moments and the discussion that shall guide the students further on the path of equities. Meditation is over, students are raring to go. Few things never change.

'Mr Jakhar, did you have a chance to find out about the wealthiest people in the world? Could you give me a couple of names please?'

'Sir, Bill Gates, Warren Buffett, and Angela Walton are the few names that I remember.'

'Thank you very much. Can you tell me more about them?'

'Sir, Bill Gates is the founder of Microsoft, one of the largest software and technology companies in the world. Warren Buffett is a legendary investor, and Angela Walton is the owner of Wal-Mart Stores.'

'How have they made so much money?'

'By running their companies,' says Jakhar.

'OK, anyone else?'

Mrs Subramanian speaks up. 'Sir, their companies generate huge profits through their operations, which has helped these promoters amass a lot of money.'

'Can anyone tell me names of the richest Indians?'

'Sir, Tata, Birla, Ambanis, Thapars, Modis, etc.,' says Gobind.

'Yes, you are right. Can you think about the source of their money as well? As Mrs Subramanian says, do they also make money by running their companies?'

'Yes, sir,' almost every one said unanimously.

'Let me ask you something. Why does their wealth keep on increasing or decreasing during the year? The profits of their companies do not change or get published on a day-to-day basis. Then how does it happen?'

'They hold shares in their companies, plus they also get salaries. As the share prices go up and down, the value of their personal wealth also changes. Let me also tell the class about Warren Buffett. He has made all his money by only investing in the shares of other companies like Coca-Cola, Washington Post, American Express, etc. His wealth is nothing but the value of the shares that his company, Berkshire Hathaway, holds in the other companies,' says Naren.

'Thanks, Naren. A major portion of the wealth of the richest people comes from the value of their shares, both listed as well as unlisted. While many rich people have made money from their own companies, Warren Buffett has made money by investing in the shares of other companies. We have a similar scenario back home. If you look at promoters of Infosys, Wipro, or the groups that Gobind mentioned, you shall find that these rich people own majority of shares in their companies. Since the value of their shares has gone up over the years, they have also become wealthier.'

'Sir, are these the same shares that you and I buy and sell in the share markets?' asks the paediatrician.

'Yes, doctor, these are very much the same shares, the same shares that we trade in, buy and sell, hoping to make a killing, the shares whose prices we track on a minute-to-minute basis. You must be wondering how the shares whose prices keep changing on real-time basis make someone so rich. Well, that's a point worth pondering. This is probably one of the most ignored realities in stock market investing. It is worth observing how the promoters of these companies have earned so much money for themselves. What is the biggest contributor to their earnings? If we closely watch the progress made by a few of these individuals over the years, we shall see very interesting things. I want all of you to focus hard here. If we understand this part well, then the rest of the journey is going to be much easier.'

Students are now deeply engrossed in what the teacher says. A few of the students, like the trio, are opening up and taking active interest in the class proceedings. Earlier they felt they were groping in the dark; now they can see the shape of things more clearly. They see a sense slowly setting in. The diverse background of the students added to the perspective of the class as a whole. They have a doctor, a student, a bureaucrat, a chartered accountant, a couple of businessmen, and a salaried person among themselves; this means a lot from a learning point of view. The master is aware of this fact. He wants his students to think and apply their thoughts to the reality of life and dynamics of investing. He wants to simplify things for his students, for he believes that investing is simple, learning is simple too. He knows no books can teach what real, practical learning can. Unfortunately there are no courses that can teach students how to invest and be successful. There are books that provide lot of theoretical knowledge but investing is beyond reading books and theory. Investing affects life; it can bring a positive change to one's surroundings if done properly, yet it can have a devastating impact on one's life if done arbitrarily.

'Let's forget about Bill Gates, Ambanis, and Birlas for a minute. Let's look at our own lives. Can someone share his own experience with the class, someone who has either run a business or seen a business grow?'

Gobind and Simmi raise their hands.

'Please go ahead, Ms Kharbanda. Gobind, we shall hear you after Simmi.'

'Sir, my father started his business way back in late '80s when he was only twenty years old. He started as small shopkeeper in West Delhi, who often found it hard to make both ends meet. He tells us that his monthly earnings were only a few hundred rupees to begin with. He went through a lot of hardships in the initial days. Sometimes he did not have customers. Sometimes he did not have money to buy enough stock for his shop. But he kept on going despite all the troubles he faced. He was focussed to make his business work despite all the obstacles that came in his way. Slowly the number of customers increased and his funding capacity increased too. Today after fifteen years he has a large shop in Chawdi Bazaar, he has money and obviously lot of customers. He also has purchased few properties here and there, including the large house in Lajpat Nagar where we stay currently. For me, summarizing his journey may be easy, but it hasn't been easy for him. Living this story on a day-to-day basis, seeing change come only at its own pace gradually over a period of time must really have been painful for him and our family. He always says **there is no shortcut to any place worth going to**,' says Simmi.

Gobind gives an account of his life too. He tells the whole class how he started from a small unknown workshop in one corner of Delhi to reach this stage of owning car dealerships across Delhi. He agrees with Simmi that the change really comes at its own pace. But keeping your focus and compassion is very important to reach your goals.

Chaitanya is really pleased to hear this. He says, *'Let me ask you something. If you were to put a value on your small workshop that you once owned, what would be it? I ask the same question to Ms Kharbanda also.'*

Gobind says, 'Sir, my father had left me a small piece of land on which I started the workshop. If I were to look at it in terms of value, the value would not have been more than, say, Rs. 1 lac at that point in time.'

'And what is the value of your empire today?'

Gobind is little bit surprised at this question. But he answers it. He says, 'I think the value of my showrooms, the service stations, my dealerships, etc. would easily be more than Rs. 100 crores.'

Simmi also says that her father's assets have swollen from a paltry few thousands when he started his business to more than Rs. 50 crores as of now. The class is slowly getting an idea about what the master is trying to arrive at. Why is he discussing these examples? No one speaks or tries to jump to conclusions. They all are in unchartered waters, probably only toe-deep right now, but they are definitely in. They want to go waist-deep, neck-deep and then swim leisurely too. But right now, they are quiet. Finally, Balwant Jakhar speaks in his husky voice, 'Sir, can I ask you something?'

'Yes.'

'If Gobind and Simmi's fathers had issued shares to shareholders twenty years back, would the price of those shares have gone up by now?' he asks.

'Don't ask me. Ask the class.'

Adarsh speaks up for the first time. 'Yes, if they had issued shares at that time, their prices would have definitely gone up now. Since they haven't issued the shares, they are the 100 per cent owners of their companies and hence have benefited from the growth of their respective businesses. However, I may add that they might not have seen their business from a shareholder point of view, because they are the owners, they are responsible for running the business. But all of this doesn't change the reality that they are the only shareholders in their companies. Technically speaking, Gobind and Simmi's fathers have been holding on to their shares since inception of their businesses, a time period of almost twenty years,' he says.

'Thanks, Adarsh, you have hit the nail on the head. You have given a new viewpoint to the class. Seeing the business from a shareholder's perspective definitely helps. Now we need to reverse this argument and think hard. When a shareholder starts seeing business from a promoter's perspective—what happens? I want all of you to remember the stories told by Gobind and Simmi and think along the new line of thought, i.e. thinking like a promoter, and see if it helps. We shall end our session here only.'

Another day comes to an end. Chaitanya feels strongly attached to this group of the butcher, the baker, and the candlestick maker.

19

What Works in Life Works in Stock Markets Too

Everyone turns up on time yet again. This means that the students are enjoying the class. They always come prepared for their lessons. They browse the Internet to find information on investing. They are enjoying the meditation sessions too. They feel a mystical calm fill them from inside. They are able to concentrate much better now, leaving their day-to-day worries outside this classroom. The master starts talking immediately after the meditation is over.

'Let's rewind the tape a little bit and think about what Simmi's father says about shortcuts. Simmi, can you please repeat the statement for all of us?'

'Yes, sir. **There is no shortcut to any place worth going to**.'

'Thank you, Simmi. I want all of you to pause here for a minute and think about this saying. Go back to the history and mythology books and see how people struggled for years to achieve something worthwhile. Remember those saffron-clad yogis who went to forests and meditated for years before the gods appeared and blessed them with two or three boons. By the time the gods appeared, these yogis were buried deep under anthills and years of turmoil.

'I remember the story of Vishwamitra who competed with Rishi Vashistha to become a Brahmarishi. It was after years of meditation and prayers (called Tapasya) that Vishwamitra was blessed with the title of Rajrishi but he wanted to become Brahmarishi like Vashistha. He was grossly disappointed. He went to the forests again and came back after a few years to claim the coveted title (called upaadhi) of Brahmarishi, but all he got was a title or upaadhi of Maharishi. He did not feel let down and went to the forest for a record third time. When he came back this time, he was awarded with Brahmarishi's upaadhi finally. Attempts were made to disturb his meditation by sending female dancers known as apsaras, but he was not deterred from his path and completed his Tapasya. He became so powerful through his yoga and meditation that he almost created a new universe one day. He challenged Indra Dev, god of rains, who did not allow Trishanku to enter the heavens or Swarga.

'When Indra kicked Trishanku out of the heavens, he started falling down towards earth; Vishwamitra stopped Trishanku in between and made him hang in the air as he began to create a new Swarga for Trishanku. These powers came to Rishi Vishwamitra only after long arduous years of discipline and meditation.

'Let me ask you a few questions here.

'Can a newly born baby start walking the next day?

'Can a student of nursery grade be admitted to engineering college the next day?

'Can a multistorey skyscraper be made overnight?

'Can businesses turn profitable on day one?

'Was Rome built in a day?

'Try to answer these questions in your mind and think about the shortcuts. You shall find that shortcuts often do not work in life. Systematic and disciplined hard work has to be put in, for achieving something worthwhile. This is true in life, sports, studies, and stock markets too. The examples are in front of you. Microsoft was started from a garage some thirty years back. Warren Buffett started investing at the age of eleven and today he is more than seventy years old. That's almost sixty years of investing. As all of you know that he is one of the most disciplined investors across the world, you would appreciate what these sixty years of disciplined investing have done for him. He is the second richest person in the world after Bill Gates. So when we talk about businesses and their success, please remember that the sustainable success comes only after long time periods. I may add here, what works in life works in stock markets too.'

At this, Sumant Mishra raises his hand and seeks the master's permission to say something. Permission is granted and Sumant says,

'Dheere Dheere he mana, Dheere hee sab hoye.

Mali seeche sau ghara, ritu aaye phal hoye.'

'Sir, Saint Kabir says in this couplet (Doha), that everything has a time. It is important to be patient as things happen over a period of time. The gardener may water a plant hundred times but the plant shall bear fruit only when the season comes. I feel equity investing is one of such things, isn't it?'

'Yes. Sumant, you are bang on in making this point. Patience is of paramount importance when it comes to investing. There are moments when you want to give up, when you aren't happy with the results or progress, when things aren't exactly *going your way. At such times, one has to exercise patience. Sometimes you may have to even start from scratch but don't hesitate doing it. By all means do it. You must be wondering what we are trying to achieve through these discussions about business growth, patience, shareholders, and promoters. What is this all leading to? Frankly speaking I do not know. This may confuse and disappoint you for a while, but we may have to live with it. Equity investing is no classroom teaching, it has no fixed curriculum that a teacher can follow. We are dealing with nothing but life which is highly uncertain. Consistent hard work is very important in this battle fraught with uncertainties. When we talk about shortcuts, it's not that the shortcuts are bad or they do not work. They may work sometimes but most of the times they do not lead to the desired results.'*

'But what is the desired result here, sir? What is our goal while investing in equity?' asks Mrs Subramanian.

Before anyone can speak, Sumant blurts out, 'Our aim is moneymaking, what else?'

It seems to be a premeditated answer but no one questions this response. No one thinks hard enough about this casual answer except Chaitanya, who chooses to be quiet, while Sumant looks at the class to find any supporters for his argument.

'Who all agree with Sumant?'

Most of the hands go up involuntarily as if they all are members of a political party seeking refuge in a self-sustaining ideology. This gives a fair amount of idea about how the class thinks, how the investors think, how they behave, and what they expect out of the markets. While the master is aware of this thought process of investors, he finds the class highly polarised towards moneymaking, about which the master knows nothing. He feels as if the class has gone back to square one. He decides to ask all the students one by one. Everyone, including the trio, Mrigendra, Simmi, Balwant, the paediatrician, Mrs Subramanian, and Mridula, says that they have a bee in their bonnet. This also makes the game more challenging and the journey more worthwhile, although the students do not realize this. The teacher has to figure out the future course of action carefully. The foundation stone needs to be laid perfectly in order to support the building. He has to somehow move the students away from the notion of moneymaking. If their objective is moneymaking, then they cannot reach far from here, and this worries the master. He has tactfully handled the class so far, he has led them down this path quite successfully, making them think aloud. He wants the answer to come from the students themselves, so that the learning becomes permanent. He wants to sow the seeds so deep in the crust of their minds that the spring blooms eternally, irrespective of the environmental changes happening around them. He thinks hard about how this should be done. He looks at the class once and decides to call the day off. However, before calling the class off, he asks Mrigendra Biswas to recapitulate what they have studied so far. Mrigendra makes the following points:

1. Investing in shares means ownership in companies

2. Shareholders should think like promoters

3. There is no shortcut to any place worth going to, and

4. Equity is a large component of the money earned by the richest people across the world

'Thank you, Mrigendra, for summarizing this succinctly. I request each of you to ponder over these points and assimilate them before taking the next step forward. With this we end today's session. Good night.'

20

Don't Make Money—
Create Wealth Instead

'Today we are going to discuss something which is a figment of my imagination, something neither discussed nor taught in any school. It may be merely my observation, but I feel it's an important aspect of investing. Over the last few years, I have met many equity investors during my working years. I asked everyone "What is your objective of investing in equity?" Most of them said, "I want to make money." My basic contention to this notion of making is "You can make money in so many ways, why equities?" One can simply open a restaurant or sell tea from a roadside stall. We know many betel leaf sellers or paan waalas who have raked in moolah by doing their jobs. I have nothing against any profession. I am making a simple point, if one wants to make only money, then there are many things that can be done, one doesn't necessarily have to invest in equities. The objective of investing in equities should be far more superior to than just making money. I feel equities are a perfect tool for wealth creation.'

Simmi interrupts Guruji and says, 'But, Guruji, isn't wealth creation similar to moneymaking?'

'I am glad that you asked, Simmi. I shall not answer this question. I would rather ask the class about the difference

between money and wealth. Tell me what you understand by these two terms. Have you ever thought about these two, or do you feel both mean one and the same thing?'

Chaitanya looks around at the 'fresh from meditation' faces trying to think hard. Yesterday most of them had raised their hands, indicating that they wanted to make money in the markets. Frankly, the students have never ever bothered to think about wealth. They think of money and only money while investing. Their eyes show that they are clueless on this subject. Some investors never bother about differentiating between moneymaking and wealth creation. To these investors, wealth is synonymous with money.

Naren raises his hand and says reluctantly, 'Sir, I shall be honest with you. I have seen both good and bad times in my life. I have started new businesses, made huge investments, bought and sold companies, and took big bets in markets too, but I never thought about money and wealth. Now that you have mentioned these two terms, I have a faint idea of what you are talking about, what you want us to ponder about. Let me try to explain the difference between the two. Wealth has a sense of permanence while the idea of money is temporary. Although one may argue that nothing is permanent in this world, wealth still would outlast money. Many people claim of having made money, but only a few can claim to have created wealth. When we talk about a paan wala, we say he has money. We don't say he has created wealth. Similarly when we talk about Warren Buffett, we don't say that he has made money. To me, wealth is leaving behind enough money that helps your next few generations to survive without having to work at all. I think of wealth as something that empowers an individual to create a huge difference for his family, society, and the country. Everything else would come close to money. As I speak, I realize that the richest persons in the world have not earned money for themselves but have created wealth and they surely have enough today that puts them in different league.'

Naren sits down after making his point.

'I couldn't agree more with you. You have made a very relevant point about money and wealth. Although it is difficult to assume that money is temporary, wealth definitely has a dimension of permanence attached to it. Let me ask others if they agree with you.'

Everyone seems to be in sync with Naren, who has made them more alert. They nod their heads in affirmation and also clap hard for Naren for making this point. Chaitanya asks all of them to think of more differences but no one comes forward. He decided to speak himself again.

'I would like to add to what Naren has said. I feel wealth has a sense of positive abundance attached to it. Let me quote the definition of wealth from a dictionary to all of you. Wealth is the abundance of valuable resources or material possessions. The word wealth is derived from the old English weal, which is from an Indo-European word stem. An individual, community, region or country that possesses an abundance of such possessions or resources is known as wealthy. Abundance differentiates money from wealth. This abundance makes wealth creation far more serious pursuit than mere moneymaking. There is actually a promoter/businessman in India whose wealth has been estimated at Rs. 76000 crores. If he converts his stock holdings into cash and decides to do nothing else but enjoy the fruits of his wealth, he can sustain for 76,000 months or 6,333 years, even if I assume his monthly expenditure is Rs.

1 crore. *That is wealth. If we assume 100 years as the average lifespan of one generation, then this gentleman can rest assured that his next 63 generations have nothing to do, without even bothering to put this money to use. I am not even trying to consider the overlap between two generations. This may sound funny, unreal, or surreal to some of you but this is wealth, sheer wealth. Everything else may pass for money.*

'Another point that I would like to make is the long-lasting impact of wealth creation. **Wealth may impact a few generations.** *Once a generation creates wealth and protects the same, the impact is felt for years to come. We see not only the wealth creator benefiting from it but also the next few generations tending to reap the benefits, owing to the empowerment that comes with it. One may look at leading business families or successful financial investors and realize this. Money, on the other hand, at best helps sustain the means at the same or slightly higher level which is more a reflection of the social environmental changes than sanguine effect of resource generation.*

*'***Wealth also means financial uplifting***. Wealth is synonymous with financial uplifting, a change in league which reflects not just on the material front but also on the social front. Wealth may permanently change the way we live, do business, approach our own life matters and how we see society. Wealth may bring a far superior empowerment as compared to money. Money, to my mind, can only bring short term cosmetic changes in lifestyle.*

'Yes, Mrs Subramanian. Do you want to add something?'

'Sir, can we say that money is like the title of Rajrishi and wealth is Brahmarishi?' she says.

Everyone laughs. Guruji is amused too.

'Yes, dear, we can say that.'

Mrs Subramanian continues, 'I would like to make another point too. I think wealth is a greater enabler compared to mere money. We see some of the leading riches of the world contributing to philanthropic causes. Bill Gates runs a foundation for eradication of polio. Similarly we see many businessmen in India allocating a part of their wealth for social causes. Tata Group is believed to be devoting a large part of its profits toward charity. J. R. D. Tata once said, "What comes from society must go back to them many times over." I am not saying that every wealth creator has contributed towards society across all the countries but wealth has that enabling power in it which can effect changes at a much broader level. Wealth doesn't only enable us to contribute to philanthropy, but education, sports, medical facilities, and business innovation itself. Maybe this enabling aspect of wealth is what makes a few people seek it.'

'Thanks, Mrs Subramanian, for enlightening all of us. I am in complete agreement with you. I hope all of us are clear about the difference between money and wealth now. Now ask yourself the following questions. Please be true to yourself as the answers to these could lay the foundation stone of a very interesting and meaningful journey.'

Do I want to make money or create wealth for myself?

Can I create wealth over a short period of 3/6/12 months?

Why there is only one Warren Buffett in the whole world?

Can wealth creation be done through disciplined investing?

'If the answer to first question is moneymaking, then this class is not for you and you can save yourself some time by doing something else. If your goal is wealth creation, then I can assure you lot of enrichment through this platform I chose to call Moneymentors. So if wealth is what we seek, then we are in the right place.'

The master can feel the happiness in the shining eyes of his students. Today he has touched the first milestone in this journey. He has been able to make them understand the crucial difference between money and wealth. He knows what he has achieved today. He can see a hand going up, out of the corner of his eye. He turns his neck to face the student who probably wants to say something.

It is Mridula Satija, the branch manager. She says, 'Sir, being a banker, I always thought that I understood money matters well and maybe slightly better than others but you have opened my eyes today. I never thought about wealth creation before. I thought dabbling in equities shall help me earn more and more money but it didn't happen. I shall go home today and read in detail about the wealth of the richest persons in the world and see what they have created with it. I thank you from the bottom of my heart for guiding us to this point and hope that you shall show us many more miracles like this in future as well.'

A few more students express their gratitude. They realize the difference today's lecture has brought to them. They can now connect dots going backwards and see clearly how the master has led all of them to this point. They can't help feel grateful to their guru.

Sumant Mishra says, 'Sir, Bible says—Seek and ye shall find.'

Everyone claps for him and for their guru before leaving for the day.

21

Wealth Creation Is Boring

'Now that all of you have understood the difference between moneymaking and wealth creation, I want you to know that wealth creation is a very boring process. There is no fun, no excitement, and no instant results may be available to all of us. There is absolutely no guarantee of success. We do not know how much time it takes. There are lot of risks involved, and failure may break our back at any point in time.'

'Sir, if there is no guarantee of success then why should one pursue this goal of wealth creation at all?' asks Simmi.

'Simmi, life is all about doing our karma, seeking worthwhile goals, trying new things, setting higher standards and benchmarks for ourselves. In pursuing most things, we do not know if we shall succeed. For example, when you left your home for this class today, were you sure of reaching here safely? Or when you took admission in school, were your parents sure of you going to college? When Gobind set up his workshop, did he know that he would own an empire of service stations one day? Maybe he knew that he would have to put a certain amount of money, minimum amount of hard work to reach somewhere worthwhile. Investing is like that only, you may seek the goal of wealth creation and may not reach there despite all your efforts or you may even reach there. Who knows? Our karma is to try and try till we get there. It is like any other quest that human

beings undertake. Remember what Bible says —seek and you shall find. You shall know about success or failure only in the end or, let me say, only later, not today. One may have to bear pain, negotiate risks, and give one's best and still only hope for the success. I told everyone in the beginning itself that I have no answers, I don't know about any certain way that can lead to wealth creation. Together we may find a formula. I hope I have made myself clear.'

'Yes, sir.'

Sumant speaks now and asks, 'Sir, what if we end up losing everything that we have invested in the markets and stocks? Forget about wealth creation, we may have to worry about our own survival.'

'Yes. This may actually happen, but we do not know yet. We may find ourselves on the brink of disaster and may end up being poorer. But that is true for everything in life. You may lose your job tomorrow and may not get another one for fifteen years. There is a risk in everything we do. Looking at the pollution levels in Delhi, ideally all of us should have oxygen cylinders on our back.'

The class bursts into laughter at this. Chaitanya knows about the apprehensions that his students have, especially after the losses they suffered in the markets. But he is aware of the power of equities; he knows that equities do have a great potential despite offering no guarantee. He picks up a marker and writes this on the whiteboard.

'Someone is sitting in shade today because someone planted a tree many years ago.'

He asks the students if they know who has said this. No one is aware.

'These words are said by Warren Buffett, the legendary investor, who has made his fortune by investing in shares. He started investing at the age of eleven, and later on, he felt that it was too late to start investing. Investing is like growing trees. You have to sow seeds first, wait for the sprouts to come through, watching over them like parents, taking care of them, and see them grow into trees one fine day—quite a boring thing to do, when you see it on a day-to-day basis but the results can be transforming over a longer period. Just as you can't gauge growth of a tree or a child on day-to-day basis, you can't see your wealth change positively on day-to-day basis.'

Chaitanya urges them all to look at their own lives and see how many boring things they have been doing regularly and thinks of another example.

'How many of you believe in God?'

Everyone raises hands, surprised at this question.

'How many of you go to temple on, say, every Tuesday?'

Once again almost all hands go up except Mrs Subramanian's.

'Mr Balwant, for how many years have you been going to the temple of Hanuman ji?'

'Sir, ever since I was six years old. My father used to go to this temple regularly, and before him, my grandfather also visited the temple regularly.'

'So your family has been visiting the temple regularly over the last hundred years or so, right? Can I ask you how many times has the monkey god appeared before you or anyone else in your family and blessed you with boons?'

'Not even once, sir.'

'Still you continue to go there, right or wrong?'

'Right, sir.'

'Are you hopeful of seeing God one day?'

'No, sir.'

'Because you believe in God, even if you haven't seen him. It's a matter of faith; you shall continue going for ages even if you know that the gods are not going to descend to earth to bless you. But praying is an act of goodness. It provides you an opportunity to focus and concentrate. It's a type of meditation. Investing is also like praying, seeking your dharma, doing your karma, and having rational expectations. Of course you shall try to make logical decisions here, checking your progress at regular intervals along the way. But you shall have to adopt investing like a religion, having faith all along. You may also not see all the results in your lifetime probably, your successors shall benefit from the steps you have taken, just as some of us would have benefited from the assets we inherited. Good investment practices can be a worthwhile inheritance to be given and received too.'

'Sir, can I say something?' asks Mrs Subramanian.

'Yes, Mrs Subramanian, go on.'

'Sir, I want to share a personal experience with the class. I have a nephew who is of the same age as my son. Ever since he was in seventh grade, he wanted to become an engineer and wanted to study in IIT Chennai, then known as IIT Madras. His parents planned for it very carefully and got him into coaching classes when he was in ninth standard. They got him distance education lessons called YG files from Brilliant tutorials. My nephew put in systematic hard work over these years, balancing sports, extracurricular activities, and studies too. He took a disciplined approach for almost five years of his student life and finally got into IIT Madras on second attempt. Now he is working in US earning a decent salary. On the other hand, my son adopted a casual approach. He took studies lightly till eleventh grade and then put in all the hard work for clearing IIT in twelfth grade only. He also joined a crash course for three months after his board exams. He sat for many engineering college entrance exams but could not clear any one of them. Although he is also quite successful now having done his engineering from a private college, he laments sometimes that he didn't work hard enough to get into the top engineering institute of the country. I think wealth creation is like studying for IIT. Regular hard work and discipline can definitely help one to reach near the goal. Am I right, sir?'

'Mrs Subramanian, you have given a very good example. Although IIT is not the end of the world, it definitely puts a student in a different league.'

Mrs Subramanian continued, 'Sir, I completely agree with you on the boredom part. A person who thinks long-term may have to live through times which are perceived as boring and vegetative by others, although such times can be immensely rewarding for that person.'

'Investing in equity for the long term is as boring as sowing seeds, as dull as preparing for an entrance exam five years down the line. One may not have stories to share with friends or interesting incidents to discuss over cocktail parties. One may not have any instant gratification for very long periods of time. We shall experience this shortly when we start investing in the equities. I think this experience is going to be a worthwhile one just for the sake of it. Since we are going to start investing soon, we shall be discussing about equity markets and other investment options beginning next week. Before we do that, we have to discuss a few more important things about investing.'

The master himself doesn't know much about how to proceed from here as there are no rules in this game. He has to keep his faith like Balwant and visit the temple every day even if the gods are not going to descend to earth to bless him.

22

Think Long-Term

The meditation time has gone up to more than eight minutes now. Surprisingly, students do not fidget; rather, they enjoy this session. They do not count seconds in their mind now; they let the silence take over their conscience and lose themselves in the river of calm. They find their concentration improving, span of attention increasing, and sense of peace hovering around them most of the time. They feel a strange empowerment within themselves, thanks to Chaitanya. Some of them call him by name, others call him Guruji.

It is Sumant Mishra who takes the initiative and speaks up. 'Guruji, when it comes to investing, every Tom, Dick, and Harry talks about investing long-term. But no one has ever been able to define long-term to me. Some say it's one year, some claim it to be three years, and some say five years. Can you please solve this puzzle for me?'

Before Guruji tries to say something, a hand goes up in the air. Guruji nods and Mrigendra Biswas stands up to say something. He says, 'Sumant, I do not know much about investing yet but I can say with lot of conviction that long-term is definitely longer than five years.'

'And why do you think so?' asks Sumant.

'Because five years is too short compared to life,' says Biswas.

'What kind of answer is this?' says Sumant.

'Sumant, no one knows the real answer. You must have read in your books that long term is more than one year. That's only for tax calculation purposes. I find Mrigendra's answer quite fascinating though. Think of your own life. Tell me when did you start working and till what age do you plan to work?'

Sumant says, 'Guruji, I started working at the age of twenty-three years and I plan to retire at sixty. So I plan to work for thirty-seven years precisely.'

'Can I say then, that you need to manage all your resources, including money, really well during these twenty-seven years?'

Pat comes the reply - Yes, sir.

'You have solved part of my problem and you have also endorsed Mrigendra's statement. He is right about life. It is much longer than the long term generally taught or thought about. So a person needs to carefully manage and grow his money over a much longer period than he generally thinks.'

Mridula: Sir, but that's too long a time period. Is it practical to invest the money for such long periods?

'Mridula, probably twenty-seven years is not the right answer. I agree that it is indeed a long period. Warren Buffett says that a person starts earning at the age of about twenty-five years and retires by fifty-five years or so. During this period, if he earns even a modest return like 9 per cent and avoids a big loss along the way, he has created wealth for himself. So I don't know what the right answer is but can tell you with a lot of conviction that very few investors think really long-term. Those who do, create a niche for themselves and may end up creating wealth too. Let's look at our lives first. Most pay insurance

premiums are for twenty years, we have been doing fixed and bank deposits for periods longer than ten years. Generation after generation, we keep saving through post office deposit schemes, then why can we not think that long when it comes to equity markets or investing? Let's go back to the concept of moneymaking and wealth creation and choose our objective. Before we actually dip our toes in the equity markets, I want each of you to have this thought clarity about the time period for which we are going to invest. Let's assume that we shall be investing for a much longer period than a normal person thinks about. Am I clear to everyone?'

Everyone is nodding although their body language doesn't reflect confidence.

Gobind: Sir, is it possible that one makes lot of money or, say, creates wealth before the long-term period is over but stays invested, and the markets go down before the person is able to take his money out?

'Yes, it is quite possible, Gobind. Markets are fraught with uncertainties. We do not know what shall happen in the next few years in our lives or in markets. We may make money over shorter periods and lose money over longer periods. It is entirely possible that even after investing for long periods of time, one may not create wealth and we have to be prepared for it. But historically there is not much evidence of people creating wealth over shorter periods and losing money over longer periods. This is getting very interesting. I want to throw this topic open and have an organised discussion about it. Let's divide the whole class in two groups: one group speaks in favour of long-term investing and the other group speaks against it. Are you game for it?'

This sounds exciting to everyone, especially the students who do not participate much. They all agree to it and the class is divided in two equal groups. Group one consists of Naren, Gobind, Naresh Kohli, Mrs Subramanian and Simmi. The remaining students, i.e. Adarsh, Mridula, Sumant, Balwant, and Mrigendra, form the second group. A space is created in the centre of the classroom, where the chair for the moderator is kept. Chaitanya becomes the discussion facilitator as the students draw battle lines in their mind.

'Before we start the discussion, I have one request to all of you. Please do not discuss for the sake of winning, discuss with an objective of learning. No one shall win or lose; we all look forward to having a healthy discussion here. You have a full fifteen minutes to jot down your points.'

Both the groups go into a huddle, talking in whispers. A few students take out their notepads, write down their points, while others merely listen. Chaitanya observes them casually. He is ready with his whiteboard markers. He shall be using them more productively during the discussion, noting important points. Fifteen minutes are over. Everyone is ready. Group one is pro and the other group is against long-term. Group one starts.

Naren: Investing is not about only investing money. Investing is also about investing time, energy, and intellect in various pursuits that we undertake. Take an example of a businessman, a housewife, a student, and for that matter, an investor too. We have already seen a few cases of investing discussed here over last few weeks. Most of the areas in life see very little changes over shorter periods. A business shows volatile results in the beginning, and then with application of resources and time, it starts stablising. For the sake of convenience, I am assuming that the market environment is supportive to this business. Slowly this steadiness leads to economies of scale and business profits start increasing. One factory becomes two and two become four. More often than not, this is achieved only after many years, just as it happened in my business. When I look at it closely, I find that my business has seen more than three economic cycles that lasted over five years each. So long-term works for business. As equity investors since we invest in businesses, the long term definitely works.

Naresh Kohli: I agree with Naren. Even my practice became steady after a long period of time. Initially I had to work as an intern with an established dentist for only a few hundred rupees per month. I gained experience over time, became more confident, and took the plunge. I purchased a shop in an up-and-coming shopping complex. This area was so new that no one imagined that the place would throng with people one day. I have spent days sitting alone in my clinic without a single patient visiting me. After fifteen long years, I am in a position to work on my terms. So, long-term works for me as well.

Simmi: Since I have seen my father's business develop, grow, and stabilize over a longer period, I have no reason to disbelieve the theory of long-term.

At this, group two seeks permission to intervene; permission is granted.

Adarsh: I agree about changes happening over a longer period and possibility of gains. But for every one businessman like Naren, Gobind, or Simmi's father, there are probably thousands of failures who could not make it big. Moreover, we are talking about investing in equities, where fortunes change by the minute. Here, just as generations can benefit from long-term gains, generations can get wiped out in a jiffy too. I don't believe in long-term when it comes to equities. I sincerely feel that one has to be smart enough to know his way in and out of the market.

Sumant: I completely support Adarsh. We are talking about stock markets here. You have bulls, bears, arbitrageurs, short sellers, mutual funds, and many other players in the market, each one trying to make his fortune. All of them put together create such a drama in the markets that no one knows how the prices shall behave. All theoretical assumptions are blown to smithereens the moment the markets open. I don't think long-term is the way. I feel it is too boring, dull, drab, vegetative, and an extremely defensive way of handling the markets. I can show you thousands of examples where even after staying put for ten years, people did not make money. How do you justify that?

Mrigendra Biswas: I agree with my team. Who knows what shall happen tomorrow? So today is the core, the nucleus of life, and my mantra too. If you have profits in your hand today, go book them and enjoy the fruits of gains, or else everything shall remain on paper. Long-term is crap.

Group one wants to rebut, is given permission to.

Gobind: I appreciate the views of my opponents, but I tend to disagree with them. Even if one person succeeds in the long term, it is good enough for me. There are probably lacs of car workshops in Delhi, whose owners shall die as workshop owners only. But look at me. Could I achieve all this over a short period? I don't think so. It happened over a longer period on its own. Yes, resources came on time; I got help from my friends, my family, and other supporters too. But imagine someone who has resources, access to technology, and also the money to back his efforts; can he not create a meaningful difference over a longer period? He can surely set an example to be emulated by millions.

As if Adarsh is waiting for this chance . . .

Adarsh: Then why did you, me, and Naren lose a fortune in the market?

A sudden hush falls over the class. Adarsh realises his mistake, feels it's too late to recover from this point. He has unintentionally unleashed the horses that were tethered until now. He cannot look into the eyes of Naren and Gobind. Humiliation enshrouds his expression, making it evident that a barrier has been breached. Guruji realizes the fragility of the situation and jumps into action.

'Adarsh, you have made a relevant point. How does group one want to counter this? Let's continue with the tug of war in the next class.'

Adarsh carries back a load on his heart; he doesn't know how the words came out. Naren is showing no sign of annoyance though, even Gobind is normal. Adarsh catches them, huddles them in a corner, and apologises. Both of them smile and hug him tight. Frowning on their friend is not going to be helpful; what Adarsh said today is true to the last bit. So they have no complaints or grudge against him. Naren would have blasted Adarsh if this had happened couple of years back, but not now. He doesn't want to waste his energy in fighting with a friend who has been by his side in good and bad times.

Like others, the trio also look forward to being here again tomorrow. Gobind looks forward to meeting and teaching the eleventh student of this class.

23

Why Is There Only One Warren Buffett?

The next morning, students are raring to go; they expect an aggressive and high-voltage discussion today. They feel that Guruji shall have to play the referee or else things can go out of control. Discussion starts again after the customary meditation that has become an integral part of this class. The time of meditation now a day has reached between ten to fifteen minutes already; soon it shall reach a constant value, never to change after that, like a straight line drawn till infinity.

Naren asks Mrs Subramanian to start the discussion.

Mrs Subramanian: Picking up from where we left last night, I want to say that the long term is relevant to our lives, even if it doesn't guarantee sure-shot success. Just because something has happened in a particular fashion in the past doesn't mean that it shall repeat itself in future too. I think we are losing track of our thoughts. We are discussing markets and the long term; we aren't saying that the long term becomes relevant because it ensures success. Long-term definitely works. Instead of seeing many people fail despite the long term, why don't we look at examples of people who have created a difference because of their discipline and long-term thinking? According to me, ahimsa practised by Mahatma Gandhi was long-term. Warren Buffett's wealth creation is a result of long term. Wipro's successful journey to become a MNC from a mere soap-making company is long-term. Infosys becoming one of the largest companies in the world from a tiny mole in the early '80s is long-term. Most successful companies and investors have been there because they stuck to their beliefs over a much longer period than most others. Warren Buffett himself was driven to the point of bankruptcy couple of times during his investing stint, but he kept faith and kept moving forward. Look at Dhirubhai Ambani, who took his company to stratospheric heights from a modest cloth trading company in the early '70s. The long term is relevant even if doesn't ensure success.

Simmi: Why should we worry about success or failure at all? We have to do our work, follow our instincts, and set out our path, don't we? If a student worries in advance that he won't be able to clear a particular exam, and stops all his preparations, then he is going to fail anyways. As Guruji said, the idea of this discussion is not to win over the opponent but learn. Let us focus on learning. Guruji, why don't you say something?

'I think this discussion is far from over, you are moving in the right direction, and I am sure shall find yourself a lot more enriched in the end. So I shall stay quiet. Group 2, why don't you carry this discussion forward?'

Mrigendra Biswas: We understand the importance of the long term, but long-term thinking in equity markets does not exist. Most investors act on news, insider tips, and their hunches. Even if we are thinking of the long term, the stock prices are impacted in the short run by the actions of various market participants. So if everyone else is playing a short-term game, then what would one achieve by investing for the long term? I have a relative who is a stockbroker, he advises clients only to make them buy and sell regularly and earn brokerage every time the client transacts. I assume there would be thousands of brokers like him, so I am not sure if the long term is the answer.

Adarsh: A few things only exist in theory; the long term is one of them. It is only for professors, lecturers, and writers. Practical life is totally different. The equity market is a jungle, and the rule of the jungle is the only way to survive in it. If we follow bookish methods, then we shall be wiped out even before we begin this journey. I am not at all convinced. The ratio of success to failure suggests that only a few investors succeed here; the rest all are butchered like innocent lambs on the altar of insanity on daily basis. I am sorry but I am not in for the long term, to me timing is everything. I have seen investors losing everything, including their shirt, in the market.

Balwant: Adarsh is right. We as lay investors do not know anything. We don't have information on companies. Anyone can take us for a ride. And when the market itself moves on short-term news, then what is the point of the long term?

Decibel levels are going up; the classroom slowly becomes Indian parliament, pandemonium beginning to build up. The students only stop short of breaking chairs and hurling shoes at each other. Guruji must stop this and guide them all.

'When we say we should think long-term, we are not saying that short-term is bad. I agree with group 2 that the market does react to the news in the short term, but it adjusts to fundamentals in the longer term. I have written a few points from your discussion on the whiteboard. I request all of you to please read them and think:

1. *Naren: Investing is not only about investing money*

2. *Adarsh: For each successful person in business or markets, there are a thousand failures too.*

3. *Sumant: There are very few takers for the long term.*

4. *Gobind: Even if one person succeeds in the long run, it is enough.*

5. *Mrs Subramanian: The long term is relevant even if it doesn't ensure success.*

6. *Simmi: We have to do our work, without worrying about success or failure.*

'These thoughts are interesting and carry deeper meanings for investing. Look at these points one by one, try to assimilate their essence and apply them to the world of investing or, for that matter, your lives. You shall really see the shades of relevance in them. Now see what we are trying to achieve through this discussion. Reset your goal to creating wealth and see this discussion in this new light.'

The discussion resumes after Guruji's divine intervention.

Naren: Thank you, Guruji, for intervening and showing us the right path. If seen from a wealth creation perspective, the long term becomes even more important. Simmi made an important point by laying emphasis on doing our work irrespective of the success and failure. I think investment is not a one-time process; it's not a zero-sum game. Investment goes for generations, lasting beyond time itself. It is quite possible that even after staying invested for longer periods, one generation might end up in losses but that doesn't stop the next generation from investing or aiming for wealth creation. It's like the promise of a horizon that can be seen but not achieved finitely. It's a responsibility that passes on and on from one generation to another. Let's keep the profits, losses, success, and failure out of it as we do not have any control over them. In fact no one has control over them. So why worry much?

Naren looks at Adarsh, who seems a little calmed down now, slowly synchronising his thought process with that of group one. Mrigendra Biswas picks up the baton now.

Mrigendra Biswas: Guruji, I am not a great admirer of mythology but I find this shloka from Srimad Bhagavadgita very relevant to life and think that it can also be applied to the field of investments:

Karmanye vadhikaraste, Ma phaleshu Kadachana,
Ma Karma Phala hetur bhurmatey sangostva akarmani

When Arjuna declined to fight the battle of Kurukshetra, Krishna urged him to perform his duties. In this verse, 'Karmanye vadhikaraste, Ma phaleshu Kadachana' means

'You have the right to perform your actions but you are not entitled to the fruits of your action.'

'Ma Karma Phala hetur bhurmatey sangostva akarmani' means 'don't let the fruit be the purpose of your actions and therefore you won't be attached to not doing your duty.' I do not know if one can really be detached from the fruits of the action but if one can assimilate this lesson deep within him or her, one can make a huge difference at least to himself. Guruji, do you find this interesting too?

*'Mrigendra, I completely agree with you. Some of the verses or shlokas from the Gita are relevant from our life's viewpoint and one can draw a parallel to the stock market also. These simple-sounding verses have a deeper current of meanings flowing beneath their surface. But we shall return to these later. Right now, all I can say is that this verse is relevant from an equity investment perspective too. I see this discussion about the long term shaping up really well, with all the students actively taking part and appreciating the views of the opponents. Remember long-term and short-term are only relative and not absolute. Each of them has its own relevance. From a wealth creation perspective, from an equity market viewpoint, the long term assumes a great importance, as equity investments are really about investing in businesses where, over the long term, changes become permanent, where generally bigger things do not happen over shorter time periods, hence the stock prices also move decisively over very long periods. Over these long periods, one can also experience some sharp short-term movements in prices on both upside and downside, but that needs to be taken in stride. **Long-term is nothing but an unbroken string of short-term movements.** Investments cannot all be for either the short term or long term; one has to*

have a judicious mix of both. As far as equities are concerned, the long term definitely works. The following are reasons that favour long-term investing in equities:

1. Rome was not built in a day

Life is a long arduous journey full of dreams, aspirations, and goals. Imagine a second grader saying, "I want to be an engineer when I grow up." Can this child get an admission to a prestigious engineering institute the next day, next month, or say, next year? Or a management trainee who aspires to become the chairman of the company in one month's time where he/she has joined only a few days back. We all have heard the stories of management trainees who have risen through the rank and file and attained the top slots after twenty to twenty-five years but not a single case where a worthwhile post was achieved overnight. We all have long-term goals which are specific to all of us, and to achieve these goals, one must work hard through the years, cope with ups and downs to finally walk down the golden shores of the destination. To my mind, wealth creation is a long-term goal. Now go back to the names that we mentioned in the previous chapter and see if anyone of them achieved the feat they have, over a short period.

2. We need to grow our money over much longer periods

As some of you already discussed, we need to grow our savings over a much longer period. An average person needs to manage his investments efficiently from the day he starts earning till the day he finally passes away. Assuming an average life span of eighty years, I would say that we all need to take care of our money for almost more than fifty years, and then it passes on to the next generation, who shall have to do the same thing. So investing is nothing but a continuous process extending up to infinity. So we better think long-term.

3. Businesses grow over the long term

As I mentioned earlier, investing in equity is investing in businesses that tend to grow over a long period. They go through the economic cycles of boom and bust. They bear the pangs of right and wrong decision-making. Sometimes, managements change, and good businesses become bad and vice versa. We can look at the businesses around us and we can easily find these examples. Various businesses started small and, over a long period of time, have grown really big, and if we observe their share prices, we could easily relate to the wealth part of it.

- *According to one estimate, if an investor bought 100 shares of Wipro in its IPO @ Rs. 180 per share, after 30 years these 100 stocks are worth a whopping 374 crores after adjusting for splits, bonuses, and dividends. This may sound crazy but this is true. At least the promoters have held on to their shares and today they figure among the richest in the country. It may be interesting to see how the business has grown over this period. You shall see that the growth in sales, revenues, gross, and net profits over this long period has been exceptional. This growth has made itself manifest in the share price movement.*

- *An investment of just Rs. 1 lac in Infosys IPO (initial public offering) has grown to over 20 crores until now.*

4. Bottoms shift and markets get rerated

This is especially true for the equity markets and real estate. Since the markets rerate themselves over a longer period and keep shifting their tops and bottoms, the share or asset prices also shift their bottoms and hold. We can apply this to any other asset class and we shall find that this hypothesis holds true almost everywhere, e.g. real estate, stocks, gold, art, etc.

A simple formula for wealth creation then is to try to capture a few market reratings in your portfolio. These shifts in bottom and peaks of the markets happen only over very long periods.

5. Probability of losing money goes down

By staying invested for a longer period, one is slowly insulating one's portfolio from being sensitive to short-term gyrations. It is generally experienced that the probability of losing big money goes down as we keep increasing the time period. What I am trying to say is that you may have greater chance of making losses in, say, six-month periods than five-year periods or, say, ten-year periods. You also have more time on your hands compared to investors who try to time the market all the time; therefore, you can take corrective actions that are more effective, thus reducing your chances of losing money or increasing your chances of creating wealth.

6. It's your money

Making money is one of the most difficult things in life. Without money, one can't sustain one's dreams. Life may not be easy in the absence of this precious resource that comes to all of us in a very hard way. Respecting money and treating it with caution is bare-minimum hygiene that one needs to have if one aims at growing money over a period of time. To have more money means to have more power to effect bigger and positive changes not only on one's family but also on society at large. I am not talking from a materialist perspective but a basic practical viewpoint here. We need money for almost everything from sustaining a respectable lifestyle to meeting our simple day-to-day needs. Therefore, putting the money to more productive use, making it grow seriously over a longer period should be our dharma, especially when we think about investing in equities.

'Next time you ask yourself why long-term, think hard and try to answer this one—why there is only one Warren Buffett in this world?'

24

Go Gabbar's Way

It's been only a few months and students feel that they have been attending this class for years. They feel attached, involved, and concerned for each other. They speak, they laugh, and they mingle too. They feel more confident, although they haven't started investing yet. Most of them have been out of markets for almost a year and half now. Making them invest in equities is going to be a big task. Before they start investing, another battle needs to be won— the battle of fear. The master has arranged for a projector as he wants to show them a Bollywood movie clip. This sounds strange, out of place, and weird to some students. But they are excited, anxious to see what is coming through. Fifteen minutes of meditation have become a source of peace and enjoyment for most of them. They don't struggle to focus now. Once the meditation is over, the excitement starts.

'Do you know what is that holds most of us back in life? What prevents us from doing new things? What is that which keeps a lid on our courage? What is that which keeps the best buried inside us and prevents it from coming out?'

Gobind says, 'Sir, we lack the courage to take chances. This is what stops us in life. That is why we can't do bigger things.'

'I am asking about the emotion that exists in all of us. I am afraid this is not the answer.'

Students are thinking, their minds racing, their focus shifting from the question to the projector and then back to the question again. This doesn't seem to be a difficult question; still they aren't able to find the answer. They look forward to Guruji, who is busy setting up the projector. Sumant Mishra gets up and helps him in adjusting the controls so that the image falling on the wall is a near-perfect square and not an ill-shaped quadrilateral. Speakers are connected next and placed in the front corners of the room.

'I am going to show you a movie clip that you must have seen many times. If not all of you, I am sure many of you might have seen it. This movie is a jewel in the crown of Indian cinema and probably this clip is the most watched part of this movie.'

Sumant presses a key on the laptop and the movie starts. The scene is set in rocky mountainous surroundings. The main character is a notorious dacoit, who is pacing up and down, burning with anger yet not showing it. The sound of his boots on the rocks is enough to scare his coterie. Three of his men stand next to each other facing the leader, who stares in their eyes, aggravating their plight and asks them, 'Kitne aadmi the?' (How many men were there?)

One of the men speaks, trembling with fear, his voice nearly failing him, 'Sardar do, do aadmi thhe.' (Sir, there were two men.)

Hearing this, the leader's eyes become bloodshot with insult as three of his best men just returned from the village empty-handed, that too because of only two normal men.

He shouts again, 'Sooar ke bacchon, woh do thhe aur tum teen, phir bhi wapas aa gaye, woh bhi khaali haath.' (You bloody piglets! They were two and you three; still you came back empty-handed.)

The leader's rant continues, the background tune adding to the sombre setting. Fear creeps up in the nerves of three men, who haven't been able to get the loot from the village. The scene is from the movie *Sholay*—the greatest Bollywood flick ever produced. Some of the students, like Mrigendra Biswas, know the sequence verbatim, yet he is not able to associate this scene with the class he is attending. What does Gabbar Singh have to do with the world of investments? The scene progresses as Gabbar shouts at the top of his voice, giving a spiel about how the nearby villages are terrified by his name. These three men have brought shame to his name because they were chased away by two ordinary men. The drama continues for a few more minutes, tension mounts, and finally the leader Gabbar Singh shoots these three men and spits on the ground saying, 'Jo dar gaya, samjho mar gaya.' (One who is scared is as good as dead.)

Lights are switched on and the projector is switched off. Some students remember seeing this movie in cinema halls with their parents. They still feel the fear climbing up their spine just as it had when they saw the movie for the first time.

'*Focus on what Gabbar Singh said in the end:* Jo dar gaya, samjho mar gaya. *If you are scared, you are as good as dead. Stretch your imaginations and extend this thought to any field of life, you shall find it relevant. Imagine a student scared of maths or any other subject; he can't score if he is scared. A person scared of water can't swim till he gets rid of his fear. It is this fear that holds us back. Once the fear is out, we are a free bird of wishes that can fly in a dream-filled sky. Fear is one of the greatest enemies of mankind. Do you agree with me?'*

'But, sir, fear is natural. It is an integral part of our persona. Each of us is scared of something or the other. That's natural to human beings. How can we get rid of it?' says Mridula.

'Mridula, fear is a state of mind. People who are completely fearless are rare. These people often reach far in their lives. Look at what Mahatma Gandhi achieved, where Lance Armstrong reached, what Nelson Mandela could do for his society. All of them moved ahead of their fear and became heroes. Look at our movies where heroes mostly lead a fearless life and conquer the evil. There are many fears, both known and unknown, and all of them are capable of limiting our efforts. This is the emotion that lets terrorists terrorise us. Fear's extent depends on an individual's willpower and determination. I believe one can get rid of fear to a great extent if not completely eliminate it, and that is enough for us. Now coming back to markets and equities, tell me what are the investors afraid of? Does fear play a negative role here?'

'Yes, sir, definitely fear plays a big role in undermining our efforts in stock markets. It sometimes stops us from taking the right action and sometimes it forces us to take wrong action,' says Simmi.

'I agree with you. Fear affects our judgement not only in equity markets but in everything we do. Sholay's Gabbar has given us a great maxim to think and ponder about. I feel if one can move beyond fear, he is bound to be victorious. There is a saying in Urdu that goes like "Tu aatishe dojakh se darata hai unhe, jo aag to pee jaate hain paani karke." (You are trying to

scare someone with hell, someone who can drink fire just like water.)

'For those who do not understand Urdu, aatishe *means fire and* dojakh *means hell. Let's focus on equity investing. What are we afraid of?'*

'Sir, we are afraid of losing money,' says Naresh Kohli.

'Anyone else?'

'We are also afraid of being perceived as inferiors if we lose money. We are scared of not only losing money but also the respect among our colleagues, relatives, and even our own family members,' says Adarsh.

'Good point, Adarsh and Naresh. This is what I was looking for. The fear of loss holds us back. Imagine if a batsman is afraid of getting caught at the boundary, will he be ever able to hit a six? Or a person who is hydrophobic, can he become a world champion in swimming? This fear of loss can then lead to loss of self-respect, loss of money, loss of comfort, and so many other things. Yet people become swimming champions and conquer the highest mountain peaks too. If they are scared of falling in a bottomless valley, then they can't achieve these feats. With respect to equities, it's only a matter of conquering our fear of loss, and everything else shall fall in place. Having said that, I must add that it's not easy. Conquering fear is no mean task; it takes courage, determination, and lot of discipline to overcome fear. Once fear is overcome then life becomes easy. I know what you are thinking. You must be thinking that Guruji is only giving us a lecture. Well, it is a lecture only until we actually overcome our fears.'

'But how do we overcome our fears, Guruji?' asks Kantha.

'Take a sip and stay cool.'

'Take a sip? What does this mean, sir?' asks Balwant Jakhar.

'I shall explain to you later. For the time being, let us know that we can reduce our fear to a great extent with application of discipline and common sense. One needs to cultivate simple habits and follow them regularly to have a fear-proof mind. To my mind, equity investing is a simple business, while most of the investors believe it to be a complex thing. So, first thing that we need to assume is that equity investing is simple.'

'Sir, I am a little confused now. There are millions of people who participate in markets. Some invest for the long term, some trade on a daily basis, making stock prices go up and down like a yo-yo and you are saying it's a simple thing. I think one needs to understand markets thoroughly and keep track of prices on a real-time basis to make any sense out of equity investing,' says Mrs Subramanian.

'Mrs Subramanian, we invest our money in businesses and not in stock markets. Prices going up or down do not make any business a good or bad investment. We have to invest our money for the long term, so short-term price movements should be ignored.'

'Sir, how do we apply the principle of simplicity to the stock markets?' asks Gobind.

'It is true that businesses are complex and one may not necessarily understand them completely by sitting outside. So one has to either develop a basic understanding of these businesses on his own or one has to trust the fund managers whose full-time job is to manage money only. One may also choose companies whose business activities affect our daily lives, for example, banks, retail, vehicles, utility companies, telecom companies, etc. Sometimes we deal with these companies as

consumers, suppliers, or business associates. For example, Mr. Gobind deals with car manufacturers. It may be relatively easier for him to associate with these companies as he is selling their products through his showrooms. He can understand their business better than an outsider. The growth of his business and his parents', i.e. car manufacturers, are correlated. If his parents produce good vehicles, then he would see his business flourishing too. He can analyse the basic sales trends and get a rough idea about how this business has done over a period of time. If he thinks that this company shall grow over a longer period, then he may start investing in this company over a period of time.

'We go to our bank and we find their services are good. Because of these good services, the number of customers has gone up, over the last few years. Number of their branches is also steadily going up. The mailers that the bank sends to us from time to time tell us about this growth. Slowly, the brand establishes itself. Now most of this information is available to us in routine, we haven't done any complex research on these companies. This may give us an idea about the quality of their business. This may be helpful in guiding us in investing in these companies' shares.

'Over a period of time, we may also find more information about these companies and help ourselves. But if someone does not have the wherewithal to invest in individual stocks, one can always invest through mutual funds. There are quite a few in India now. One thing we may do is to ask ourselves before investing, if this company is going to be there ten years down the line and will it have more customers than today?'

'Guruji, can it be made simpler than this too?' Adarsh asks softly.

'Yes, it can be. Hire a good fund manager and enjoy your life. It's a serious business, Adarsh, but it can be done in an uncomplicated manner, we shall soon see that. Meanwhile, please remember what Gabbar Singh said.'

Everyone laughs and leaves for the day.

25

Going Nowhere

The year is 2002, markets are calm and there is absolutely no buzz around them. No one is talking about equity markets these days. The Bombay stock exchange index is hovering around 3000, half of its peak value in the year 2000. The CNX IT index is trading at approximately 13000—80 per cent down from its dizzying heights of almost 65000. Equity investing has become a stigma because whatever investors had invested in has gone down like water off the back of an elephant. Markets have become boring and no new issues are coming, unlike the time when the infotech sector was blossoming like spring. Getting one to invest in the equity market these days is like asking a goat to happily opt for a slaughter. It is in this environment Guruji has to make his students invest in the stocks. Virtually every stock has fallen, only the extent varies. Most of the stocks in the infotech sector have plummeted by more than 90 per cent. Everyone including Guruji has made losses but that is not the matter of concern now; the point of concern is about the future losses that one can suffer by investing in equities again. Guruji has to think of something to convince his students. He decides to play on and see what happens.

'Dear all, I think you are ready to take a plunge in the equities now. Can we start investing tomorrow itself? I don't

think we should waste any time sitting outside the stock markets. Let's dip our toes together.'

Nervousness is evident in the class. Although students are prepared to invest, they didn't expect investing to start so early. They don't seem to be ready. They look at each other and find a blank expression everywhere except on Guruji's face.

Mridula says, 'Sir, isn't it too early to start investing?'

'Mridula, it's never too early or too late to start investing. Remember Warren Buffet, who started investing when he was eleven and felt it was too late.'

'But, sir, markets are virtually flat over the last three years. No one is taking interest in the markets,' says Balwant Jakhar.

'Why do you say no one is taking interest? We are taking interest. Aren't we?'

'Sir, there is no activity in the markets. Prices have fallen to such a great extent that it shall take years from here for prices to start moving,' says Simmi joining the chorus.

'Are we investing money in markets, prices, or businesses?'

'But, sir . . . um, shall we not take too much risk by entering at this stage when we don't know when the markets shall start moving?' asks Mridula.

'For a minute, forget about stock markets and the indices. Just focus on the businesses. Most of the old economy stocks are trading below their intrinsic value for last couple of years, which practically means there is a sale going on in the markets and no one is ready to act. Isn't it contrary to our normal behaviour?'

'Guruji, there is a difference between buying clothes or other merchandise on sale and shares. Merchandise once bought is bought, it cannot fall in price further,' says Mrs Subramanian.

'*How do you know that it doesn't fall in price?*'

'Sir, a shirt's price is not quoted on real-time basis, whereas a share shall show its price every minute,' Naresh Kohli submits.

'*If the price isn't quoted, it doesn't mean that the price cannot fall. Try to understand a simple thing. We know a Van Heusen shirt costs us say Rs. 1000/-, the same shirt is now available in Rs. 750/-, we immediately buy it because we know the discount and the real price both. When it comes to stock, generally we are not aware of the real price. We see only the price at which it is quoting in the market and then there is a fear of this price going down too. There is one more thing that affects our decision-making regarding buying a stock trading at discount. Often investors feel that the stocks that have fallen in price or the stocks whose prices haven't moved over last few years aren't worth buying as they are out of fashion. There is a stigma attached to them, which to my mind is not an appropriate thing. Buying a cheap shirt is smart, buying a stock available at discount isn't common, so it's considered a dumb job by the normal public.*'

'Sir, I think all of us are afraid of losing money by investing in the equities at this stage,' Naren speaks at last.

'Sir, yesterday you spoke something about taking a sip. What is it all about? Can you please explain?' asks Mrigendra.

'*Equity markets are like a glass of sherbet, you must consume it sip by sip. That's what I meant by take a sip. One must enjoy the experience rather than worry about losses. Losses can be handled easily. I ask you to do a simple exercise. Take a piece of paper and write down an amount that you can spare for equity investments at this stage. Please be honest and write the amount.'*

Everyone writes an amount, not knowing what is about to come. Naren writes a whopping amount of 25 crores, Adarsh 2 crores, Gobind 3 crores and the others also write according to their individual capacities.

'Imagine that the stocks that we are going to buy can fall by 50 per cent tomorrow morning, will you still invest this amount?'

'No, sir,' everyone speaks in a chorus.

'Now do another thing. Divide this amount by 25 and imagine that you shall invest only 1/25th amount each month for the next 25 months. Now assume that the price can fall by 50 per cent the very next day. Will it trouble us as much it did in the first case? Suppose I have to invest Rs. 10 lacs over the next 10 months and I decide to invest in ten instalments, then I can insulate myself to a great extent against large losses if the prices fall quickly. It shall also mean that I shall get less benefit from the price appreciation too. One can choose the amounts and the number of instalments accordingly.'

'Sir, we extend a facility of systematic investment plans to the investors. By using this facility, investors can contribute a fixed amount every month to a mutual fund scheme, although this facility is not quite popular with the investors currently,' Sumant Mishra speaks.

'Yes, Sumant, I am aware of this facility. It is an excellent tool that everyone can benefit from. Now that we have a tool to tackle the losses in our hands, are we ready to take the plunge?'

A few students speak firmly this time and express their concurrence to take the plunge in the equities, although there is no agreement on the number of instalments yet. But everyone seems to be aboard the equity bandwagon. Guruji smiles, he knows that the initial firewall has been breached; slowly he shall instil more confidence in the students.

'Now the best part is that I don't know which shares you should invest in. I also do not know which mutual fund schemes we should be investing in. I give you one month's break to find out a little bit about investing options and come back after one month. I shall also use this time to educate myself and find out about various investment options. I hope this break shall bring you a lease of fresh energy before embarking upon such an exciting journey. You may choose your own ways of finding out about investment options. See you after one month.'

Everyone is surprised at the one-month break, but they welcome this move. They shall be able to prepare themselves well before actual investing. Some students are excited, others are puzzled. The trio is focussed and is quite happy about this opportunity.

'Guruji, will you be available during this period, should we need any guidance?' asks Adarsh.

'No, I shall not be available during this one month. You shall have to work it out on your own. Remember you have to just list the options, not start investing until we meet here after one month. Please do this independently so that each of you gets to learn as much as possible.'

Everyone packs up and leaves. Guruji decides to stay back to think and introspect. He thinks of the day when he started these classes. In a few months' time they have covered quite a distance.

Sometimes he also thinks of Sonia and wonders where she would be.

26

Seek and You Shall Find

Each student has a job on his hands. They have to find out about investment options on their own. They desperately want to contact each other but Guruji's instructions are clear, so each of them pursues in his own way. Naren gets in touch with his banker. There is a new relationship manager who has replaced Sonia. He has asked him to come prepared with lot of information on mutual funds and individual stocks, especially the old economy stocks that have not fallen as much as the technology stocks have. The banker promises to get back to him with all the information as soon as possible. Adarsh seeks the help of his wife Rachel to find out where he can invest the money. Gobind finds it tough without Naren and Adarsh but tries on his own. He decides to visit the eleventh student and seek her guidance.

Sumant Mishra digs deeper into the information provided by his own fund house. He also contacts many distributors who sell his funds. Mrs Subramanian uses this opportunity to visit her home town and find some information too. Her cousin is an independent financial advisor. Balwant Jakhar finds it tough to find information as his previous broker had shut his shop and run away. He tries to read the business newspapers and educate himself a bit. He also surfs the Internet to find out more and more information. So does everyone else. Simmi comes across a book called *Common Sense on Mutual Funds* by John C. Bogle. She reads it thoroughly, although there are a few things that she is not able to understand. Naresh Kohli goes to a bookshop in Connaught Place and purchases a few books on investing. He picks one of them, *One Up on Wall Street*, written by the famous, legendary fund manager Peter Lynch who managed the largest mutual fund in the world, the Fidelity Magellan fund. Mrigendra Biswas speaks to a few of his colleagues in his office, but no one is able to help him as they themselves do not know anyone who can provide investment advice. Mrigendra finds it strange though. He decides to do more searching on his own. He visits offices of a few mutual funds and stockbrokers who provide him with some investment advice. He picks up mutual fund fact sheets from each office he visits and reads them religiously. Mridula is not able to find much as no one knows anything about investing in her office; she is no better than Mrigendra. She resorts to Internet surfing and viewing the websites of various mutual funds operating in India. Everyone is on their toes to get maximum information on their own. As directed by Guruji, they avoid talking to each other and sharing the information.

Chaitanya himself is busy. He has to find information too. He needs to pick up from where he left three years ago, to bury a past that still haunts him, to get rid of the guilt held deep within. He has to become a student again. He has to scan the market for potential investment opportunities, open old books again to brush up on his fundamentals, and revive his network of information again. He knows this game well but the challenge is to keep things simple, to keep the jargon out and teach his students once for all so that they can adopt equity investing as an everlasting habit. He is determined to do it. He has to read between the lines, update himself on the latest numbers on the markets and a few stocks, so as to enable him to make informed decisions. He can sense a great opportunity in the market as country's social fabric is undergoing a change. People are aspiring like never before and lifestyles are changing fast. Branded clothes, mobile phones, bigger cars, rush on the airports and shopping malls tell Chaitanya a lot about the shape of things to come. He doesn't need to read books to understand what is going on around him; India is slowly gearing up for a big economic boom. The pent-up energy is about to unleash itself, the revolution at the base of the pyramid of population is quite palpable, and it's only a matter of time before the ripples are felt on the stock markets too. Indian markets haven't seen a broad-based rally yet. On a few previous occasions when the markets went up, very few sectors or shares participated, but all this shall undergo a change soon, if Chaitanya's hunch is right. He makes a list of people to be spoken to, a list of books to refer to, a few sectors to be tracked, and a few mutual fund schemes to be studied.

Equity markets crashed globally in the year 2000, making investors suffer huge losses everywhere in the world. Interest rates started easing up considerably after the terrorist attack on the twin towers called the World Trade Center in New York. This attack had a significant impact on the US economy that was already reeling under the pressure of a slowdown. The central bank in the US started cutting interest rates at an unprecedented rate to boost consumption, and some of this money was bound to find a way to Indian stocks as well. While the equity funds and stocks across the globe were being rejected by the investors for poor performance, bond funds (mutual fund schemes that invest in bonds) were having a spectacular run because interest rates were going down. While equity funds were receiving no money at all, bond funds were having a wild party on the street. Was this leading somewhere? Did this mean anything? Just a couple of years back, no one even knew about bond funds, and now investors had developed apathy towards equity funds. This also meant that people were selling equity shares/funds in desperation and moving their money to bonds/bond funds. This was not going to stay like this forever.

Chaitanya needs to find out more. While browsing through the Internet, he comes across an article—'Everything you wanted to know about the universe . . .' by the legendary bond investor Bill Gross. The article makes a strong case for asset price bubbles after the interest rate cuts, and the situation across the globe is similar to what is mentioned in the article. Real interest rates have gone down, which means that slowly the returns on the fixed-income instruments like bonds and bond funds shall go down. Money is becoming cheap for individual investors as indicated in the downward movement of interest rates on the various loans like vehicle, personal, and home loans. People can borrow cheap and buy cars and houses. While the individual investors are spending on home, food, clothes, cars, bikes, and gadgets, the industrial consumers are leveraging themselves and buying out companies, expanding their operations locally as well as globally. The demand for their goods is going up, meaning that their income shall also increase in future.

India is on the cusp of an investment revolution. Economic liberalisation that started in the last decade is gaining momentum now, and the government has done its bit to keep the economy open to other countries to get a slice of foreign portfolio and direct investments.

Chaitanya is surprised how most of the investors are not able to read the writing on the wall. He starts touching base with his contacts from the past. As he looks all around him and compares this scenario with that of the years prior to the stock market crash, he finds an amazing similarity between the two. He sees the crowd moving in one single direction, a compulsive herd phenomenon taking place for bonds, just as it happened for infotech shares few years back. He has read in many books that in stock markets, the crowd is always wrong. If nothing else, he shall at least teach his students to be ahead of the crowd, just as a leader is. Chaitanya starts visiting various stockbrokers just to gauge the optimism at their counters, visiting mutual funds' local offices to see which schemes are they receiving money in, reading mutual fund industry mobilisation figures from a few websites, scanning a few balance sheets and company reports over the next few days. His reading is right; virtually no money is going in either the equity shares or equity funds, which means that it's become a buyer's market, and at such times, good bargains are available in every market, the stock market being no different.

Retail counters of stockbrokers where individual investors usually trade are vacant; day traders are gone forever. Mutual funds are receiving money only in the bonds funds, and equity funds have by and large become untouchables. Chaitanya has picked up a few application forms from the mutual fund offices and from the stockbrokers. He shall need to open a few accounts with stockbrokers as well.

Naren no longer runs the broking business; he came out of it after making obscene losses in the stock market. Gobind and Adarsh became detached too; they do not even look at their portfolios now as most of the stocks have fallen by more than 90 per cent from their peak values.

Chaitanya has also met up with a few analysts who used to work with him in the past. They have provided him with valuable information on the general economy and a few select stocks. He has used his mutual fund industry connections to meet a few equity fund managers and seek their opinion on the markets. In a month's time he has stocked up his silos with enough ammunition for the ensuing battle. He is sure that his students would have also worked hard to accumulate information on investment options available in the market, and he is not wrong in making this assumption as most of his students are keeping their nose to the grindstone in doing so.

One month is over; they all look forward to start another phase of this journey.

27

Take a SIP—Stay Cool

Sukha Dukhe Same' kritva, Labha Labhou Jaya Jayou,
Thatho Yuddhya yujyasva, naivam papam avapsyasi.

'Having an equal mind in happiness—sorrows, gain—loss, victory and defeat, engage in the battle and you shall not incur any sin. This shloka from Srimad Bhagavadgita is very pertinent when it comes to life and investing too. It says we must maintain equanimity under all circumstances and keep ourselves engaged in our karma. For an investor, the karma is investing with focus, passion, and discipline, hence we as investors must maintain mental balance all the time, as we have no control over profits or losses. Sometimes external forces can drive the prices in any direction, making an investor doubt his/her capabilities for reasons beyond his control. Let's remember this shloka while we engage in the battle of investment and we shall emerge victorious like Pandavas who decimated Kauravas in the end. Before we start investing, let us be clear that we may have to meet profits and losses, joys and sorrows, good, bad, and the ugly down the road. We may face trying times, even moments when our own conviction washes away, making us question our decision-making. But despite all this, we must go on and on.

'Remember, no gain is permanent and no loss is final, so gains should not result in egomania and losses should not lead to

depression. Profit and loss are the results of the actions taken in the past. We must analyse our actions and modify our approach accordingly. The joy of gain and the stigma of loss should not deter us from the path of karma, i.e. investing for the long term, investing for the wealth creation. The Gita has emphasized the importance of karma. By following his karma, a person can become a Karma yogi and be in a state of bliss—a state in which a person is detached from the fruits of action. If we simply apply this principle to money management or investing, one can become a moneyogi, which is an evolved state of not only investing but also self.

'I have no tools to guarantee you a profit. I have no means to teach you on how to avoid losses. I urge you to embrace both these imposters, i.e. profit and loss, and treat them equally. They are our partners on the road to wealth creation. Being focussed is important, doing the karma of investing and the detachment from the fruits of our action is important too. We can't become saffron-clad yogis as we have responsibilities on our shoulders, we have families to take care of, we have to shape our careers up, and keep doing what we have been doing in our personal lives. We only have to change the ways of investing to lead much more peaceful lives. We have to invest in way that we do not incur huge losses at any one single instance. As human beings, we can stay happy if we aren't making profits, but not when we suffer big losses.

'So we should first focus is on investing to minimise our losses. How do we do this? Can anyone help me with an answer?'

Students are spellbound. They are looking at a new guru today. They look at each other, hoping someone shall answer.

It is Mrigendra who speaks up, 'Guruji, the only way to avoid making big losses is to invest in small amounts. But then what should we do after a loss has been made?'

'Follow your karma. Analyse your losses and if you feel you have invested in a good portfolio or stock, invest more. Remember what I told you a few minutes back—equanimity in all circumstances and no loss is final.

'But, Guruji, losses can keep happening over a very long period, being detached over such a long period may be difficult,' says Simmi.

'Simmi, handling losses can be challenging for all human beings, especially when these losses are financial in nature. If we do not know losses, we cannot appreciate our gains. There is no business, no investment in the world where losing is not a possibility. You need to take losses in your stride. You can't avoid losses; you can keep them at a tolerable level though. We shall shortly discover this. How many of you did go to various mutual fund offices during the past month?'

Almost all hands go up in an instant.

'What did the mutual funds tell you? What did they have to advise you?'

'Guruji, they have given us information about their schemes, especially the bond funds. These funds invest in only bonds and have given very good returns over last two years or so,' says Biswas.

'What else?'

'Sir, they also told us about something called SIP through which a person can make regular investments at a monthly interval. But these plans are not very popular with the investors,' admits Mrs Subramanian.

'And why are they not popular?'

'Because investors haven't made money in them,' speaks Mrs Subramanian again.

'Does anyone else know more about these SIPs?'

'Guruji, SIPs work on the principle of rupee cost averaging. As a person keeps on investing regularly in a mutual fund scheme, he ends up buying through the lows and highs and thereby achieving an average price, which is quite helpful as against buying the units at one single instant. For example, an investor might have bought a particular MF scheme at a NAV of, say, Rs. 10 in 1998 and today the NAV is Rs. 20. He has earned an absolute return of 100 per cent. However the NAV of the scheme had gone down below 10 in the year 2000 and stayed below 7 for a very long period too. If the same investor kept on buying these units per month, instead of investing his money at one go, he might have invested in these units even when the price was lower than 10. This way he could have brought down his average price to 8.50, thus gaining 125 per cent instead of 100 per cent,' says Sumant.

'Thank you, Sumant. Let us not complicate our discussion at this stage by getting into technical details. Just know that mutual funds allow you to buy units of a single scheme regularly on a particular day every month through a facility called SIP. The investors need to give instructions only once. But they have to provide the mutual fund with post-dated cheques, so that the mutual fund staff can bank them every month. This is a good facility for all the investors.'

'Isn't it a savings tool meant for small investors, Guruji?' asks Adarsh.

'*Yes, it can be seen as a savings tool meant for small investors also, because it allows investors to buy units worth as low as Rs. 500 every month. But there is no upper limit.*'

'But, Guruji, what is the relevance of SIP to our discussion? If it's a tool for only small investors, how shall it help us in creating wealth?' asks Naresh Kohli.

'*Naresh, I shall come to your point later on. Let me first explain to you what Sumant was talking about. He talked about two investors: one who bought his units at Rs. 10 and the other one who bought these units regularly over a period of time, thereby reducing his cost of acquisition of units to Rs. 8.50. Now just for once, imagine the NAV falls to Rs. 6.5 somehow. Our first investor shall suffer a loss of 35% ((10-6.5)/10) and the other investor who bought units through the SIP shall only suffer a loss of ((8.5-6.5)/8.5)= 23.53%, which is better than a loss of 35%. Do we agree?*'

'Yes, sir,' almost everyone says in sync.

'But, Guruji, if one understands the markets and can wait, he can buy all his units at Rs. 6.5 only. Then he can make a killing when the NAV reaches Rs. 20,' says Naren.

'*That is quite possible, Naren and there are people who do it. But since we do not know with certainty about the lowest and highest prices, the decision-making becomes a little difficult. We don't know if 6.5 is the lowest and 20 is the highest.*'

'But still I think the SIP doesn't work for large investors, who have got huge surpluses and don't need to save every month like salaried individuals,' says Naren again.

'I don't think so, Naren. The law of averages works for all investors, big or small, doesn't it, Guruji?' asks Mridula.

'*Mridula, both Naren and you are partially right. SIP essentially is a savings tool mostly meant for investors who get cash flows on regular intervals like salaried individuals. Businessmen, on the other hand, are not certain about the timing of their cash flows so they may find this tool inappropriate sometimes, but as you say—the law of averages works fine for all investors, whether big or small. Having large sums of money when the markets are trading at lower levels can be a very big advantage, and at such instances, lump sum investment can work better, should the markets move up suddenly over a short period of time. But our aim is to invest for a longer period in order to create wealth, so I think we shall do better by investing our money in a staggered manner than by investing in one shot. For big investors, an SIP shall work just as fine as it works for the smaller ones. If you look at the concept of SIP at a broader level, you shall find that most of the successful equity investors have been SIP investors because they kept on buying even when the prices of their shares fell.*

'There is another facility provided by almost all Mutual Funds which is known as STP or Systematic Transfer Plan. In this, an investor can park his money in any one scheme of a mutual fund and sweep his money into another scheme on a particular day of a month. Unlike SIP, here you don't have to give post-dated cheques to mutual funds. Investors who have large surpluses may use this facility. Now can anyone help me with the investment opportunities available in the market?'

'Sir, from an equity market perspective, there are only two ways to invest. One through the mutual fund schemes and the other is to invest direct in the stock market through stockbrokers,' says Balwant Jakhar.

Most of the students know about only these two ways, so there is no disagreement with Balwant.

'We shall explore both of them. Each student shall invest in mutual funds and also in the stock markets. I believe it is not where you invest that matters, but the manner in which you invest. This journey of investing is as important for me as it is for all of you. I shall be investing along with you people and try to keep my mental balance as well.'

Another session comes to end; students feel like a battalion standing on the border waiting for their commander's signal to attack and conquer, and restore their lost pride. The excitement is building up slowly but surely. Who knows what comes next?

28

Don't Chase Popularity

Another day begins with the custom of first losing oneself in the calmed depths and then finding the self in the depths of meditation. Students go completely blank when they meditate now; some even fall asleep and have to be woken up at the end of fifteen minutes. But they all feel this experience is worth its while. It has changed them at some subconscious level; they feel galvanised, energised, and positively inclined towards life in general. A strange energy fills their lungs these days. Even during their one-month-long break, they have continued to meditate every day.

'I think we have to start with a few mutual fund schemes and stocks that I have identified for you. The mutual fund schemes I have chosen are not glamorous, they are not popular either, and they aren't the biggest schemes too. But I liked their portfolio quality even though they haven't been the best performing funds during the last bull run of 1998–2000. Incidentally, a few of these schemes did not take any large exposure to the infotech sector during that period. Similarly the stocks I have chosen are into traditional businesses that make sense from a futuristic perspective. The sectors I have chosen are banking, housing finance, pharmaceuticals, capital goods, power, and engineering, as I think these sectors shall benefit

from the growth the country is expected to witness in the years to come.'

Guruji draws a vertical line on the whiteboard, writes names of the stocks on the left-hand side and the names of mutual fund schemes on the right-hand side. There are about ten stocks and five mutual fund schemes. Students look at these names and stay quiet. Guruji is right; none of these schemes or stocks is even remotely popular. Barring one scheme, all other mutual fund schemes are boring diversified equity schemes that invest in five to six sectors and have at least thirty stocks in their portfolio. The one scheme that's different from others is a dividend yield portfolio, where the fund manager invests in the stocks that pay a higher dividend compared to the others. Students like Naren who understand a bit of this investing game squirm at these names. They feel these names are not worthy of being in their portfolios. But they stay quiet so as not to show any disrespect towards Guruji.

'Since we are going to invest our hard-earned money in these mutual funds and stocks, I want everyone to study them over the next couple of days and come back with their observations and viewpoints. I am providing everyone with some basic information about these. This is an important step in our journey which shall make a huge impact on not only on our investments but also our lives. To be on the safer side, we shall make our investments in a staggered manner over a period of time. We shall adopt the SIP route while investing in mutual funds. Any questions?'

Guruji hands over a few printed sheets and application forms to everyone. These sheets carry information about the stocks and the mutual funds where they are going to invest their money. Students keep these sheets on the top of their desks, some excitedly and some reluctantly. One hand goes up.

Naren says, 'Guruji, my first impression of these stocks and portfolios is not very great. You are right in branding these stocks as boring as no one seems to be buying them. Most of the companies are in traditional businesses and these mutual fund schemes seem to be completely neglected too, none of them is above 100 crores in size. Should we not buy larger mutual fund schemes and the stocks that have fallen more in the prices in the recent crash. I don't mean to disrespect you, but these do not seem to be the right choice for investments at this stage.'

Guruji is smiling ear to ear as if someone has cracked a joke that he only understands. He knows that such questions shall be asked by the students. It is difficult to avoid popular stocks in the stock market, and his students are proving this right.

'Naren, you have made a pertinent point and I was expecting this question to come through. I am glad that you asked. Look at these stocks carefully. They are all in the businesses that can be understood easily by all of us. We all are familiar with a bank, an automobile company, and probably an engineering business too. None of them is into any esoteric business that requires a special skill to be understood. So let's say we are going for simple businesses, and there is nothing wrong with that. Before 1998, stock market investors did not know much beyond three to four stocks and the infotech sector came from nowhere and took the lead. Few of the infotech stocks did exist in 1995 as well, but they weren't popular at that point in time, they became popular when their prices started moving up.

In stock markets, popularity has a price and most of the investors end up paying that price quite dearly sometimes. While picking these stocks, I looked at their core business strengths, the quality of their management, the dividend track record, their balance sheets, and a few other ratios. A few of these stocks have a market capitalisation lower than the cash that they are holding on their balance sheets.'

'Sir, please explain this googly to all of us. What is market capitalization?' asks Gobind.

'Market capitalization (or market cap) is the total value of the issued shares of a publicly traded company; it is equal to the share price times the number of shares outstanding. As outstanding stock is bought and sold in public markets, capitalization could be used as a proxy for the public opinion of a company's net worth and is a determining factor in some forms of stock valuation. Simply put, the market cap is a rough measure of how a company is valued by the market. For example, one of the companies that we are proposing to invest in has cash of Rs. 200 crores on its balance sheet and the total market cap of the stock is only 50 crores today. The management is good and the company has been paying a dividend for last five years. To my mind, it's a no-brainer to invest in such a company. Unpopular stocks are not necessarily bad and popular ones aren't compulsorily good, so we are going for good stocks and not the popular ones. Similarly the mutual fund schemes that I have chosen are not popular. They are diversified equity funds which have not caught investors' fancy yet. Some of the stocks that I have selected can also be seen in these mutual fund portfolios. Having said that, Naren, we can still end up making mistakes and losing money.'

'But, Guruji, even if I assume that these stocks are good and are cheaply priced today, how shall they move when no one is buying them?' visibly puzzled Naren asks.

'Naren, as investors, we have control only on our investment decisions and not on the others' action. Each stock or mutual fund scheme which becomes popular one day has been unpopular at some point in time and probably for a long period of time too. But people or investors who buy these stocks or mutual funds after they have become immensely popular generally buy them at much higher prices compared to the time when they were unpopular. If their quality is good, then ultimately the market finds the right price for them. To my mind, the biggest challenge for all of us as investors is to have conviction to buy when no one else is. What do we do when we buy real estate? We buy a piece of land which is available cheap today and there is a scope of development on or around this piece of land in future, say a new highway coming up, or a big supermarket or a railway station being planned near this land, which hopefully shall take its price up. We buy the land before the development takes place, not after it has taken place, don't we? And we do not worry about the land price for a very long time period too. We want to buy this piece of land before the market comes to know, not after everyone knows about it, right? We need to apply the same principle here as well. Remember we talked about detachment in our earlier sessions. We need to detach ourselves from the fruits of our action as we have no control or right over them. While the Gita talks about following the path of Karmayoga, I am asking you to practice Moneyoga in order to create wealth over a longer period than just make few bucks here and there. Peter Lynch, in his book One Up on Wall Street, *lays emphasis on picking up the boring but good-quality businesses as against*

something in vogue. We must strive to find quality and value before anyone else. This shall help us create an alpha of huge proportions and bring in the element of permanence in our wealth too.'

'Sir, you mean there are companies in today's market that are available at low prices and are being ignored by investors?' asks Simmi.

'At any given point in time, there are companies that are good but ignored. Investors fail to see value in them as it may not be fashionable or chic to do so. This is what creates opportunity for the long-term wealth creators. If you want to understand this better, just try to find out what Warren Buffett and Jim Rogers were doing when infotech shares were going through the roof.'

Naren is quiet. He is slowly getting the point. No stock is good or bad; you just need to look at it dispassionately. You need to keep your calm and take your bets rather than chasing the popularity blindly. As against chasing the fashionable and talking about it in the cocktail parties, one should aim at spotting good businesses, buying them quietly, and discussing politics or sports when it is party time. Discuss anything but stocks. He looks back and thinks about the mistakes he made in the past. Memories of haughtiness and pomp come back rushing to him. He looks at the ground and seeks solace in the silence again. He stares at the whiteboard where Guruji has written a few boring names. Although he is not fully convinced yet, he knows that there is some relevance in what Chaitanya is saying.

'Before we wind up, I would like some of you to consider bringing your family members to this class, especially your children, if you wish to. See you in the next class.'

29

Rudyard Kipling Was a Stock Market Guru

'Before we actually take our first plunge, I want all of you to read this wonderful poem by Rudyard Kipling called "If". Whenever I have found myself in any mental or emotional trough in life, this poem has rescued me. If you read it carefully, you shall see this poem is apt for all stock market investors too. Here it is for all of you.'

Guruji switches the projector on and students read the poem.

If you can keep your head when all about you
Are losing theirs and blaming it on you,
If you can trust yourself when all men doubt you,
But make allowance for their doubting too;
If you can wait and not be tired by waiting,
Or being lied about, don't deal in lies,
Or being hated, don't give way to hating,
And yet don't look too good, nor talk too wise:

If you can dream—and not make dreams your master;
If you can think—and not make thoughts your aim;
If you can meet with Triumph and Disaster
And treat those two impostors just the same;

If you can bear to hear the truth you've spoken
Twisted by knaves to make a trap for fools,
Or watch the things you gave your life to, broken,
And stoop and build 'em up with worn-out tools:

If you can make one heap of all your winnings
And risk it on one turn of pitch-and-toss,
And lose, and start again at your beginnings
And never breathe a word about your loss;
If you can force your heart and nerve and sinew
To serve your turn long after they are gone,
And so hold on when there is nothing in you
Except the Will which says to them: "Hold on!"

If you can talk with crowds and keep your virtue,
Or walk with Kings—nor lose the common touch,
If neither foes nor loving friends can hurt you,
If all men count with you, but none too much;
If you can fill the unforgiving minute
With sixty seconds' worth of distance run,
Yours is the Earth and everything that's in it,
And—which is more—you'll be a Man, my son!

'Rudyard Kipling found the inspiration for this poem in a failed war, fought in the late nineteenth century. It was first published in 1910 in a book called Rewards and Fairies—a collection of short stories and poems by Kipling. If you read this poem carefully, you shall find the thread of karma running right through its core, similar to what the Gita says. I have highlighted a few lines as they seem quite pertinent to me from a long-term investing perspective. Every time I read it, it shows itself in a new light providing a new perspective to look at* *life. This poem is pinned on every cadet's desk in the National Defence Academy, Khadakwasla, for the sheer inspiration it brings to any human being. Can you see the deeper message in here?'*

Students are mesmerised. They are sunk deep into this masterpiece. They find a subtle resonance rising deep inside them; they hear the echo of these words ringing in their ears. Guruji's voice softly alters their state of mind as they find themselves coming to the classroom from a state of divine hypnotism.

'Sir, this is an excellent poem. Each verse holds depth of wisdom in it, yet it conveys the message with utmost simplicity. I am deeply influenced by this poem and shall read it again and again to completely absorb its essence,' Biswas says.

Other students are also charmed by this piece of poetry. Guruji has taken a few printouts, which are passed on to every student. Each printout carries today's date and the student's name too. This surprises the students, makes them smile too. Adarsh says, 'Guruji, I have heard a lot about this poem but had never read it. I really like it. The first stanza itself sets the tone for the entire poem. It seems that Kipling knew a lot about stock investing too, especially when he talks about having faith in one's actions when others have doubts in their mind. And not being tired of waiting, this is simply the essence of long-term investing that you have been teaching us about, isn't it?'

'Yes, Adarsh. I am glad that you are already reading between the lines to get to the deeper core of this masterpiece. Please pay attention to the first verse, where the author says, 'nor look too good or talk too wise'. This talks about humility along

the way, being down to earth, adopting a balanced approach, acting normal despite the market gyrations or vicissitudes of life. Would anyone like to talk about the next stanza?'

'Sir, this stanza says the same thing as the Gita's shloka you taught us. Treating victory and defeat in the same manner, keeping your cool as these two imposters try to throw us off balance. This also talks about starting afresh even after everything has been blown away. This applies to a lot of equity investors who first lose their money and then their willpower. Some of them do decide not to come back ever again. Like Adarsh, I am also mesmerised by this poem,' states Simmi.

Naren speaks now. He says, 'Sir, I can identify with the next stanza really well. In fact my two friends Adarsh and Gobind are also in the same boat. We saw a time period when everything was hunky-dory and soon everything started falling apart as if a storm had chosen to visit a house of cards. We not only lost money but also lost the hope, the will to do anything at all. Yet there was something in our spirit that wanted to fight back, to come back and redeem our pride. Our coming to this class is a stroke of destiny only. I am glad that we came. Thank you so much for helping all of us. Thanks to you, our will to hold on became stronger and stronger. I have read this poem earlier but I never saw it from a stock market perspective. On a deeper level, it says a lot that's relevant from the viewpoint of investing. This poem is like a guru mantra to me now.'

'Dear all, the last stanza is the crux of this poem. Once again you shall see an overlap between the Gita and this poem here. It emphasizes the importance of karma again. One needs to keep doing one's work, one's karma and filling the

unforgiving minute with the scent of his spirit. The karma without expectation of the fruit shall fill the fleeting minute with the essence of the purpose and then everything shall belong to you, as you would have risen above victory and defeat, happiness and sorrows, and loss and gain too. I don't think this poem can work as a minute-to-minute guide for the investors, yet it provides enough meat for thought. Its deeper currents carry an important lesson for all of us and can help us all to lead a meaningful life through a compassionate discharge of our karma. If you notice carefully, the whole poem talks about equanimity, about keeping one's head steady on one's shoulders even in the time of distress. We shall be tested time and again. There shall be moments of celebration and despair too. We shall have to keep our cool, as someone just said, keeping in touch with the ground, yet staring at the stars that twinkle in the galaxy of wealth, thinking pure long-term and taking the current results in our longer-than-life stride. There is probably much more in this poem than we can comprehend. I keep coming back to it whenever I feel the need to do so, and this poem has never disappointed me. It always shows me the right path that passes through my own self, my own karma and deeds.

'We shall be starting our investments tomorrow. I hope all of you are as excited as I am. I hope it shall be a worthwhile journey to embark upon. I look forward to meeting you all tomorrow.'

Students gather their belongings and begin to leave, looking at their printouts as if there is really a mantra of wealth creation written on it. Just like Guruji, they are also eager to take the plunge now. They want to create wealth not only for themselves but also for their next few generations. These students who come from various backgrounds have similar needs, same goals and identical dreams too, only the extent and aspirations differ. Their unity in this class has resulted into a unique like-mindedness that may culminate into a grand synergy on the road to wealth creation. Most of them feel better now compared to how they felt a few months back. Their once-casual viewpoint towards investing is slowly changing into a more mature, long-term perspective, which augurs well for their future. Rachel (Adarsh's wife) shall be joining these classes soon, just as a few more members from other students' families have agreed to come along. Managing them shall be more fun than an administrative challenge for Guruji. This is what he has been looking forward to, having kids in his class. He firmly believes that children can become more responsible if they are taught about money and investing from an early age. He is happy that he is getting an opportunity to do so here. Excitement is in the air and everyone is thrilled about what the future is going to bring their way.

30

Welcome, Kids

'Dear kids, welcome to Moneymentors. I hope your parents haven't forced you to be here. Money is very important to all of us. Our objective is to learn about money and investing. I promise you that there is going to be lot of fun for all of you in these classes. Along with fun we shall also do some learning. I shall give you a little bit of homework sometimes but that shouldn't worry you at all. I am happy to see all of you here. Since we shall have a different curriculum from the seniors who are already attending these classes, we shall hold the junior classes at a different time and location too. Uncle Naren has allowed us to use his farmhouse for holding these classes, which means that you don't have to cope with a dull ambience like this. Your classes shall be held on weekends so that you have ample time for your studies too. We shall begin from the coming Saturday. I have kept some stuff for all of you in the adjoining room; you may please take it from there. Aunt Rachel has voluntarily agreed to help me with junior classes and I am thankful to her. Can we please have a round of applause for her and our juniors too?'

The whole class makes productive use of their palms to make a resonating sound of applause, which makes children giggle and smile. Each of them is given a bag which is full of goodies for them. There are a couple of T-shirts, one cap, one pencil box, a few drawing sheets, crayons, pens, a smiley ball, and a book named *Rich Dad Poor Dad* by Robert Kiyosaki. They shall be required to read this book at some stage, as they understand. No one is clear right now how these children are going to be taught, but they know at the back of their minds that Guruji might have thought about it already. Rachel shall be their coordinator and Guruji himself shall give classes. One thing everyone is sure of is that the classes shall be lot of fun for the kids. Chaitanya has kept a few board games for the kids in the next room, which keep the children busy while their parents are taking lessons in wealth creation. The children's class shall begin with very basic stuff about money and slowly graduate to investing and wealth creation. There is a lot of work that needs to be done for the juniors and a detailed list has been provided to Rachel. She in turn has outsourced some of this work to the seniors who are attending this class.

Naren has done his bit by letting his farmhouse being used, arranging a transport for ferrying kids from their home and back, and organising home-made hygienic snacks for the kids every time the class is held. Biswas has to write a few poems on money, income, expenses, barter system, savings, etc. These shall be simple poems that children can sing together much like the rhymes that they did in their schools. Simmi has taken the challenge of creating colourful props for these sessions. Sumant has organised some basic literature that mutual funds provide on savings. Some mutual funds also run schemes especially for children; Sumant has also arranged for their application forms, should there be a need to invest in them. Most of the children are in their early teens so they are kept in a single batch. They shall spend two hours each on Saturdays and Sundays in learning about money and investing. Rachel along with Chaitanya shall conduct these sessions, although Guruji has some other ideas in his mind too. He shall ask all the seniors to teach the kids by rotation to run this initiative in a more cohesive manner.

'I know that we have to start investing from today. But we shall do it from tomorrow. Today let me just spend some time on what we intend to do with the juniors. We want them to learn everything about money, respect money, and understand the impact it can make on their lives. We want them to know that money is a scarce resource and is limited in nature and that they should not be taking it for granted. Our objective is to make them start investing from an early age, so that by the time they reach college, they have enough resources on their own to fund their education. We want them to be self-dependent at least in the matters of money. This way they shall find many more opportunities available to them than the students who follow the traditional path of education. We want them to become the wealth creators of tomorrow, to treat and handle the money in a way that we couldn't do ourselves. All of you shall be helping me in this.'

Mridula Satija speaks up. 'Sir, isn't money a boring subject, too boring to be taught to kids?'

'Depends on the way you teach it. Rachel has worked very hard to make this subject very interesting for the children. I am sure they are going to enjoy it. Whether all kids would like it, I am not sure, but whoever likes it and keeps learning shall have a very different growth path in front of him/her, especially in a country where one billion people are living.'

'Sir, why can't we hold even the adult classes in Naren's farmhouse?' asks Adarsh.

Guruji looks at Naren, who is already smiling, nodding his head affirmatively.

'It shall take me about a week's time to do the alterations and other arrangements. We can start there from the next week,' says Naren.

There is a round of applause for Naren and virtually everyone is thanking him. Not that they don't like this place, but moving to a new place brings excitement, a welcome change for everyone including Guruji.

'I have prepared some notes on the investments that we propose to take from tomorrow. You may take them with you, study them, and see if we need to make some changes. Basically each one of us shall take a systematic investment plan with a mutual fund for a minimum period of five years. Each one of us shall be buying a set of stocks every month on a particular day. I have mentioned the names of the stocks, based on my understanding. If someone wants to add or delete any stock, I am happy to discuss. We shall monitor the progress of our investments once a month and take corrective actions if required. Along with these investments, we also have the option of doing lump sum investments, should anyone be interested. But the rules of monitoring shall remain same. We shall continue to learn, discuss, debate, and deliberate too. We shall not buy any stock for a period less than five years and I would prefer you to hold some of these stocks forever, if possible.'

'Sir, what if we need the money in between?' asks Balwant Jakhar.

'We are not going to invest everything in stock markets or equities. So we shall have some money kept aside for our

long-term and short-term needs. When I say five years, it may be longer than five years and it may be shorter too. If we have a need that requires every penny from our investments, then one should not hesitate to liquidate everything and cater to that need. Investments are not more important than our life, although they can help improve its quality. Let's not make the kids wait any longer. Please take your note sets and proceed. I shall see you all tomorrow.'

Everyone leaves. Chaitanya decides to sit alone for some time. He stares at the bunch of papers on his table. He isn't sure of the results but he is quite sure of the quality of efforts that he has put in for his students. He is happy about the fact that many kids have come forward to learn about money. These students have become a part of his life. He doesn't have many needs beyond this group. His life is all about Moneymentors now. He has enough savings to take care of his paltry expenses. Although his students keep on insisting that he charge them a fee, Chaitanya hasn't agreed to their demands. Following the path of karma has been spiritually fulfilling so far and shall continue to be so going forward too. At least he hopes so. He looks at his classroom; a tear appears in the corner of his eye. He is attached to it; he has decided to purchase this place.

31

Indian Economy on a Song— Take the Plunge

Students have gone through the notes. Guruji has suggested that they start a SIP (systematic investment plan) in an unnoticed diversified equity fund. They haven't heard much about this scheme, fund house, or fund manager. Guruji has further suggested that they invest in ten stocks which come from the infotech sector, automobiles, engineering, capital goods, banking, oil refining, pharmaceuticals, power, and entertainment. He has provided a brief note on all these stocks to the students. Guruji has also suggested that they make lump sum investment in a new mutual fund scheme launched recently. This scheme proposes to invest in shares of the power sector. The initial public offering (IPO) of the fund hasn't done as well as some of the IPOs were doing in the era of the infotech boom. This doesn't matter to Guruji; in fact, he is quite happy about the fact that not many people are subscribing to equity offerings as this means that prices are still reasonable as the crowd is still away from the market.

Interest rates have gone down globally over last few years; this has resulted in increasing consumption across the segment of consumers. Individual consumers are buying mobile phones, cars, homes, branded goods, consumer durables as their surplus income has gone up. The decisions that were considered very big—like buying a car, TV, or fridge—are becoming a matter of routine for most Indians. The Indian consumer no longer asks the advice of friends and relatives before buying a simple household item. Buying second-hand cars is passé, thanks to aspirations of Indians. India has the maximum percentage of youth in the world, which makes this market a mouth-watering prospect for all global players like Coke, Pepsi, Nike, Casio, global carmakers like Hyundai, Toyota, and Mercedes, and global electronics players like LG and Samsung. Everyone is looking at India. New roads are being built; Delhi is going to get a Metro Rail soon. Big shopping malls are coming up all over the place. People from smaller cities are moving to larger cities in search of jobs and opportunities, demanding more facilities and infrastructure from the central and state governments. More and more airports are being planned as air travel is coming into vogue. A low-cost airline has been launched in India, where people can buy a ticket for as low Rs. 500; a consumption boom is on its way. Indian software companies are being used for outsourcing by the large players in USA, Europe, and other Asian countries. Many call centres are being set up in Gurgaon, a small town on the edge of Delhi, Hyderabad, and Bangalore—the electronic city of India. Construction is in full swing everywhere, and no town in India is left untouched by this revolution. Growth in infrastructure is slowly leading to job creation for everyone, leading to higher incomes in more hands, meaning more consumption and more earnings for companies. Guruji's thoughts are very simple. He can see this boom coming through. He has selected certain sectors that shall benefit from this boom, and luckily for him, the prices are still very attractive as investors are still recovering from the shock of the stock market crash that happened in the year 2000. He has chosen companies with good managements that have a sound track record of business and earnings growth. Most of these companies are available at dirt-cheap prices, and Guruji and his students have ample time on their hands to purchase these companies. It's like going to a big sale and being the only customer in the store that's full of goodies.

New TV channels are getting launched; global media players are eyeing the prospect of coming into India, a country of one billion people. The total market capitalisation of the entire media sector is less than 5,000 crores, which means one dollar per Indian. Since India is slated to go up in global rankings, the media sector is virtually available for no cost. Outsourcing of back offices for global banks and research companies has suddenly put India on the global map. The country of snake charmers and beggars is slowly becoming a country of globetrotters as more and more Indians are opting for foreign holidays and embracing new ways of living. There is a social transformation underway as Indians are becoming more open in their culture and thinking. A few Indian girls have already made their mark globally by bagging Miss Universe and Miss World titles; as a result, the global cosmetic giants like Revlon and L'Oréal are setting up their counters at every shopping mall opening across the country. Aspiring Indians are ready to take a giant leap, and sooner rather than later, this shall reflect in the bottom lines of corporates, making their share prices go up through the roof, sky, and the stratosphere too.

In the field of pharmaceuticals, India has a certain distinctive advantage over rivals like china. Indian genes vary from state to state which makes the medical research more effective and cheaper in India. More and more pharma companies want to set up a research base in India because of the local skill sets, cost-effectiveness, and the biological diversity of Indian population. Engineering companies are getting more and more orders from not only foreign countries but also from the Indian government, who wants to emulate the Chinese model of growth. Cheap money, soaring aspirations, young population, and genuine demand for infrastructure and services are the right recipe for an economic and stock market boom. One has to slowly get into the market and wait for things to happen. The Bombay Stock Exchange Index—SENSEX—is trading close to 3000, which is seen as the bottom of the markets by the pundits, yet people are afraid to take the plunge as the memories of last crash are still fresh in their memories. Guruji always believes that if one is to achieve something big, he has to separate himself from the crowd and take his initiatives in a focussed manner. A leader is always alone in the beginning; slowly the crowd starts pouring in and follows the leader. That's why in life and in stock markets, being ahead of the curve really helps. Guruji is doing the same thing by making his students take equity market exposure at this stage when everyone and his mother-in-law are scared of the E word. Each student has signed up a SIP for five years and bought some stocks as well. The plan is to take the stock market exposure in a disciplined, systematic way. Each student has committed a certain amount per month to this exercise. Thanks to Naren, Adarsh, Gobind, Simmi, and Naresh

Kohli, the total corpus that this group wants to invest in the markets is more than Rs. 50 crores, more than 60 per cent coming from Naren himself. He has decided to invest his lifetime savings in the markets, with a renewed focus and fresh perspective. He has the power of Guruji behind him now and he is confident of success this time. Adarsh and Gobind are with their friend as usual, notwithstanding the comfort that Guruji's presence brings. Other students have also chipped in with whatever they can spare at this stage. A large bank has started offering the services of online trading in the stock markets and all the students and Guruji himself have opened an account with it. This way they can purchase shares at the click of a mouse. It takes a couple of days to complete the paper formalities for the investments to become operational. Post-dated cheques for next five years have been provided to mutual funds, and the SIPs are operational now. A few days have passed and students aren't able to resist the temptation of checking the stock prices and NAV (net asset value) of their mutual funds.

'Dear students, thank you very much for making this beginning and taking the plunge in the equity market. Let us resolve to stay committed to this journey, no matter what. I hope I can count on you in this. I have also committed my lifetime savings into this expedition, so we all are together in it. Going forward, we shall be holding our class on monthly intervals, so that you can have more time for our daily routines, work, and family.'

32

Psychological Pitfalls— Finding the Best Performers

One month is now a long period to pass without meeting for the class. Students are in touch with each other though. They long to meet again in the classroom, discussing and learning with Guruji. They aren't sure why Guruji has decided to reduce the frequency of the classes; maybe he wants to devote more time for kids, and maybe he has some personal agenda that he wants to attend to, maybe something else. They are eager to be under the roof of that classroom again. What they don't know is that Guruji wants to teach them patience; he wants to teach them the subtleties of investing by telling them that investments are just one part of their life and not life itself. He wants them to focus on their jobs, businesses, and other avocations, now that they have started investing. He has requested them not to track the prices on a daily, weekly, or real-time basis. He wants them to adopt investing just as any other routine of their life, so it is necessary that the frequency be reduced. This way they can be more independent as well. Prices haven't gone anywhere in the last thirty days; in fact they have fallen a bit. The NAV of the funds they have chosen have also gone down marginally.

The students have learnt their lessons well; they have started reading business newspapers and they meditate for fifteen minutes without fail every day. They have started taking their money matters more seriously now, which is indeed a good sign. Sumant buys groceries regularly. Balwant Jakhar has taken all money-related matters in his hands. Mridula is making sure that not a single penny in her household is idle or goes to waste, Naren has become more mature and patient in the investment department, and Adarsh has started listening to Rachel more carefully.

Finally one month is over and they are meeting Guruji again, this time in a more colourful, cosy, and lavish ambience of neatly manicured lawns, trimmed hedges, and rows of swaying tulips. Naren has invested a lot of money and time in developing his farm, which reflects in everything from the grand entrance to the plush interiors. Naren feels as if everyone is visiting his home only, so he has arranged for delicious snacks and other eatables for everyone. The room which has been converted into the classroom has modern audiovisual equipment; it has swivel leather chairs arranged around a few round tables with Naren's servants available for serving while the classes are going on. They all like this surrounding, and Guruji is happy as long as his students are happy.

'Dear all, welcome to Moneymentors once again. Some of you must be surprised at the new schedule of our classes. I have done this change to make the investing seem like just any other thing in your life. All of us should take it really easy. Now tell me who has been tracking the investments regularly?'

Few hands go up religiously, others stay down. Guruji looks at the raised hands and smiles.

'I know it's tempting to track our investments regularly but I shall request you to avoid seeing them on daily or weekly basis. Today we shall discuss the common myths prevailing in the investor fraternity. These myths not only undermine the purpose of investing but are also a big hurdle in the way of wealth creation. They often play the spoilsport in the game of investing by shaping our psychology in a particular manner, and when things go the other way, we become disheartened.

The first myth is related to investing in the best performing stock / mutual fund. Fixation with the best is a natural human phenomenon—who doesn't want the best car, best home, best husband, best wife, best friend, or anything that comes with this superlative tag? Then why not have the best performing investments too? Let me tell you that there is absolutely nothing wrong with this notion or desire. But how do we define the best performing stock or mutual fund? Can anyone answer?'

'Sir, the best performing stock or mutual fund scheme is a scheme/stock that has given the best performance over a particular time period in the past, say one month, one year, three years, five years, or any other period,' says Sumant.

'But how does past performance help, especially when my investments have to perform in future? I don't want my investments to be done in a fund or stock that has the best performance in the past; I want something that shall be the best performing in the future.'

'Sir, traditionally we judge a mutual fund scheme or a stock by its price movement in the past. This gives us an idea about its quality and consistency also. Moreover, if we do not look at the past performance of a fund or a stock, then what is there to analyse, what do we base our investing decisions upon?' says Sumant again.

'I agree with you, Sumant. We can analyse a fund or a stock with its past performance. But does it mean that this fund or stock is going to be the best performing fund in the future too? Moreover, how do we choose the time period? I mean best performing fund over what period? What about a fund or a stock that hasn't done well in the past or a fund that doesn't have a history long enough to have a trustworthy track record? Can this stock or fund not become the best performing fund of tomorrow?'

'Sir, past performance of a scheme or a share is definitely speaks volumes about fund management strength of a particular fund house or a company. A consistent past performance over longer periods does carry a lot of weight in investment decision-making,' says Simmi.

'Yes, Simmi, I am with you. All I am trying to say is that the best past performance doesn't mean that the performance delivered in the future too shall be the best. The best performing stocks of yesterday may lie in dust tomorrow. The great mutual fund schemes of yesteryears may become the laggards of tomorrow. How do you ensure that you invest in a fund or stock that is going to be the best performer of the future?'

'Guruji, the only way to ensure that we invest in the best performing fund of the future or a stock is that we are able to predict which sectors shall do well in the time period to come, which is no easy thing to do. It shall be a mix of having acumen and bit of guesswork too. Then on the top of it one has to be lucky as well,' Adarsh says.

'That's where the karma of investing comes into play. One has to reconcile with the fact that one can't spot the best performers consistently on prospective basis. Historically best performing stocks or funds mean little in the forward journey.

Historical performance is important though because it means that there was a fund manager who chose a particular stock or a sector when others didn't.'

'But, sir, most of the investors and advisors base their investment decisions on the historical performance only. Is this a wrong practice then?' asks Kantha Subramanian.

'It's not wrong at all but it serves a limited purpose from a wealth creation perspective. Let me explain this with two examples. Suppose a mutual fund scheme is the best performing scheme for the past year, investors start buying more and more of it, meaning that the fund manager is receiving more cash in his fund. Now the fund manager has to deploy this cash equally efficiently, deliver performance to keep attracting more money from the investors as the markets keep moving up. From a practical viewpoint this is not sustainable. We experienced this during the infotech boom. Most of the infotech funds kept on getting cash from the investors, till the tide turned against the tech stocks. The prices tumbled, NAVs fell, and the best performers became the worst performers in a few months' time. The buyers' market became a sellers' market as no one wanted to own these stocks. However, if one chose an average performing fund, say a diversified equity fund that did not have a 100 per cent exposure to one single sector, one might have been able to ride this storm better. Remember no fund, no stock can be the best performer forever, if it could be so then there shall be no market. Most of the successful investors have repeatedly said that average performance over a longer period is preferable to a superlative performance over a shorter period. Yet psychologically it could be demoralising not to hold the best performers in your portfolio. So in a nutshell even if you have invested in the best performing stock or the best performing

portfolio, there is no guarantee that this stock or fund shall not become the worst in the future.

'Moreover, best performer over what period? A fund may be best performing in the past year, but not in the last two years. It may be the worst performer in the three-year category and an average player in four-year. Then what do you do? Performance of an MF changes on a daily basis, and stocks change on a real-time basis. If we are invested in good MF schemes and good companies, we shall be able to capture their good and bad times over a longer period. All I want to convey is that the best performing portfolio or best performing stock over a certain period doesn't ensure success in future. An average performing company or a portfolio shall do equally well over a longer period. Over a very long time period, the power of compounding comes into play and shows its magic. So if you are in a cocktail party and don't own the best performing stocks or MFs, talk about weather.

Everyone laughs heartily at this subtle joke in the end. They enjoy a nice cup of tea after the lecture is over and depart only to meet again after one month.

Chaitanya spends some time in isolation after everyone leaves. He has started thinking about Sonia a little more these days. He wants to know where she is, but doesn't know where to start from.

33

Markets Are Not Risky

The first class for the kids is held at the farmhouse on the next weekend. Rachel has read Robert Kiyosaki's book as instructed by Guruji. She has found out information about financial literacy for kids from the Internet and prepared notes for the children. She has written a few stories, made couple of presentations which talk about basics of money. With the help of Naren's servants, a model of the bank is prepared in one room using the tables, chairs, and other furniture available at the farm. Fake currency notes have been arranged as well.

In their first class, children learn about the concept of money and banking. Guruji and Rachel talk about the barter system, stamps, coins, etc. to teach the children about basics of money. They are shown pictures of coins from the ancient times and how money has evolved over a period of time starting from barter system to present-day credit cards. They are taught about the concept of consideration and the necessity of money in our present day lives. They also learn about the function of banks. Rachel has written a few short poems on money; kids recite these during the class, Rachel sings along with them. The kids enjoy the session; they hardly know how two hours have already passed. They seem eager and excited to come back again tomorrow and learn more about money just like their parents are to learn about wealth creation.

The adults have spent their time in mulling over the stuff taught in the last class. Some of the students, like the trio, think about their last investing stints when they were fiercely chasing the best performers of the past only to lose everything in the end. They do not know what Guruji is going to talk about today. They are enjoying the fine Darjeeling tea that Naren has arranged for them today along with low-fat crispy spring rolls prepared by Lavanya at home. Even Guruji takes a sumptuous dig at them before starting the class.

'How many of you hate the stock market?'

Students are almost shocked with this question; they are still thinking about it when Guruji repeats his question.

'I am asking how many of you hate the stock market, or let me ask you, what is that you do not like in the stock market?'

This sounds better; a couple of hands go up.

Naresh Kohli says, 'Sir, I hate market volatility. It adds so much risk to this business of investing and wealth creation stuff.'

'I agree with Mr Kohli. If only the markets could be less volatile, it would be a better place to be in,' says a smiling Mridula Satija.

The same view is echoed by a couple more students and slowly the whole class except Rachel is saying the same thing.

'Rachel, what do you say? What is that you don't like about the stock market?'

'Sir, market is a market. To me there is no difference between a vegetable market and stock market as far as volatility is concerned. I don't think there is any market that isn't volatile. In fact I feel if it isn't volatile, it isn't a market at all,' says Rachel.

Students, including Adarsh himself, are stunned with this smart response. They are lost in her words even before their brains start processing what she just said.

'Why do you say if it isn't volatile, it isn't a market?' asks Sumant.

Rachel hears the question patiently and responds, 'Volatility is an essential characteristic of any market, be it a local vegetable market or global currency market. The volatility represents the difference of opinion between various investors which creates an active price in the market. Volatility is a result of difference in perception of various investors and I feel it is actually good to have volatility in the markets because it means markets are alive,' she adds.

'How is volatility related to perception?' asks Mridula.

'Assume there are two investors: one feels the prices shall go up, the other feels the price shall go down. The latter one sells the stock, and the former one, who believes prices shall go up, buys it. Imagine this phenomenon with a large number of investors who have different objectives in the market and you shall easily get your answer,' Rachel utters.

'Rachel is right. Volatility of price is a function of perception, demand-supply, and individual views of the investors. To add to what Rachel said, imagine now there is an investor who feels prices shall fall over next few months, and then stabilize before moving up. He shall keep buying the stock as long as someone is selling it. A few investors work with price targets. They have their own strategies of operating in the market. Volatility, Warren Buffett says, is a friend of a long-term investor. Most of

the investors think volatility is akin to risk. It is not. It is merely a reflection of the price movement at a particular juncture. This difference of opinion is a healthy sign for the wealth creators. If everyone has the same view then there is no market.'

'But, sir, if the prices keep fluctuating, then the risk factor comes in automatically, doesn't it?' asks Gobind.

'Would anyone like to respond to Gobind?'

Naren speaks. He says, 'Gobind, the risk is not in the price movement. The risk is in the business itself. If the business is good, then it shows in the prices over the long term. Markets are markets. Remember we discussed about this. We are buying shares, participating in businesses, not investing in markets. The market is only a representation, a medium to discover the prices at any moment. The price of a stock may fall for many reasons. Some can be technical reasons related to demand-supply and some can be fundamental reasons related to the business itself. By buying regularly or in a systematic way, we can negate the fluctuations in the prices to some extent.'

'Let us assume that this whole class is the market. I divide it in two groups. One group has the shares and the other group has the money. Both the groups feel that prices shall go up tomorrow. The group with cash wants to buy the shares today but the group who is holding the shares will not sell as they also feel the same way. Similarly if both the groups expect prices to fall, then the group with shares would want to sell and encash, but the other group won't buy as they know they can buy the stocks cheaper tomorrow. In both the cases, there is no market as no buying or selling takes place. But does it change the fundamental reality of business? If there was no stock market for, say, two years, will the businesses close down? No. The market is merely a place

where buyers and sellers meet. It can be an actual, physical place like a building or it can be an imaginary place held on a computer server somewhere. The market is not risky, businesses are. Markets may not reflect the reality of business all the time, and this is what creates opportunity for the long-term investors. When one of the large software companies came out with its IPO way back in 1994, there were not enough buyers and the IPO devolved. That means that investors did not believe in the potential of this company at that point in time. They might have thought that the price was too high to be paid for owning a share of a new company or they did not believe in the business at all. Whatever may be the reason, the markets reflected the perception of the investors in form of the issue going bust. Five to six years down the line, the company became a multi-bagger. I am told Rs. 10,000 invested in this share became almost 27 crores in a period of ten years. There are investors who ignored the market and bought this share because they believed in what they were doing. Remember, markets shall do what they have to, we shall do what we believe is correct in our opinion.'

'Sir, by the way, onion prices are going up and down every day but we do not realise it because we have not bought onions worth lacs of rupees,' speaks Biswas and everyone bursts into laughter.

The onion prices are behaving like a yo-yo that has forgotten its downward movement; there is a fear that the state government may fall because of the high onion prices. The sessions are gradually becoming more participative, productive, and spiritually more fulfilling to the students. Gobind and Adarsh have taken places near Naren's home and now the three of them have started going for their morning walk together. Yoga and meditation have become a permanent part of the students' lives. Guruji has added a meaningful dimension to their lives already and now he is teaching the kids too. They all feel so grateful to him.

'Dear all, I hope I have been able to make myself clear and all of you have understood that markets are not risky, businesses are. Markets shall do what they have to, we shall follow our karma. We shall discuss about another fallacy of investors in our next class.'

Although a few students have already checked the prices, they keep quiet. The stock prices have gone up, the mutual fund NAVs have also moved up a little. They have begun on a positive note; they have a reason to feel happy.

34

Crowd Sees the Risk— Leaders See Opportunity

Naren has arranged a bank trip for the kids. Since Naren is still a privileged customer of the bank, the bank has obliged him by arranging this trip. Kids are shown around the bank branch, told about various services that a bank provides to its customers. Most of the kids are in early teens. They are familiar with the concept of interest, which helps them understand bank deposits. In fact, the bank manager has helped them by opening a bank account for each of the kids. Parents have gladly deposited some money as well. They all are provided with chequebooks and are taught how to write a cheque. This simple thing brings the children closer to the money, teaching them what most of the kids do not get to learn until they start earning money.

It's weekend time; Chaitanya has kept a very special topic for the class this time.

'Dear all, we shall talk about something very interesting today. Let me start right away by asking you the meaning of crowd. *What do you mean by the word* crowd?*'*

'Sir, crowd means a large group, large number of people gathered somewhere for some specific purpose. They may have been called to a particular location for some purpose/ cause in a public gathering, or they might have been there as a matter of routine, like a crowd at the railway station or bus stops,' says Mrigendra Biswas.

'*What is the identity of the crowd?*'

'Sir, I don't think crowd has an identity as such. The purpose for which they have gathered may give them a collective identity though, for example, a political rally organised by a party, or an agitation called by, say, government employees,' says Mridula Satija.

'*What does the crowd do?*'

This time, Balwant Jakhar speaks; he says, 'Sir, the crowd does many unruly things in a country like India. The politicians use common people for organising rallies and showing their political strength. The crowd mobs, loots, litters, destroys, and does many other inappropriate things like rioting too.'

'*What else does the crowd do?*'

'Sir, the crowd does what it is told to do, especially when they have gathered for a specific purpose. They follow the instructions of their leaders,' says Kantha.

'*Thanks, Kantha, this was what I was looking for. The crowd follows. As rightly said by Mrigendra, the crowd doesn't have an identity. It's a group identified by the purpose. But this crowd consists of people, who have their own identities, goals, dreams, and aspirations. Each individual has a unique identity and wants to lead a purposeful life, yet when he/she becomes part of the crowd, the individual identity is gone. In stock markets, a crowd is considered to be a group of foolish followers who are being herded here and there by market forces. They follow smart investors in stock markets, just as they follow smart leaders in real life. In order to have a meaningful existence in the stock markets or in life, one needs to separate oneself from the crowd by one's actions, which may be difficult sometimes.'*

'Sir, everyone can't be a leader,' Kohli speaks.

'But everyone can choose not to become a follower, can't they?'

'Got it, sir,' says Kohli smilingly.

'It is actually our choice to be a leader or to be a follower. The stock market gives this opportunity to everyone, but only a few like Warren Buffett take the difficult path of being a leader. The junta or the crowd takes the downtrodden path of followership. Being a leader is not easy. It takes lot of conviction in oneself to do so. A leader usually begins alone in life and stock markets too. The crowd follows him with a lag; it is this lag that creates the financial edge for the leader, which finally leads to wealth creation over a longer period. Remember Mahatma Gandhi was alone for the initial few years in South Africa, getting beaten by the police and the other English men. But slowly the Ahimsa movement caught on and became a revolution in itself. Even after it became a revolution, it took a few decades before India could get freedom. Mahatma Gandhi was like a long-term equity market investor who invested in the shares of Ahimsa before anyone else could and kept on investing in it. Since the idea was strong, the public latched on to it, and as is commonly said, it finally led to freedom making Gandhi a hero of the masses. But being a Gandhi is not easy either. As long as you are investing in the good companies and MF schemes, you should not worry about being alone. Sometimes, investing in equity is like stepping into a dark room which everyone is afraid of. Suddenly you decide to step in, initially nothing is visible but gradually you find your way around things, whose

*shapes become clearer each passing moment. Finally the dawn lights up the space around you and the crowd joins you in your journey as there is more clarity now. Remember—the leaders love uncertainty and the crowd dies for clarity. By the time clarity comes, one part of the cycle is already over. In equity market parlance, the crowd is like the police in Bollywood movies—*coming always late.'

Guruji makes everyone cackle with his remark. Students are having a good time; their investment is in positive territory and soon the next tranche of money shall go. Markets are still dull and boring; not many investors are looking forward to equities. Bombay Stock Exchange Index has hardly moved up, by a couple of hundred points to 3200, when the third instalment of the investment goes, but that hardly matters.

'Another important aspect of investing is to observe how the crowd looks at the risk and the opportunity vis-à-vis a leader. Tell me, what do these words mean?'

'Sir, risk means losing money and opportunity is a chance in a person's hand, as far as stock markets are concerned,' a beaming Biswas says.

'At any given point in time, the crowd sees things in a different way from a long-term investor. Where a long-term investor sees opportunity, the crowd sees a risk and vice versa. Am I right?'

'Yes, sir,' most of them say.

'When the markets are trading at lower levels like these days, where has the crowd gone?'

'Sir, they are staying away from equity markets as they perceive there is too much risk in the stocks. When we met various mutual fund officials and stockbrokers during our one-month break, we found out that there were hardly any investors who were investing in equity markets or equity mutual funds,' says Naren.

'*The crowd sees only one thing at a time. They either see a huge risk in the markets or they see huge opportunity in the markets. When markets were booming, everyone was making money. The crowd didn't want to stay out of the markets because they spotted an opportunity just as everyone else had. They did not see the risk at that point in time. Similarly they are looking at only risk today, completely ignoring the huge opportunity present in the markets. They are scared today because they think they may lose more money.*'

'But, Guruji, how is it different with the leaders or the wealth creators?' asks Simmi.

'*Good question, Simmi. For a long-term investor or a leader, the risk and opportunity always go hand in hand. A leader always sees these two in conjunction not in isolation. Risk and opportunity are two faces of a coin; one can't exist without the other. When markets were booming, indices were going up like a rocket heading for the moon, the opportunity was still there but it came at a huge premium or a great level of risk. Similarly today the size of the opportunity is much bigger compared to the risk. But look at the poor crowd who is blindfolded by the losses they have suffered in the past.*'

'Sir, suppose the markets start going up tomorrow, I assume that the crowd shall start building up in the market, but how do we know that the crowd is there?' asks a puzzled Kohli. 'I don't think they show this crowd on the TV.'

'*You make a strong point here by saying that this crowd is not shown on the TV channels. I am 100 per cent with you. You won't certainly see a crowd outside the stock exchanges these days as most of the trading happens online, over the Internet. People can place their orders over phones or invest online using a few Internet sites, which are slowly coming into vogue. One can only see this crowd in the price movement and a few parameters related to a share.'*

'What are these other parameters, Guruji?' asks Kohli.

'We shall cover some of these parameters later. At this juncture, let us know that the crowd builds up slowly and a wise investor is easily able to sense the presence of the crowd in the marketplace even if there is no physical marketplace. The prices move up crazily, the volume of shares go up, the breadth of the market goes up, and at some point in time, even phony company shares start moving up. That indicates the crowd's presence. Technically a leader should do exactly the opposite of what the crowd is doing, but it is not easy, one has to be extremely disciplined to do that.

It has been almost six months since the students started investing. The BSE has moved to 3400, a gain of 13 per cent. Students' portfolios are in green; they are happy.

35

P/E Ratio

'Dear students, as we move forward into our journey, I would want you to know about this ratio called P/E. PE stands for price–earnings ratio.'

Guruji walks to the whiteboard and writes these two words one upon the other. He writes *price* in the numerator and *earnings* in the denominator.

'P/E ratio is a simple, commonly used and time-tested tool for evaluating the equity shares. This depicts the ratio of price (market price of one share) to the EPS (earnings per share) of a particular company. Let me explain it in more detail. Every listed company has a certain number of shares held by its shareholders. If we divide the total earnings of a company by the number of shares that this company has issued, we arrive at the figure of earnings per share.

'Suppose a company has issued 100 shares to its shareholders and has a total earning of Rs. 100. Then its EPS shall be 100 divided by 100, which means Rs. 1. Understand?'

The chorus of 'Yes, sir' is heard.

'Now let us assume that the stock price of this company is Rs. 500 per share. What does this mean?'

'Sir, it means that the investors have to pay Rs. 500 per share to own this company's shares,' says Biswas.

'You are right. But there is something else too. Who shall help me?'

Guruji spots a smiling Rachel, who says, 'Guruji, this also means that investors are paying Rs. 500 for each rupee that the company earns. This is too high a price to pay.'

'Let's calculate the P/E ratio of this company. As most of you would have already calculated, the P/E ratio is Rs. 500 divided by 1, which equals 500. As Rachel says, this means that investors are ready to pay Rs. 500 for each rupee that the company earns. Now let us assume that the price of this share is only Rs. 10 and the EPS is Rs. 5. The P/E ratio of this stock shall be 10 divided by 5, which is equal to 2, meaning that investors are willing to pay Rs. 2 for each rupee earned by this company. This ratio indicates whether the stock is undervalued or overvalued. For an investor's perspective, a lower P/E ratio is preferable to a higher one, because a lower P/E would generally indicate that the share price is undervalued and a higher P/E means the opposite.'

Rachel asks, 'Sir, is a lower P/E sufficient enough to gauge the quality of a company? I mean, can we make our buying decision on the basis of low P/E alone?'

'Good question, Rachel. Although a low P/E is indicative of undervaluation of a stock, it is by no means the ultimate tool for decision-making. We need to look at the P/E of other stocks in the same sector. One may also compare the P/E of the stock with overall P/E of the market to get a fair idea of relative valuation. We may find an undervalued company within an overvalued sector and vice versa. This also doesn't mean that a high P/E stock is a bad investment idea. P/E is generally the starting point. There are a host of other factors that one must look at before buying the stock.'

'Sir, you mentioned something about the P/E of the market itself, what does it indicate?' asks Gobind.

'P/E of the market is calculated in pretty much the same manner as the individual stock P/E. Long-term average P/E of the Indian stock markets is 16, so if the current P/E of the index is below 16, then the market is undervalued, and if it above 16, then the market is heated up. For example, today the thirty companies forming the SENSEX have a weighted average earning of Rs. 310 and the SENSEX is trading at 3000 points. So can we now calculate the P/E of the index?'

Simple questions bring excitement even to the grown-up students. Everyone raises hands to make Guruji smile. Simmi is asked to give the answer. She divides 3000 by 310 and comes up with the right answer of 9.6, making everyone wonder at the extent of undervaluation of the markets.

'But, sir, if the markets are so underpriced, why the hell the investors are not coming forward to buy?' asks Naresh Kohli.

'Investors aren't buying shares because of fear. They are part of the crowd, hence not used to lead but follow. While P/E ratio is a good indicator on absolute and relative basis, it needs to be seen in light of the other factors such as price to book ratio, dividend yield, the quality of management, etc. I would urge all of you to study about these a little bit before we meet for the next session.'

'Sir, if one doesn't want to study all these ratios and the related stuff but still wants to create wealth, is it possible to do so?' asks Biswas.

Almost everyone laughs except Guruji, Rachel, Adarsh, Naren, and Biswas himself.

'Certainly, one can create wealth by simply investing in mutual funds. Most of the mutual funds have qualified investment teams who work round the year to evaluate securities and make investing and divesting decisions for a very nominal fee per year. The objective of mutual funds is to help people who either do not have the wherewithal to understand the markets or do not have time to do so. It basically means that you can hire a fund manager to manage your money by paying a small fee. Do you agree with me, Sumant?'

'Absolutely, one can hire a good fund manager by paying as low as 2 per cent per annum,' says a smiling Sumant.

'By investing through MFs, you can ensure yourself a good night's sleep while a smart fund manager takes care of your money round the clock. This is a good way to participate in markets, especially when one doesn't want to take the headache of doing investments oneself. Although many investors do not see the mutual funds this way, they lose the sight of the long-term objectives and the services provided by MFs in the short-term fluctuations of their NAVs. One must take a holistic view of the services provided by the MFs and seek to benefit from them. Mutual funds, to my mind, are the ultimate answer to the woes of investors, should they chose to act with discipline. Apart from providing diversification benefits, mutual funds also provide certain tax benefits to the investors, thanks to our government. Ideally, I think an investor can do justice to his portfolio by keeping a judicious mix of mutual funds and shares in his portfolio. Moreover, mutual funds have schemes for investing in both debt and equity. From a wealth creation perspective, investing in equity mutual funds can be worthwhile if one invests systematically over a longer period. One may simply start an SIP.

'Coming back to P/E ratio, I would say that it is a useful parameter if seen in conjunction with other ratios. Also a low PE is not necessarily good and high PE is not essentially bad.'

'Sir, what do you mean by low PE not being good and high PE not being bad?'

'A low PE may not always mean a steal. Low PE may also mean that the market is assuming that a particular company's earnings may not grow much. These may be established companies which are in a mature phase of growth. On the other hand, there may be certain high-growth sectors like technology where the market is assigning a higher PE multiple to the stocks because of the growth expectations. That is why I said that we need to see relative PEs, say, finding a low PE stock within a high PE group. Once spotted, we test other parameters to see if the company is really available cheap as compared to the peers. If yes, then we start buying.'

'Sir, what is the rule of thumb for using P/E ratio?' asks Simmi.

Guruji looks at Rachel, who seems to be keen to answer this one. He nods in the affirmative to let her handle this question.

'Simmi, generally a single-digit PE is considered to be manna for the stock investors. Single digit means less than ten. So one may say, if a stock or the entire market is trading at a single-digit PE, it is a good starting point because the price is low. Cheap price in the stock market brings an automatic margin of safety. But as Guruji mentioned, a low PE is always not good. Certain low-growth industries like manufacturing, textiles, or sometimes commodities may have low P/E ratios. On the other hand, some high-growth industries like software, technology, media, and entertainment companies may exhibit higher PEs owing to the growth potential they may have. One needs to see the growth potential in the company or a sector before making a buy decision. An ideal stock could be the one which has low PE compared to its peers, has lots of cash on its balance sheet, and has a good growth potential. I hope I have answered your question,' says Rachel.

'Let me say that Rachel has answered this question better than I could have.'

This makes Rachel blush and Adarsh feel proud, as everyone claps for her.

'Guruji, why don't you tell us about the basics of the other ratios as well?' asks Gobind.

'I shall tell you in brief about a couple of more useful measures in the next class. Meanwhile, I request everyone to find out about these on their own too.'

36

Be Anything But a Pig

'Someone once said bulls make money, bears make money, pigs get slaughtered. For an investor to be successful in the market, he needs to identify himself, needs to know himself better than he thinks he knows. One can be a bull or a bear; there is nothing wrong in taking a position. The real risk is in not knowing which side of the fence you are on. You shall then be rolling here and there with the crowd, making yourself meat for the beast of volatility. Warren Buffett says if you do not know who you are, then the stock market is going to be a costly place to find out. Knowing yourself, as you should, shall help you chart the path to reach your goal. Know yourself so that you are not labelled a pig.'

The class is silent, listening with concentration to Guruji, who is flowing smooth like a river in its youth. Guruji continues.

'We have discussed a lot about fear in the past, today we shall also look at the emotions of greed and hope that dominate investors' minds from time to time. It is believed that these emotions surface at the wrong time. For example, investors become greedy when the markets are going up every day, and they put more money at higher levels, which fuels the euphoria further, taking stock prices higher, attracting more investors like a magnet pulling the poor iron filings from a heap of dust.

Similarly when markets are down or flat, investors do not want to invest out of fear of losses. Then they just hope that their prices shall come back someday. Has anyone been through this experience of fear, greed, and hope?'

Everyone is looking at each other; no one is willing to raise a hand except Naren. Naren gets up, clears his throat, and says, 'Guruji, probably no one knows this better than I do. I have been so deep in this trap that I almost know everything about it. I made so much money that it stopped mattering to me. I hated to count it, there was a feeling of too much, and yet I was not willing to quit. I was watching markets go up like a gas balloon in the sky; I didn't want to lose any opportunity of participating in the madness that was taking place around me. I was so confident that the thoughts of markets ever falling didn't cross my mind even once. I had bought those stocks really cheap and I believed they could never ever fall below my prices, no matter what. I felt I was on the top of the markets, knowing a few fund managers and others who were in the markets with me. Because I had made money, I believed I was an expert on these stocks. I found myself in love with my stocks, which were going up by the minute. I did not realise when this feeling of closeness towards my stocks turned into greed. Greed ruled my mind, making me go for more and more, probably more than anyone else on the earth. I must confess that I didn't realise it then. When the fall came, it blew away everything, every shred of belief I had in myself, each mole of confidence that ever existed in me, and more importantly, it also blasted away the edifice of arrogance that I was protecting myself with. In the beginning, I was so sure that the prices would come back that I invested more money when the prices fell, not realising that I was trying to catch falling knives. Finally, I got tired of investing more. But still I didn't want to sell my stocks as they had fallen so much that it would dent my ego to have liquidated them. I was worried about what people would say. Slowly the hope for recovery of prices dwindled away and the fear set in. I wanted to protect whatever was remaining with me, while no longer hoping for recovery. What was worth a thousand crores at the peak wasn't even worth a few lacs now. I completely stopped looking at my portfolio as it reminded me only of my losses and failure. I fell in my own eyes and finally decided not to invest in equities again because of the losses I suffered. Having attended these classes, I can now comfortably look back and analyse my own behaviour. I really didn't know my identity at all.'

There was a tinge of sadness in Naren's tone. Guruji decided to interrupt him.

'*Thank you, Naren. You brought another emotion to the fore, the indifference after the loss—the apathy towards the portfolio, which has fallen from the peak and is worth a lot less now. Remember, each penny is important and we must value it because one can buy a good stock or some other security with this money. Now the question is how to break this trap of fear, greed, and hope. One way is to invest regularly in the markets, doing simple things like SIPs that may seem boring and dull in the beginning but have potential of creating wealth over a longer period. Second is to watch the behaviour of the crowd and do the opposite.*

We can break this trap of fear, greed, and hope easily. By knowing that you don't need to make all the money in the world, you get rid of greed. To realise that you can't lose all you have earned in a single day makes you steer clear of fear, and once you are clear of these two evils, you need not bank on hope as you certainly know what you are doing in the markets. Fear and greed are for the crowd. An investor who knows himself really well doesn't need to worry about these two devils. While dealing in equities, one can buy good-quality stocks regularly, and when investing in mutual funds, one can simply use this dynamic tool called SIP. One can SIP his way to success through mutual funds. Most of you must have heard about Brahmastra in Indian mythology, which is the most powerful weapon used by Brahma—the creator of this world. I consider SIP to be the Brahmastra in this battle for wealth creation. This is a wonderful tool, and in future, more and more investors shall use it to create wealth.

'But, Guruji, is SIP a tool for smart investors too?' asks Sumant.

'SIP is a tool that can be used by anyone as the rules of money do not change for anyone. Every investor, no matter how big or small, fool or smart, can use this tool efficiently to help himself create wealth. I know these days SIP is not popular among investors who search for instant nirvana. SIP/ STP teaches us patience and discipline. Moreover, it helps break the trap of fear, greed, and hope.

It has been more than nine months, and students are regularly investing in stocks and mutual fund schemes. To their satisfaction and pleasure, the initial results are enthralling. Markets are slowly inching up on the back of good earnings from engineering, construction, infrastructure, and banking companies. These are the few sectors where their investments have been focussed. They have begun on a good note; this increases their confidence further. Most of their investments are up by almost 25 per cent. They have resolved to keep investing this for a very long period irrespective of the results, because Guruji has told them to do so, because they have also started to believe in investing this way.

37

Time Flies

Days have become months, months have rolled into years. Four long years have passed since the students took the plunge. The stock markets have grown multifold. Rachel has become a mini Guruji for all the students. Sometimes, Guruji gives her a topic to conduct a lecture for the adults' section, and she does it diligently. Markets are roaring. Cheap money across the globe has led to the business of leveraging. Dollar and yen carry trades have become buzzwords for the common equity investors. Guruji's students have not only recouped their losses but also are handsomely in the money now. Naren is sitting on obscene gains as he had made huge lump sum investments initially in stocks too. The memory of the past is slowly fading away, making way for a spiritual prosperity that prevails over his mind, heart, and soul. He doesn't count his money on real-time basis. TV has been removed from his cabin; he does not need to track the prices daily anymore. The same thing is practiced by Adarsh, Gobind, and others. Their happiness comes more from the way they are investing now than the windfall they have made in the markets. This is what Guruji wanted to do. He has taken away the price fixation that used to haunt his students. He has taught them that the businesses are more important than the price, which is understood so very well by his students.

Guruji is happy about the transformation that he has been able to bring about. The students have shown tremendous spirit throughout this journey till this point. They know that this sojourn has no end; this shall continue. The seeds of discipline that they have sown in their lives shall continue to bloom for generations to come. Their children shall follow their footsteps in the field of investments, if not profession. Naren has decided to fold up his business and become a full-time investor and investment advisor. He has made enough to secure his next few generations and now he wants to focus only on wealth creation through equities. His daughter Kanishka has gone to study for an MBA. His son Kshitij is preparing to appear for entrance exams for admission in engineering.

Life is cruising along fine for most of the students. Mridula Satija is now an evolved investor and regarded well by her colleagues in the branch. She is now guiding the bank's management in setting up distribution channels for selling financial products to the bank's customers. Naresh Kohli is prospering as usual. He is religiously putting one part of his earnings into equities every month and has been able to get his wife and children to attend these classes. Sumant is doing reasonably well. He has just bought a flat in the western suburbs of Delhi, thanks to the gains he made in equities. He checked with Guruji before divesting a part of his investments to purchase this house. Guruji was perfectly fine with his decision. Simmi has been able to convince her father to attend the classes too. Kantha Subramanian couldn't be happier. She has peace of mind and money too.

She looks forward to teaching her son about investing and wealth creation. Mrigendra Biswas has started writing on investing and stock markets in Hindi in a local daily now.

Rachel has found a purpose in helping Guruji in conducting these classes. Her time is being utilised more productively now. Gobind has opened a few more showrooms. He is now envisaging opening a multi-brand dealership which shall be the first in India. Like Sumant, Gobind also has divested a part of his gains to purchase property, of course with Guruji's permission. Adarsh's business is flourishing too. For the students, these classes have become a permanent part of their life. It has been an experience which has brought spiritual enrichment and material prosperity to them.

The Bombay Stock Exchange Index which was languishing at 3000 levels had gone past 20000 now. Equity mutual funds NAVs are soaring once again. More and more fund houses are launching infrastructure- and power-sector-oriented schemes now. The crowd is building up again in the marketplace and excitement is palpable. Guruji had advised the students to make good investments in the infrastructure and power funds launched way back in 2003–2004, apart from doing their regular monthly investments. Students have made more than 80 per cent returns for each of the last four years. Many stocks that were considered to be untouchables in the era of infotech boom have become the market favourites now. Guruji and his warrior students identified these stocks and mutual funds at least three years ahead of the crowd; hence, they are sitting on a pile of gold now. Since the excitement is too good to be true, Guruji has started identifying the sectors and stocks which are being ignored by the investors in the current rally. Many of these companies are doing well, clocking good revenues and profits, yet their prices are not moving in line with the prices of the infrastructure and capital goods stocks. This rings bells with the students. The market seems to have fallen in love with a few sectors just as it had been with the ICE (information technology, communication, and entertainment) sector way back in the year 2000. This time around, it is the turn of infrastructure and power-related sectors. Guruji knows that one day the tide shall turn, but he doesn't know when, as there is no way of knowing it too. He doesn't know when the frenzy shall end. Although he has made the students invest in good-quality stocks, he knows that even these stocks shall bear the brunt of the bears' ire one day. He has suggested that the students liquidate most of their infrastructure-related investments and focus on a few ignored sectors like software, pharma, and FMCG.

Naren plans to take up a certification, which shall help him become a qualified investment advisor. The students have become a single group of like-minded people; they know each other so well now. They help each other beyond investments too. Naresh Kohli has become the family dentist for most of them. Balwant Jakhar often arranges fresh milk and butter from his village for most of the students. Anyone purchasing a car gets a hefty discount from Gobind's showrooms and Adarsh is helping them with taxation-related matters. Mrs Subramanian is helping Lavanya learn South Indian recipes and Sumant helps all the students in coordinating for their mutual fund reports.

Guruji is quite happy to see this progress. He is quite satisfied with himself; he often thinks of now focussing on his larger goal, which no one knows except him. Life is back on track once again; happiness and prosperity have found a way back to all of them. They are slowly becoming better investors, which they always wanted. They are more like a closely knit family now, with Guruji a permanent part of it. They couldn't have asked for more.

38

The Last Lecture—May 2012

'Friends, as they say, all good things come to an end. So our association shall also cease to exist in a limited way that I shall not be giving these classes anymore. Rachel shall carry on with the good work we all have done together. I am extremely happy to have got this opportunity to work with you all, which brought a wealth of different perspectives to me. I don't think I deserve the tag of guru or a teacher, as I firmly believe that I am a student myself. The world of investing is vast and endless as an ocean. One can't hope to know it all; there are no perfect ways to ensure achievement of your goals here as a lot depends on external environment. I still hope that I have been able to add some value to all of you and your families. My objective was to show you the path and walk along with you to reap the fruits of the seeds that we have sown.'

There is absolute silence in the classroom, as if one has dropped a bomb and annihilated everything. One can see more frustration than surprise on the faces that are staring and blank. Guruji's words are searing through their skin like shards of broken glass piercing through the epidermis. How can Guruji leave them? Why is he leaving them? How will they survive without him? What shall they do now? So many questions hang in front of their eyes, and they have absolutely no clue about the answers.

'I know all of you so well that I can see the questions that are troubling you right now. Don't worry about the questions. Time shall provide you all the answers. It is not an easy decision for me to make, but I have to follow my karma of taking the financial education to many more investors and their families. I need to work with more people who can not only benefit from my efforts but can also take this message of disciplined investing to many more such persons. Investing is neither science nor art; it is not a practice too. To me, investing is our dharma. Just as we pray in temples, mosques, churches, and gurudwaras, we need to be religious about investments and keep on investing with utmost discipline and dedication. It's not about making money or making more money than your neighbours or relatives. It is about participating in the larger change that's happening around all of us, especially at a time when the global economy is slowing down and the whole world is looking at India.'

Gobind can feel a tear rise from within to reach the edge of his eye. He can't control his emotions. Naren, who has a lump in his throat, is unable to think of anything right now. He has forgotten everything that has happened over the last few years. He knows in his heart that Guruji is going for certain; what he is not able to negotiate is how this loss shall be recouped. Adarsh's eyes are wet too. Silence engulfs the entire class, including Rachel, who has no clue about what's happening. They all were enjoying these sessions so much. Guruji became a part of their life, their subconscious, and now he is leaving them. This is unfair. They will not let it happen.

Gobind quietly slips out of the classroom to make a call. It's time to bring the eleventh student to the class now.

'Remember that simplicity is a virtue. Simple things done with great passion and discipline may lead to miracles in life. Investors who embrace simplicity need not fear about anything in markets. Stock markets are nothing but our own lives. Continuity of efforts, no matter how simple or stupid, shall lead to the doors of wealth creation. Every evening when I went back home, I used to write my diary. I have written about my life, my experience with stocks, markets, and all of you in this diary and I hope to publish it in the form of a book someday. When I look back, I feel happy about everything that happened to me and all of you. There is always a larger purpose behind everything that happens.'

Simmi is feeling lost. Tears are flowing down her cheeks like someone has left a tap open. She is sobbing; Rachel walks up to her and hugs her tight, crying herself. A pall of gloom has fallen over the class, and the evening suddenly appears to be darker and heavier. Mrigendra Biswas cannot believe what Guruji is saying. He can't imagine Guruji not being there in this classroom ever. He too is crying silently without realizing that his shirt is completely soaked in tears. Balwant Jakhar, who has been more or less a silent player in the class, also feels something tugging at his heart. He feels like breaking down too.

Life is all about movement. I wasn't with you all the time. Our meeting each other was for a purpose, for a specific objective, and I am glad that we have covered a significant distance on this path. My going away shall also prove a cardinal point in the field of investments—no one knows it all. There is no master and no student. You shall see that you shall do just as fine without me also. My physical presence here in this room can anyways not be assured forever, just as yours can't be. The game of investing shall continue, players can come and go. I know we have come so close to each other that going away shall disturb the rhythm of our life but change is the only constant in our lives. Nothing stays forever. I want you all to grow more independent and responsible in the ways you invest and carry your lives.'

'Guruji, where shall you go?' asks Sumant.

'I do not know yet. I have some unfinished agenda to take care of. This may take days, months, even years. I do not know where my life shall take me. But wherever I go, each one of you shall remain in my mind and heart. You all are a fruit of possibility grown on the branches of my hope. I must thank all of you for bearing with me all this time. I shall leave my contact coordinates with you, so that we can get in touch with each other whenever we want. Please note that the work is still unfinished. This journey of investing needs to be continued for generations to come, and I shall be disheartened if any one of you discontinues doing so. I told you in the beginning that I do not have all the answers, I say it again. No one has all the answers except your own self. You know yourself, your goals, objectives, dreams, ambitions, and longings. All the answers are within you, so you are the true guru of yourself, and not me. I am only a means, a medium, or maybe a tool that can help you for some time. In the longer run, you have to negotiate the tides yourself.'

Students are holding each other's hands, needing strength in this hour of difficulty. Everyone is crying without any fear of being noticed. The classroom becomes a saline ocean at this juncture. Guruji shows no sign of emotions.

'Be with each other and more importantly be with yourself. Never ever lose sight of your goals. You shall do fine. Rachel and

Naren are talented persons with tremendous thought clarity, and I am sure you shall enjoy being taught by her. Let me tell you that I am not guiding her on how to take this forward; she has to find a way on her own, of course with your help. I am sure you shall cooperate with her. May God bless you all. Thank you, everyone. If I have hurt any one of you knowingly or unknowingly, I apologize from the bottom of my heart.'

Everyone is on their feet, not knowing what to do. Gobind, who has come back to the classroom, takes the first step towards Guruji. He hugs Chaitanya, who hugs him back with equal compassion. Gobind's tears know no bounds as he mumbles, 'Guruji, please don't go. What shall we do without you?' Chaitanya feels a lump rising in his throat too. He stays silent though, holds Gobind by shoulders, and looks into his eyes. With his fingers, Guruji wipes off Gobind's tears and urges him to smile. Next one in line is Naren, who owes so much to Chaitanya. If it were not for Guruji, his life would have been devastated by now. Normally, Naren would like to keep his emotions to himself but today he has lost so much that tears don't matter. If only his tears could keep Guruji from going, he would fill an ocean with them. He puts his head on Chaitanya's chest and cries aloud like a child. He has no inhibitions today. His saviour is going away, leaving them in midstream, abandoning them for some unknown reason, and he can't do anything about it. He feels so helpless and dejected. Chaitanya asks him to gather himself and take care of the other students who are not as mature and able as he is. Naren promises to Chaitanya that he shall take care of the class like his family and make sure that they follow the path shown by him.

Guruji walks up to everyone and hugs them passionately. They are a permanent part of him now. They aren't just students; they are his creation. Biswas, Sumant, Kantha, Mridula, Naresh Kohli, Rachel, and Balwant, all of them are soaked in emotions, their wet cheeks and soggy eyes bear the testimony to the grief that they are experiencing right now. Chaitanya holds each one of them like a guru should.

Rachel is apprehensive about the future, she doesn't know if she shall be accepted by the students as well as Guruji has been. She walks up to Chaitanya and stands in front of him, looking straight into his eyes where she can see a definite wetness. Chaitanya holds her cheeks in his hands and wipes off her tears. Despite being younger than her, he feels more grown-up and responsible towards her. He gives her half a hug and reassures her that she will do fine in future. Everyone gets a chance to embrace Guruji, and slowly tears dry up as reality sinks in.

'Dear all, hills are calling me. I am going back to the ashram near Simla where Gobind and Rachel met me. I have purchased a small piece of land on which I plan to construct a school for financial education. I shall be teaching investments to the schoolkids, housewives, and others who feel a need for it. Also I need to search for someone.'

Before Guruji can speak further, Naren interrupts him, saying, 'Guruji, sorry to interrupt you like this. You have taught us for the last five years and we haven't paid you a single dime in return. I know you won't charge us a fee but you have to allow us to help you set up that school of yours. Please do not say no or our hearts shall be broken completely. Allow me to take care of this hereon. I, along with Adarsh, Gobind, and anyone else who wishes to contribute for this noble cause, shall pay for the land, construction of the school, and the running expenses of that facility, since we know that you shall not be charging the students there also. Please do not even try to think of convincing us. Thanks to your help and guidance, we all have enough resources to help you in this mission of yours.'

Everyone heartily claps for Naren and commits to help Guruji for this cause. Chaitanya is overwhelmed with this unexpected response. If he says no to them, it may seem disrespecting to all of them.

'This is a great help to me, Naren. I gladly accept it. As I know what it means for me, I won't say thanks and dilute the impact.'

'Guruji, there is one more gift that you have to accept from the three of us. We have been thinking of giving you this gift for a long time now but didn't get an opportunity to do so. Since you shall be starting a new phase of your life now, I feel you need a partner who can walk along with you on this noble path. You don't have to search for her, she is right here standing outside this classroom,' says Gobind.

Everyone in the class is confused except the trio and Rachel. Even Chaitanya isn't able to understand what Gobind is saying.

'Guruji, when you took a big turn in your life a few years back, you left her behind. The poor girl is still standing on the same place while you moved on. She has taken a lot of pain and sorrows in her stride and made huge sacrifices that you are not aware of. She has worked hard to lead a meaningful life just as you wanted her to,' Naren speaks.

'Sir, she has paid a huge price for her mistakes by losing you for all these years. She went in search of you but came back empty-handed. She corrected her mistakes by returning us the money that she had taken from BBC as commission and she has been diligently learning about stocks and investing all these years with our help. We all have been taking notes by turns and transmitting it back to Sonia. She has also followed all your teachings and techniques by investing whatever little she was left with. We want you to accept her and start a new life,' says Rachel.

Chaitanya is barely able to absorb the intensity of this situation as Gobind walks in with Sonia. Her face, although not as youthful as it was few years back, still shines with hope. Her hair seems to have acquired a bit of grey here and there. She walks slowly in a repentant, hopeful manner, still unsure of her future. Tears have never stopped rolling down her cheeks ever since Chaitanya walked away. She looks up to face Chaitanya, who by now has become as cold as a stone in the Himalayas, unsure of what he should do. His head hangs down as he feels burdened within himself. He suddenly feels selfish that he never bothered to check about the girl whom he intended to marry once, while this poor girl has been waiting for him to come back.

Suddenly he becomes unaware of his surroundings; he walks towards Gobind and looks straight into Sonia's tear-filled eyes. He takes her hand in his hands and hugs her passionately. Tears come out aplenty from his eyes as well.

'I am sorry, Sonia. I am really sorry' is all he can say.

He releases Sonia from his arms and turns to face the trio who have returned the favour to him in a priceless manner. He hugs Naren, Gobind, and Adarsh one by one and thanks them profoundly. They have paid him the fee not only for this life but also for the next seven generations.

'*Dear students, it's time for me to move on. I shall be in touch with all of you shortly again. Please know that I shall never ever be far from you. Whenever you need me, just drop me a line on moneymentors@yahoo.com and I shall immediately do the needful. I won't say goodbye as I am not too strong in saying it. I shall just say, "See you soon".*'

Guruji pauses for a few seconds, wipes tears off his cheeks, and orates in Urdu:

Sitaron ko aankhon mein mehfooz rakhna
Bahut door tak raat hee raat hogi
Mai har haal mein muskurata rahoonga
Tumhari dosti agar saath hogi
Musafir hoon mai bhi, musafir ho tum bhi
Kahin na Kahin, fir mulakaat hogi.

Keep the stars safe in your eyes
The night is going to be long
I shall keep smiling forever
If your friendship is with me
I am a traveller and you are a traveller too
We shall surely meet somewhere.

39

July 2014

It has been some time since Chaitanya and Sonia left Delhi to start a new chapter in their lives. They stay in a small town near Shimla away from the din and bustle of a large city. They run financial literacy schools across Himachal and in Delhi, teaching investing to whoever needs it—housewives, students, businessmen, doctors, and others. They also facilitate online learning through their website.

Naren and Rachel have been conducting the classes Chaitanya had started way back in 2002. A lot of water has passed under the bridge since then.

Chaitanya and Sonia stare at the wedding invitation sent by Naren. Naren's daughter is getting married next week. Chaitanya shall be attending the same. Sonia picks up an envelope from Chaitanya's table and gives it to him. It's a courier from one of his students. Wondering what could be inside, he tears it open and finds a poem handwritten by one of his students, a poem dedicated to 'Our Stock Market Monk'.

I am a bull's roar—
asking for more.
I am the fear
that creates a bear.

I am the greed
going beyond need.
I am the hope
slipping down the slope.
I am the happiness
inside the spoken finesse.
I am the silent realisation
in the failure's exasperation.
I am a dream
I am a mirage
I am the song of profit
and
the lament of the loss.
I am the itch for the money
I am the life in each penny
I am known yet unknown.
I am nothing
but your own reflection.
I am the stock market.

It's signed Rachel.
Chaitanya smiles and passes the paper to Sonia.

Key learnings

- Investing is not about only making money.

- Shareholders are owners of a company to the extent of percentage of their shareholding.

- When you own a share, think like a promoter. Focus on the business and not the price. Stock price is only a by-product of earnings.

- Promoters are shareholders who hold their shares for extraordinarily long periods of time. Few of them have created phenomenal wealth for themselves.

- There is no shortcut to any place worth going to.

- Wealth and money are two different things. Wealth is a greater enabler compared to mere money.

- The long term is boring, but it can make a meaningful difference to our lives.

- The long term is longer than our lives.

- Fear is the greatest enemy of a stock market investor. There is nothing more demeaning than the stigma of the loss.

- SIP (systematic investment plan) is an excellent tool to help investors rise high above their fears and enjoy the journey of wealth creation.

- Equanimity is a virtue; profit and losses are part and parcel of investing.

- Rudyard Kipling's poem 'If' can be applied equally to life and stock markets. It offers valuable lessons for both.

- Investments are a part of life and not vice versa. Enjoy life and avoid the temptation of checking your NAVs/stock prices on a daily basis.

- Teach your kids about investments; apart from providing them with good education and values, this can be one of the greatest favours we can do for them and our families.

- You can't invest in tomorrow's winners by just looking at past performance. Past performance doesn't guarantee successful future.

- Markets aren't risky, businesses are.

- The crowd follows the leader with a lag and sees risk and opportunity in complete isolation.

- Price–earnings (P/E) ratio is a simple yet powerful tool when it comes to stock market investing.

- Know yourself. Be anything but a pig.